CW00515360

PETRICLYSM

AMANDA ROSS

ISBN: 978-1-09835-688-0 (print)

ISBN: 978-1-09835-689-7 (eBook)

To my students who always encourage me to write more. This one's for you.

PROLOGUE

September 23
Chaos. Turned. Order. That's how it all started. One minute I'm in school trying to stay awake in class and the next minute they're sending me home. Why? What's happening? I didn't have a chance to really ask these questions. Not until I walked through the door of my home and saw my parents sitting around the table, both their heads were stooped in quiet, intense conversation. My dad was never home this early. Was he sent home, too? And my mom, was she off from the hospital today?

Even after a few months I still didn't have any answers. The news was on a repeating loop saying the same thing day in and day out. Even alternative news sources couldn't give me much more information. It was mostly speculation and attempts at fixing the problem. Isolation seemed to be the best cure, but intense, extended isolation made the cure worse than the disease to put it mildly—even the most introvert-hardy have a limit as to how much alone time is too much. Then they took away our holidays and asked us to give up more of our autonomy "for the sake of the vulnerable." I laugh. It's always "for the children" and now they're just expanding their reach, but since when have I benefited? I'm glad I have my parents. I don't have any siblings. The tax on an extra child was too much at the time my parents would have considered one. Now, siblings are a rarity and only the richest of the rich can afford more than two children. Population control, environmental issues, yadda yadda yadda.

Eventually I got to go back to school but was sent home several weeks later. Again. And now? I don't go to school at all. They won't let me even though the majority of the population is now free to do so. I can't go to the movies. I can't leave Anvac. That's where we eventually moved after things started settling down into what the authorities called, "The New Norm." My parents had to give up our house and most of our belongings. We were instructed to take only the bare necessities. They took our phones and our computers. I was allowed to keep my old iPod, an ancient bricklike thing that can only play music. Sometimes I feel like I'm living in the Dark Ages. Maybe I am.

Every night at precisely 9pm they cut off our power. It doesn't come on again until 6am half an hour before all the adults jump on buses and head to work. The old yellow school buses now army green wait just inside the gates each morning for them. My parents work a 10-hour shift in some kind of factory before being bused home. I don't know exactly what they do. They're kind of vague about the whole thing and don't like to talk about it. I guess I will find out when I come of age and have to work for my own food rations.

Me? I get to stay home all day. It's not quite the vacation it sounds like. Even though I found high school dull, it was definitely more entertaining for a 16-year-old than wandering the two rooms my family now occupies. I stay inside most of the time. It's safer not getting too familiar with others. I mainly try diverting attention from my growling stomach or the fact that I am now able to count my ribs; I stay busy doing things that don't require a lot of energy. We subsist on government rations which are never enough, especially for a growing teenager. Thankfully, I don't think I'm going to grow much more. "Short people unite!" was my rallying cry at school when someone brought my height to my attention. Like, gee, thanks I had no idea I was short. [Insert eyeroll here.]

Anyway, I spend much of my time trying to keep our apartment clean which isn't hard, document as much as I can here, and read books from the library. When the government created Anvac they accidentally included a public library within the fences. They only realized their mistake after it was fenced in and never bothered to remove the books or block us from entering the building. We have a self-appointed librarian who helps us find useful things to read using a very old card cataloguing system. I mostly read books on survival, how to live off the land, how to build a shelter, and so on. They're some of my favorites. Why these books in particular? I'm planning for my future; our future. A future where we're able to leave the city. It really is daydreaming at this point, but one can never be too prepared.

Who are the "we" in all of this? Well, me—Hazel—16, my mom and dad, and my best friend Nick, who's 17, and his dad. When I first arrived in Anvac, I would walk along the perimeter fence looking out into the rest of the city where I used to live. I liked to stare up at the tall buildings surrounding us and watch the reflection of the sky in their brilliant windows. The sun shining back, the clouds skimming from one building to the next. Anvac was blocked on all four sides so seeing the sun happened at noon and in reflections. As I walked the fence, I always hoped that a friend from school would happen by and tell me what was going on in the rest of the world, but then I remembered my last few weeks at school and decided to give up. Some people walked the perimeter of the fence at night to try and gather news, hiding in the shadows as far from the front gates and watching eyes of the guards as possible. I didn't know how difficult it would be to live without knowing what's going on in the world. I took for granted the ability to access information anytime I wanted. Same with a lot of things actually.

It was on one of my walks along the fence when I saw Nick coming from the opposite direction looking for his friends. It was exciting and kind of sad for both of us to discover we were on the same side of the fence. We've been more or less inseparable since. I know he still walks the perimeter sometimes hoping his mom will come and find him. But she doesn't and she won't.

I can always tell when he's been out looking again. The rejection is sometimes hard to hide.

Since no newspapers are allowed into our small community and no one owns a TV or radio we get news from covert operations within Anvac. Turns out a lot of the citizens are quite resourceful. The information is then passed from one person to the next telephone-style, but by the time it reaches our house I'm never quite sure whether to believe it or not. Sometimes we hear about wars around the world or outbreaks in other cities. We even heard about a new government—a government that erased all borders—yeah, right.

Sometimes people escape Anvac but are eventually brought back. If they try again, the authorities roll in a mobile guillotine and execute the individual in the center of Anvac. It's quite primitive if you ask me. And gruesome. I always avert my eyes since we are forced to attend. It's meant to be a deterrent to those of us living here. Sometimes it does the opposite, though, and those desperate enough to leave this life volunteer for a quick exit.

Once I found a newspaper rolled up and stuck through the chain link fence on the backside of Anvac. It was so well hidden that I'm sure it was meant for someone else to find. I read the headline: "First President of the World Elected". Wait? What? They were right? I didn't know what to make of what I was reading so I rolled it back up and replaced it. I told my parents about finding the newspaper and the headline later that day and they swore me to secrecy that I wouldn't tell anyone I had seen it; that I wouldn't repeat what the headline said. I asked if they ever saw the news when they were at work. Both of them turned away and remained silent.

I still have hope and so does Nick that things will eventually get better, that maybe our rations will be increased, or that they'll simply let us leave. We like to dream of such things, it's why we read and why our parents encourage us to learn as much as we can about life in the country and about our history. If we don't have hope, we have nothing. And for the record, I *am getting out of here one day.*

CHAPTER 1

The kids of Anvac gathered near the gates trickling in by ones, twos, and threes a little after six to await the arrival of the adults returning from work. This nightly ritual was punctuated with hushed conversations between small groups of friends and even smaller pairs of siblings. A lone group of three siblings—the only one of its kind in the community—stood a little apart from the others. The oddity of their existence and the palpable envy at the obvious former wealth these three represented kept them from mingling with the larger crowd even though they were now all equals. A growing air of expectancy and impatience for the meager meals that would follow permeated the atmosphere as time marched slowly toward their parents' arrival. The crowd paused at intervals to listen intently for the telltale sound of buses rumbling down the vacant streets.

Wending his way through the cumulating throng, Nick saw Hazel casually walking toward the bus stop to wait for her parents. He waved as he spotted her across the street trying to get her attention, her long reddish-brown hair swaying from side to side, her full lips slightly pursed in concentration as her dark brown eyes scanned faces. Nick, once very muscular, was tall and lean like a willowy beanpole. He could easily see over most of the heads of the growing group, his shaggy dark hair added a punctuation mark to his height. He successfully caught Hazel's eye with his dark blue gaze, and she threaded through several small groups to join Nick on the opposite side.

"Hey Hazel," he smiled broadly, his left front tooth missing its corner. "No buses, yet?" It was 6:30pm and the buses should have been rumbling down the street arriving in Anvac. They usually ran right on time. Timeliness was part of the new order. Having heard the phrase "Time is Money" often enough it wasn't surprising that a government would keep to a strict schedule.

"Haven't seen them," she smiled back warmly glancing toward the closed gates. "I hope they get here soon. I'm starving and can't *wait* to be a little less starving." She said this last with as much sarcasm as she could muster. He understood the sentiment and his stomach growled in agreement. He chuckled at the sad truth. Neither of them really thought there would be enough to eat again and counted on the fact that as things settled more into the "New Norm" there would eventually be even less. They stood there waiting, occasionally shifting weight from one leg to the other watching the guard shacks on either side of the fence for movement. Whenever the buses arrived the guards would go out and open the gates to let them in and then wait until all passengers were unloaded and the buses had driven out again before closing them. Nick and Hazel could see shadows moving inside the shacks, but the windows were tinted so not much more could be seen.

More youngsters showed up at the bus stop waiting for their parents to get home. As the arrival continued to be delayed more kids arrived. Some who normally waited inside the confines of their small apartments shyly gathered with the others. By seven the size of the group had doubled. Conversation had dwindled to a bare minimum; words were used sparingly as minutes marched on. The guards still made no move toward opening the gates.

"Where are they?" asked a little girl in a thin t-shirt with a faded picture of a rainbow and frayed jeans several inches too short. A shrug came from the boy she addressed, a little taller than she in clothing even more worn. The group remained quiet, but the tension was growing. Hazel observed the group. Here were kids of all ages quietly waiting for their parents. No playing, no fighting, no crying. All of them painfully thin in shabby clothes calmly waiting for three green buses to arrive. They learned early on the rules for waiting at the gates. If they misbehaved the guards would punish them. Some guards were nicer than others and would admonish them with a warning, other guards gave no warning and unleashed pent up anger through the liberal use of nightsticks. And now, after months of rations, the kids had no extra energy to play or fight or even cry. They simply waited.

Pariahs thought Hazel, looking around again *We've all been marooned.* She smiled remembering how she used to yell "Maaaarrrroooonnnned" just like her friend's parrot did whenever it was left alone in a room. *I wonder if that crazy bird is still alive.*

Eventually every child in Anvac was standing at the gates. Hazel recognized a few faces but didn't know any names. Even though the community was relatively small, no one talked much. There wasn't much "community" in the community. Just like communist countries or Hitler's Germany, they'd learned in the early months of Anvac that the less people knew about one another the better.

The anxiety and restlessness were growing. Seven twenty-nine and still no buses could be heard coming; the guards could no longer be seen in their shacks. The sun had already set and purple streaks painting the sky were all that remained of the day. The power would go out in little more than an hour and a half and then the only visible light came from the higher windows of the buildings surrounding Anvac. Useless for anything. The streetlights had kicked on, enveloping the silent crowd in an orange glow, the buzz amplified in the stillness.

Nick nudged Hazel and beckoned her away from the crowd, now swollen to about 100 kids of all ages. Once they were some paces away from the group he said in a hoarse whisper, "Listen." He looked back over his shoulder at the group, “No, seriously. Listen. What do you hear?” She paused, cocked her ear toward the city and away from the mumbling crowd.

“Nothing, really, maybe a few cars idling in the distance? The buzzing streetlights?” Hazel responded with a look of confusion. Then several things happened at once, cars in nearby intersections sounded like they were colliding one right after the other. In an instant, a distant drone became a deafening roar overhead. The scraping of metal bounced off the tall buildings around them. Everyone looked up just in time to see the underside of a 747-passenger plane flying overhead, its right-wing disintegrating as it skimmed the side of the nearest skyscraper sending sparks showering over Anvac. Kids automatically ducked and shielded their heads, then looked once more at the tail of the plane as it cleared the gate. In seconds the sickening crunch of the plane colliding with a building directly in its flight path resounded through the empty streets. A deep sienna-orange, black edged, cracking fireball burst into the sky like an immense thunderhead momentarily blinding the audience. A moment later soundwaves roiled over the stunned group with a flicker of heat that rustled untamed stands of hair like a warm breeze on a summer night. All the kids looked toward the explosion and then chaos ensued. They scattered to all points of Anvac crying and screaming, some attempted to open the gates forgetting about the guards in their fear, most running for home before more disaster could strike. Then all was silent. The typical city noises—cars driving, horns honking, air brakes discharging—the general hum that one typically tunes out was gone. No cars were passing by on invisible streets, no more planes flying overhead, nothing. And, ominously, no sirens rushing to greet the downed plane.

“Hazel, I don’t think the buses are coming,” Nick grabbed her hand leading her, snaking his way through the oncoming rush of bodies toward his apartment.

CHAPTER 2

All through the night there was silence followed by more silence. After a couple of hours Nick suggested they go outside to try and ascertain information that might help them find their parents. It was obvious that the stillness bothered Nick. Even though he didn't much care for the city noises, the absence of them was much more troubling.

Hazel grabbed the raggedy green sweatshirt she'd worn to the bus stop and pulled it over her head, running hands through static-y hair to catch the fly aways and then, by habit, gathering the long tendrils into a loose ponytail. She quietly followed Nick down the steps and out into the cool night air, their movements furtive and hesitant. They moved from shadow to shadow trying to go unnoticed by the kids who may be watching from their apartments or who also may have broken curfew.

It felt weird to be out after curfew. Nick looked left and right to double check that there weren't any guards. None were visible and the gates were still shut tight. Yet another aspect of all this weirdness. There were usually sentries posted at the gate each night to ensure that the citizens of Anvac stayed put; they would patrol the streets at random to keep people on guard. Nick and Hazel made their way to the tallest building within the fence. It was only five stories high, but from the roof more of the city was visible. There seemed to be fires all over the city, but still no noise. No sirens, no cars, no planes flying. No one, except them, even alert to the fact that something was wrong. Nothing but the streetlights in the city and some in the buildings were on. The power in Anvac had gone off at nine. At least some things were still working like they should.

"What do you think is going on?" Nick asked. Hazel jumped at the sound of his voice in the silence.

"I really don't know," she whispered back. "Where are our parents? They didn't come home. Do you think they're okay?"

"Who can tell," he sighed, his shoulders slumping slightly. "Maybe we should find out. I know of a weak spot in the fence that's easy to get under."

"Are you serious? What about the authorities? What if we get caught?" Hazel's dark eyes narrowed with worry, then widened in excitement at the possibility. She tried hard to remind herself of the consequences of breaking the rules but was giddy with the thought of leaving Anvac.

"I don't think we have to worry about the authorities right now," he said, looking toward the guard shacks for any sign of life. Although the shacks were kept dark at night, the usual glow of a cellphone could be seen. Tonight, nothing. He peered over the side of the building and could see shadows moving. "Look," he said quietly, pointing. Hazel snuck up next to him. She could barely make out three small dark shapes walking to the fence that ran beside the back wall of the building. They watched as one of the shapes found an opening in the chain-link fence where someone had cut it sometime in the past. It was so cleverly hidden that only those who knew it was there could see it. The other two shapes ducked under, the third following then slipping out into the night. It was that easy.

"Well," Nick started, "we aren't the only ones with a similar idea. What do you say? Want to leave Anvac?"

Hazel smiled broadly, "Yes! Let's go! So where should we start?" She looked back at the spot where the three shapes had slipped out.

"First, we should gather what we can take with us. Like food, clothes, matches."

"Matches?"

"Well, yeah, you know, stuff like that. Things that might be very important to have, just in case.

"In case of what?" she cut him off.

"In case of whatever may be happening out there. We have absolutely no idea what's going on and I want to be prepared. Like they taught in Boy Scouts. You know the motto 'Be prepared.' I mean, I was just shy of becoming an Eagle Scout before the Great Wave," he grinned.

"And you read too many post-apocalyptic books," Hazel gave playfully.

"Well, and that, too. But you don't have any room to talk either—Miss I'm-Going-to-Live-on-a-Farm," he needled her in the side. She jerked to the side and stifled a laugh being highly ticklish. "So…bring what we need, but not too much? We should be light on our feet. We're just going to find out what's going on. We might come straight back here. I really don't know," he stood. Hazel followed him back down to the street.

They got back to Nick's apartment where he filled a small black backpack with useful items including all the food rations he still had on hand and a box of waterproof matches. Even with all of the food, Nick's backpack was still relatively empty and light. He only had one thick sweatshirt and a raincoat that he threw in just in case, changing into his least worn pair of sneakers, and a dark blue trucker's hat for good measure. Hazel liked the hat; it was an added touch of incognito. At her apartment, she grabbed essentially the same things, a light blanket, her journal, a hippie book with a pencil drawing of a girl on the front called *Living on the Earth* and three ballpoint pens just in case. Nick raised his eyebrows at the book and Hazel shrugged; he has his fiction; she had her how to live eco-friendly reading material. Then they slept. Nick on the couch.

Nick couldn't fall asleep, being excited at the prospect of leaving Anvac and simply being worried about his dad, so after some time he went and roused Hazel. She was already awake, just waiting for him to get up. Before setting out they sat down for the largest meal they'd consumed in months. Even though this final meal in Anvac, as Nick termed it, used up a lot of their rations it was better starting out on full stomachs with energy and it felt really good to have eaten enough for once.

Light was barely entering the sky as Nick led the way to the far side of Anvac where the fence was easy to pull up. Hazel ducked under as Nick held the fence, pushed his bag through and followed. They were now both outside of Anvac for the first time in 18 months. Hazel took a deep breath, even the air felt freer. Hazel wanted to dance and run and skip and shout at the sheer exhilaration of being outside Anvac. But she refrained, they still had no idea what was going on. So, they proceeded with caution staying close to the buildings and walking as noiselessly as possible. The city was silent, unmoving with the exception of random buildings still on fire scattered throughout the city. Smoke was starting to accumulate at the street level, cutting down on visibility.

Several large pieces of debris from the crashed 747 littered the sleeping streets. It was a fresh reminder that something was very wrong. The charred pieces, most likely from the wing, had a sobering effect on Hazel. Between the accumulating smoke and plane debris, her mind wandered to the people who'd lost their lives, wondering how many more may have been affected by whatever was going on. She still relished the thought of being away from Anvac, but what was the price of her burgeoning freedom? An awareness that something much more serious and maybe much more dangerous going on grew to full wakefulness inside. Her thoughts turned to her parents. Where were they? And with that, all excitement at newfound freedom vanished.

Nick understood Hazel's first reaction to being on the other side of the fence, but he'd quickly reined it in. He was deeply concerned with getting to the bottom of everything before celebrating. No matter what, something—something BIG—had happened. What could cause a city to simply stop? Not the grid, the people. The first thing he'd noticed was the lack of people walking down the streets. Usually, the hustle and bustle of the early morning would permeate the atmosphere. Buses going from stop to stop, individuals looking down at their phones while intuitively avoiding other pedestrians. But today? Nothing.

Hazel kept quiet, her eyes darting now to different points along the street looking for anything that could account for the stillness. A few times she thought she saw individuals peeking out of curtained windows in apartment buildings, but she couldn't be sure. A cat raced out from behind a bush and she jumped, nearly letting out a scream. Her heart pounding long after the fright. Where was everybody?

About three blocks from Anvac, they came to a large intersection where several cars were smoldering in the middle, obviously having collided. The bodies of the drivers were still sitting behind the wheels. It looked as if no one had even made a move to get out or to help. Nick started looking around a little more and pointed to the other cars sitting at the lights. Each car was pushing on the one in front of it in succession, indicating which two lanes had a green light at the time whatever it was happened. The cars were kept in place by the wrecked vehicles in the intersection. Drivers who had been at red lights were still waiting, feet steadfastly locked on brakes, immobile. Every driver regardless of direction was still behind their respective wheels. Not a single driver had attempted to get out. Some vehicles were still idling while others appeared to have run out of gas. Nick looked toward the next intersection and could make out through the haze the same scene repeating itself. It was most likely the same across the city. All the streets were packed. It had happened during rush hour. He walked up to the nearest car and tapped on the window. The driver made no movement. After a couple of tries, Nick lifted the door handle. It was locked so he moved on to the next vehicle, tapped on the window and then tried the door. This time door opened. The driver sat staring blankly ahead, hands at ten and two, foot still firmly pressed on the brake. The man was a pale translucent blue with hints of purple around the mouth.

"Sir?" Nick said quietly, tapping the driver on the shoulder. "Sir? Can you hear me?" he said a little louder and tapping harder. He gave the driver a little shove and recoiled at the stiffness of the driver. He pushed the driver again much harder than he intended and heard a loud crack as the hands at ten and two broke free from the arms. "Oh my God!" he screamed. "He... he...he...broke!" Hazel came over to see what was going on. The driver's hands were still gripping the steering wheel.

"What in the..." Hazel looked in.

"I...I...I tried to see if he was still alive, so I pushed him—too hard, obviously—and he just...he broke!" Nick looked like he was going to be sick. He moved away and brought up a good portion of his breakfast.

"Well, he's definitely dead."

"I kind of figured that, but was hoping he had just passed out," he grimaced still bent over hands on knees. "Look at his coloring. He's somewhere between purple and blue and skin tone and pale white. It's like when people are being choked to death and turn that weird color." He looked closely at the man while avoiding the dismembered hands.

"Yes, his skin looks almost like marble. Look, his veins are black," she pointed to the man's hands where a spider web of small black intricacies were visible. She pushed up the man's sweatshirt sleeve revealing his inner right wrist. The normally blue veins looked like streaks of black running up his arm.

"Feels like marble, too," he said, gently touching the man's face looking like he was going to be sick again. "Do you think they're all like this?" he surveyed the crowded intersection.

"Only one way to find out," she raised her shoulders into a resigned shrug. They decided to check a few more cars at random and found the same scene in each one. After the first driver, Nick was extremely careful not to shove or jostle the individual, afraid of breaking them. Every driver was a cold translucent blue, stiff, marble-like statue, black veins running under the skin, the hues dependent on the individual's original skin color. "What do you think caused this?" Hazel asked getting out of another vehicle and standing next to Nick. He shrugged in response. "Do...do you think our parents are..." she couldn't finish; the thought of seeing their parents like this frightened her.

He slung his arm across her shoulders in a side hug, "They might be, but my gut tells me that that's not the case. Let's get a move on and see if we can find *anyone* alive." She nodded and started walking. Then stopped.

"Do you *know* where our parents are, exactly?" Hazel asked.

"Not really," he paused, "Did your mom or dad ever tell you where they go?"

"Ummm, actually…no. You?"

"My dad only ever said that they worked about five miles from Anvac in a sprawling one-story building. He always said they were making things, but he didn't elaborate."

"Yeah, my parents always called it 'The Factory', but wouldn't say what they made. All I know is that they hated their jobs and told me that I wouldn't want to know what they did anyway. I think they were being vague because they had to be. Like they couldn't tell me what they were making."

"I got the same feeling," Nick agreed. "Let's keep going this way, I always saw the buses turn left at the end of the street. It's our best shot right now."

They walked for about half an hour down streets that looked frozen in time. Each car that was still running they either opened the door or broke the window with a large rock Nick found, put the car in park, and turned it off. Hazel chuckled that they were doing their part to save the environment. Car after car showed the same thing. Bodies that were cold and stiff some bluer others more purple all with traceries of black veins. Some drivers had their cellphones in hands, batteries slowly dying. Nick pried one free to check the signal. It was still strong. But for how long? The hardest part was finding the kids, some had been looking out the window, others with headphones on watching a screen fixed to the back of the seat in front of them, babies who had either been fussing or sleeping—all cold, all unmoving, all a ghostly shade of blue.

After passing through another intersection Nick stopped at the corner to examine and cover an elderly man with a newspaper. The man was lying sideways on the ground, his bike still between his legs. "He looks like my grandpa," Nick offered up by way of explanation. The man's left hand had shattered when it hit the pavement. "They all remind me of the people who were petrified in Pompeii. It's like whatever happened was instantaneous. It doesn't look like anyone survived."

"Except us and the other kids in Anvac."

"Yeah. That's what's so puzzling."

They trudged down another couple of blocks, already slowing down from mental and physical exhaustion; throats dry and irritated from the smoke. There was a convenience store on the corner across from where they stood. Hazel traipsed across the intersection, weaving through the frozen traffic jam. She pushed the door open; a body was blocking the entrance; it was surprisingly heavy as Hazel attempted to open the door further. Once inside Hazel noticed that the body at the door was missing its head. She saw it lying a few feet from where the person had fallen. She shivered; it was definitely a sight she might never get used to. There were a few other customers inside. Cold. Stiff. Marble-like. Some standing, some having toppled over. The store clerk was sitting on a stool behind the register, hand in the till frozen in mid-transaction with a customer who stood across the counter from her.

"We don't have any money," Hazel said, disappointed.

Nick laughed, "Somehow I don't think it's going to matter right now. If things ever get back to 'normal,'" he threw up air quotes, "we can come back and pay for what we take. Okay?" Hazel looked at him and assented, she already had half a Snickers bar gone, having already realized the foolishness of her statement.

Nick grinned, "Well, I call that nutritious."

"Lhuvthescharcasm," she chewed. After swallowing she continued, "Besides, do you know how long it's been since I've had one of these? I'm going to take some more." She grabbed four more off the shelf and stuffed them in her bag. It was the perfect time of year where it wasn't cold outside but wasn't warm enough to melt the chocolate either.

"Well in that case," Nick reached for a package of Twinkies and ate both in about four bites. A look of supreme delight lit up his face as sponge cake filled his cheeks. He tipped the rest of the box into his backpack. "No need to worry about calories right now."

"Okay Charlie, what do we *need* to take with us?" Hazel asked putting a few bags of peanuts and a couple of protein bars in with the Snickers. Next, she grabbed a couple bottles of water just to be safe. She popped a diet Coke, drinking it greedily before moving on.

"Water is good. So are those nuts and bars," he pointed. "I'll grab some more matches, a thing of rope, here's a tarp. What else?" he said spinning around. "I don't think we need too much more right now. We still have no idea what's going on and I don't want to lug a whole bunch of stuff. Just in case we get caught. Or if we have to run." *Whatever this is, try not to panic* Nick reminded himself.

"Okay," she said reluctantly, putting a couple boxes of cereal back on the shelf. "You and your matches," she snickered. The box of Cap'n Crunch Crunch Berries was too much temptation, though, she popped the top and ate a handful before slipping the box into her backpack, checking to make sure Nick wasn't watching. The backpack was now quite hefty in weight—a delightful feeling knowing it was full of food. *I feel like Scarlett O'Hara,* Hazel thought to herself, *I'll never be hungry again—I hope.*

"I have an idea," Nick piped up excitedly an aisle over. Hazel looked over and watched him quickly slip a package of Oreos in his bag. "You see that?" He pointed to the surveillance camera in the corner, "I bet we could see what happened and when. It seems like everything stopped at pretty much the same time."

"That's a really good idea." Hazel went up to the store clerk, apologized under her breath and then dug in the woman's pockets for keys. Once in the backroom Nick got to work on figuring out the surveillance camera equipment.

"Got it!" he exclaimed after a few minutes. "Watch this," he backed up the time stamped video. They watched as the video moved forward recognizing the few customers in the store. At precisely 7:30pm everyone in the store froze, a couple customers falling over in midstride. Hazel watched the person at the door and watched the neck snap, the head roll slightly out of the frame. There was no blood. Whatever happened, it was fast. Synchronized. Simultaneous. No. Explanation. Just sudden death. Everyone becoming a Grecian statue without the sculptor.

Stunned, Nick backed up the scene again and played the clip three more times. He ran it in slow motion the last time through. Nothing could explain what they were seeing. Nothing. He sat back attempting to digest the scene he'd just witnessed. Was it only here in Seattle or was this nationwide? Worldwide? It was like someone somewhere flipped a switch. Could it be reversed? At least for those who hadn't broken. Nick cringed at the horrifying idea of whatever this was being undone. But he figured that what happened at precisely 7:30pm the night before was a permanent solution to a problem he didn't know existed. Whoever had devised and implemented this awful destruction—he figured someone, or something, was behind it—cared very little for humanity's role in the world. Nick had always abided by the live and let live philosophy, but now he may not be able to simply let live.

"It's like they all just…" Hazel started.

"Turned off…" Nick finished. He sat still for a few moments, clenching his jaw, "There's nothing here to tell us what happened. We should probably get going. Find our parents," he said with some urgency leaving the video paused at 19:30:03. "I don't want to be out after dark, and I have a feeling it's going to be a long day. It's midmorning now, but we don't know how long it will take us to find our parents." He got up quickly, refocusing on finding their parents, the video still too incomprehensible to dwell on. *Oh dad*, he thought, *please let me find you. Please.* Walking back through the store, being careful to avoid the customers on the way out, Nick grabbed a package of batteries and two flashlights before letting the door close.

A thickening haze of smoke enveloped them; visibility was lessening and breathing becoming more painful. Hoisting the much heavier backpacks to slumped shoulders they continued on in the silent, strange new world. After another mile a very large, very industrial-looking, sprawling, one-story building loomed out of the smoke. There was a high, chain-link fence all the way around with angry-looking razor wire at the top.

"I don't know about you, but I'm guessing this might be the place," Hazel stated, looking up at the razor wire. "How do you suppose we get in?"

"Mmm, maybe try the front gate," he pointed to the right. Down around to the front of the building the gate was wide open. As they walked through the gates, their hearts quickened. The green buses were parked out front. There they were all three buses that each day trundled their parents to and from their jobs. A large concrete sign out front announced the building's name: "The Virology Lab of North Pangea."

"North Pangea?" Nick grunted a laugh with a hint of incredulity. "I mean, they don't get points for originality in naming the country of the world. Right?"

"Agreed, although I'm guessing we might be just a region now. There's probably South, East, West, and Central. A whole world would be a lot to handle without smaller chunks," Hazel surmised. "But virology?" she returned to the sign. "As in viruses? What in the world would our parents be doing here?"

"I don't know, but let's hope they're here and alive," Nick said, now very worried what they would find if indeed this was where their parents worked. He doubted answers would be easy to find. He couldn't shake the sinking feeling in the pit of his stomach.

CHAPTER 3

As they walked past the guard houses on either side of the gate, Nick and Hazel could see that the guards looked exactly like all the others they'd seen. Cold. Marble-like. Dead. Hazel swallowed the lump in her throat that threatened to choke her. Hoping against hope that she wouldn't be faced with seeing her parents in the same condition, but with each new body they encountered, Hazel could picture in her mind's eye exactly what her parents would look like if the same fate had befallen them.

They ascended the five steps up to the main entrance and found the front door ajar. Nick opened it cautiously and peered in before giving the okay. The place was deserted with the exception of the woman sitting at a computer behind the large curved front reception desk; a computer screen lit up, the colorful shapes splashing the secretary's marble-like features in shades of pink, green, yellow, blue in rotation as the shapes bounced from one side of the screen to the other. The woman's hand still resting on the mouse. Nick started searching for an ID that would allow access to adjacent wings. Each door required an ID scan. He eventually found one after searching the woman, finding it hanging from her lanyard. Her hair getting tangled in the clip. That was another strange feature to these new statues. Every part of a person was solid with the exception of the hair and nails that had grown beyond the quick. A slight breeze would give the illusion that a person was moving. It had a disorienting affect.

"Which door?" he asked once he had the ID in hand. *Leila Mason* the name read accompanied by a picture of the deceased, a smiling woman in a business suit, dark hair slicked back in a professional-looking bun. Nick averted his gaze from the picture to look at the headings over each door.

"That one," Hazel pointed to the door on the right labeled *Operations*. Nick swiped the ID and a green light flashed as the locks disengaged. *Ka chunk*. The door closed slowly behind them as they heard the locks reengage. *Ka chunk*. The hallway was empty. It was a relief to see that there weren't any bodies lying around. All along the corridor were small rooms. Each delineated by the words *Exam Room* followed by a letter. Nick cracked open the door of the first room, *Exam Room A*, and looked in. Automatic overhead lights flickered on revealing a standard physician's exam room, just like a doctor's office would have. The exam table was neatly propped up in a sitting position with clean white paper smoothed over the surface. There was a sink with antibacterial soap and boxes of latex gloves in various sizes ready for use. Nothing out of the ordinary, until remembering the key word on the sign out front. *Virology*. Nick closed the door and opened random exam rooms as they made their way to the end of the corridor. The last room on the right was *Exam Room V*, twenty-two rooms in all. The corridor ended in a large steel door with a small mesh-screened window near the top. Nick peered through the window. Hazel hopped to look in, not tall enough to look through.

"It's a lab of some sort," he relayed, nose pressed against the glass fogging it up. Nick swiped the ID, green light flashed, locks disengaged, and they were in, cautiously entering, deciding at the last second to prop the door open with the backpacks. All across the large space were tables with laboratory equipment and computer screens some with family photos changing at intervals, some stock vacation photos, another with an old screen saver that always reminded Nick of Pickup Sticks, and the usual morphing shapes. As far as Nick could tell, no one else was here.

He went to the nearest desk and started rifling through the papers. Nothing. In his haste he knocked them off the desk and they fluttered to the ground and as they did so, bumped the computer mouse. A smiling baby in a bathtub disappeared and a login screen popped up.

"Well?" Hazel asked.

"Nothing. And I don't think we'll be able to access any of these computers," he indicated all the computers in the room with a general sweep of his arm. "Let's keep moving. We can come back to this once we find our parents. Maybe they can help," after a pause he said quietly, "I sure hope they weren't…test subjects…" His demeanor shifted at the thought. *Exactly what* were *their parents doing here? If this is where they worked. I really hope we're wrong about this.*

They slowly picked a path through the cluttered laboratory. It looked like a lot of people had worked here. But where were they now? Had they already left for the day? Was the lab connected to what happened? But why would it be? It didn't make sense. Nick jostled the mouse of each computer they passed. He was hoping one wouldn't require a login. No dice. Hazel rifled through more papers but couldn't find anything that shed light on what was happening. At the far side of the lab there was another door that led out to a larger empty room. At least, it looked empty until the lights came on. Nick hit the switch and the fluorescent lights flickered on buzzing to full brightness. There were tall stacks of cardboard boxes in the center of the room making it difficult to see if there was anyone else there.

"Hello?" Nick quietly shouted into the stillness. "Hello? Dad? Anyone?" He started making his way around the stack of boxes for a better look. He stopped and held out his hand to make Hazel wait, but she couldn't. "Wait, Hazel," he begged. "Wait," trying to grab her arm as she walked around him.

All along the backwall were opaque plastic bags stacked four high. They were like garment bags only larger, body sized. They could make out blurred arms pressed against the plastic, feet forming little tents at the ends. Hazel stared. *Were they dead dead or frozen marble statue dead like the others?* She decided if these were bodies, they had to be dead dead since the incident would have left no one to take care of the actual dead. Another thought came to her, *they were dead dead before 7:30pm*. She couldn't move her legs. Hazel tried to speak again, but her voice caught in her throat somewhere between finding words to articulate what was before her and a sob that threatened to escape. She was finally able to say, "Maybe those are the scientists."

"Only one way to find out," Nick replied, steeling himself against the fact he would have to look to see. He walked to the nearest opaque bag and pulled it from the top. It was heavy and moved like a large sack filled with tightly packed wet sand. It took more effort than he thought it would to get the bag down. At the last heave, his grip slipped, and the body fell to the floor with a thud. Nick held back the vomit that threatened its way up the back of his throat again. He unzipped the bag, peeling the plastic back from the face. Inside was an older man, his skin grey and cold to the touch, a slight sickly-sweet smell emanated from the bag. He zipped the bag up quickly. "I recognize him, but I don't know his name." Her legs buckled at these words and she sank, eyes fixed on the objects in front of her. She slowly shook her head from side to side trying to say something, but nothing was coming out. *No! No! No! This is some sort of dream. I need to wake up*. She moved her hands in front of her face, rubbing her eyes trying to make what she was seeing disappear.

"What about our parents? Maybe they're not here," she said losing hope fast.

"Maybe. Maybe not," was the soft, slow response. "I mean, these could be other people who just happen to ride…green…buses," he stopped. Reluctantly, "But we won't know until we check. You don't have to. I'll do it." She granted without looking up. After a while Nick confirmed their worst fears. Seventy-seven bags, all adults who left Anvac the morning before on three green buses to go to a factory he had never heard of that turned out to be a virology lab. Nick had laid aside their parents as he found them among the other bodies.

"Nick what are we going to do?" Hazel asked, not able to keep the tears from falling now.

"We need to say goodbye first," he choked, eyes watering in the light. Nick pointed to two bags. He turned away to be alone with the solitary bag lying at his feet.

Hazel slowly approached the bodies on the floor, not really wanting to know beyond a doubt that these two lifeless forms were all that remained of the parents who had loved her and taken care of her even through recent circumstances. If she didn't see those faces, never unzipped the covering, she could go on with the idea that her parents were still out there waiting for her to find them. Maybe they'd already picked a spot for them to live in the country. A large rambling farmhouse with no other visible houses nearby. A white picket fence, an old barn with a loft full of hay. Maybe a dog or two that would curl up at her feet on cold winter nights. Just like they'd always planned. Just like it was supposed to happen at the end of the world. But now her hand was reaching for the zipper pull on the nearest bag, unbidden, without command. A hand acting independently of its owner, unzipping the barrier between fantasy and reality. The hand peeled back the plastic. And there he was. One-third of her family's dream. Her father's strong features now grey, thin lips turned up at the corners in a frozen grin. His eyes slightly open revealing the light blue irises now cloudy in death. She leaned over, her tears falling freely now, and whispered, "I love you." What more could one say? Anything needed saying was no longer an option. *I have no regrets* she thought, pacified at the truthfulness. *No regrets. Daddy, I'll find our house and come back for you, you and mom. You'll be buried near me. I promise. I'll come back for you.* She bent down one more time to kiss his forehead. Raising up she took a sobbing breath and almost gagged at the decay that'd already started. "I can't," she started to say, then cried and let the sorrow take over. She watched as her hand rezipped the bag, hiding her father's face.

Finally, with a sigh and another shuddering sob, she turned to the smaller form and looked at her mother's face for the last time. Hazel felt like she was outside of herself, as if she, Hazel, were floating above this scene watching the Hazel down there, cry over her mother's beautiful form hoping beyond hope that her mother would simply wake up. Now two-thirds of the dream was shattered. Hazel lifted her hand and smoothed her mother's brown curls away from the face, tucking loose locks behind ears. A glint of gold caught in the hair and Hazel realized it was her great grandmother's gold locket with the intricate rose design clasped around her mother's neck. She removed it, undoing the tiny clasp, disentangling it from her mother's hair, refastening it around her neck—the Hazel above crashing into the Hazel below as the cold locket rested against the hollow of her throat bringing her back to earth.

As an afterthought Hazel took her parents' wedding rings, taking the holy symbols of unity; two gold bands, one larger and smooth, one smaller inlaid with clusters of diamonds and added them to the chain around her neck. She then tucked the locket and the rings inside the sweatshirt so that they were hidden.

Exhausted, she looked for Nick and found him sitting quietly beside another bag a little way from where she stood, his back to her. Nick sat solemnly by the lone body bag. His father's typically happy-go-lucky face exposed. Nick held his father's hand tightly wishing with all his might that he could warm it up and discover that his father was still alive—that he'd simply been cold and needed more layers of clothing or something. His parents had divorced when he was in middle school and his mom had chosen a very different path in life. She'd remarried, had another kid, and never looked back. She'd turned her back on all that she and his father had believed while they were married including him. When he and his dad had first been sent to Anvac, he would wander the fence perimeter expectantly searching the crowds and peoples on the other side of the fence for his mother's face. He knew he shouldn't search. Knew that each day he would be more and more disappointed. Just like when his parents were first divorced. He'd be all set to go to a movie with his mom and then she'd cancel at the last minute. Before things got really bad and a "new norm" was unleashed, she stopped calling altogether. His dad was all he had left. Had.

And now. Here he was holding his father's hand for the last time. Thinking about all the future tomorrows without his friend, his confidant. He whispered softly, "If I ever become a dad, I want to be just like you. Thanks for the memories." Nick gently replaced the arm, laying it across his father's chest, grabbing the other and putting them together. He bowed his head and said a prayer for the departed, indicating all the bodies surrounding him, thinking of all the kids who had lost a parent or parents that day, not just himself and Hazel. Zipping up the body bag slowly and pausing at his father's face, a tear escaped and landed on the grey cheek, the brief ceremony completed. Nick stood and handed a scrap of paper to Hazel. She was sitting by her parents facing him, eyes averted out of respect.

"What's this?" she asked gently taking it from him and unfolding it. *I hope someone finds this*—began the note in Nick's dad's scrawling handwriting—*They're going to drug us. The vac*…The note ended abruptly. "Where did you find this?" she handed it back to Nick.

"I searched my dad's pockets to see if there was anything I could take. A memento. Something to remember him by. I found that instead."

"What do you think he means by 'the vac'? What did they do to our parents?"

"I think 'the vac' might have been short for vaccine," Nick suggested, "I don't think he had time to finish his note. I think our parents might have been working on something or been test subjects or something or, or…"

"Or what?" she pressed. "We've never been vaccinated."

"Or they, whoever, found out that... That, that… I don't know," he stopped, frustrated. "We need to get to, to get…ugh, somewhere where they keep records of this stuff."

"Maybe one of the computers around here would have what we're looking for?"

"Maybe, but they're all password protected. Fat chance of finding a login and password. I guess we could start looking, but first I just need..."

He walked away wiping his eyes and sat against the wall, head buried in his hands.

Hazel sat eating another Snickers bar while she waited, eating slowly trying to concentrate on the flavors, but so numb, a part of her still disconnected from the reality of their situation, it was gone before she even tasted it. She watched Nick and waited. His dad was his whole life. Her parents had been hers. But somehow, for her, things had changed. Her parents had increasingly encouraged her obsession with books about living off the land and growing food. Her daydreams had taken on a new life of their own while waiting out the days in Anvac. Losing sight of the original dreams where she lived with her parents on a farm in the middle of nowhere revisiting them on occasion, her thoughts had ventured on ideas of what it would be like to go off alone. Her dad would feed her questions, "What would she do if…" She shuddered remembering one of the more recent ones:

"Okay, Hazel," her father started, "What would you do if something catastrophic happened that wiped out most of the people still remaining on earth? Another Great Wave that was greater. City or country?"

"Country," she'd said loving these games, they got her ideas flowing. An enthusiastic "Yes" was always the response. The country was definitely the right answer.

"Yes. Good," he smiled. "Now, what would happen if your mom and I were gone, too?"

She'd blinked at him. It was a question she'd asked herself before but had never heard her father articulate it. She'd paused, not wanting to seem too eager or reveal her recent daydreams, "Ummm, grab Nick and head to the country?"

"Sure," her dad had said encouragingly. "What else?"

"Or go off alone. Grab my Living on the Earth *book and figure things out as I went."*

"Yes! Never leave that book behind. I know it's a crazy old book, but it makes sense."

Hazel shivered and patted her bag. The book was there now. It dawned on her dad hadn't been playing, he had been trying to relay a message, get her prepared. For this. *He knew! He knew something was going to happen*. "Nick!" she exclaimed a little too loudly. His head popped up from his hands. "He knew! My dad knew! I bet my mom and your dad did, too." She walked over and explained the recent conversation with her dad. "I think he was preparing me. Of course, this doesn't make it easier…" she trailed off glancing at the body bags on the floor. Then continued, "But he knows we'll be okay and that's got to be worth something, right? Did your dad ever say anything?"

"No," he said, running through his memories. "Wait. Maybe he did. Just the other day he asked if I knew what caused the Great Wave and he asked me things about why he chose to come to Anvac and that if I really understood. I just gave a thumbs up. We've been over that a million times. Freedom. He was exercising his freedom," he paused. Then, getting up, "I don't know anything else about what my dad would have been doing here. He worked in factories all his life, so maybe it was the easiest lie he could tell and make it seem like the truth. He might have convinced your parents to say the same," He pondered this for a few, then gathered his energy. "If we're going to do this we should get started. I don't want to spend the night here. This place gives me the creeps and now it's a tomb. I don't want to be outside after dark either." He walked to the door of the lab and picked up his dropped backpack handing Hazel hers, turned one more time to look at the bodies behind the boxes. "Goodbye," Nick whispered and flipped the switch. He secured the door and turned his attention back to the lab.

"None of the computers in here are going to be much help," he surmised. "Maybe we should go to the other wing of the building. The other door was labeled *Offices*."

"Sure," Hazel agreed. Nick double-checked that they still had the ID card and made their way back through the main entrance. The sun was already waning. "What time is it?"

"Umm, let's see," he looked at the old analog clock on the wall, "four-thirty. Wow. I didn't realize we'd been here that long," Nick grimaced.

"Grieving takes time. It's okay," she felt a wave of sorrow wash over her like an electric rush. She shivered and continued walking.

"We need to hurry if we are going to find some other place to stay tonight," he determinedly swiped the ID, the green light flashed; the door unlocked. Once through, it was surprising to find that this section of the building was much smaller with only a few doors leading to offices. The lab, exam rooms, and the room with their parents must've taken up the lion share of the space. Nick tried the first door and found that it was locked.

"Well?"

"Let's just keep trying the doors. If we can't find one unlocked, then I will bust it down. Flex some muscle," he tried to make light. He continued trying doors as they walked down the hall. Finally, the door at the end of the hallway turned easily. "Ah-ha! It's the big kahuna's office. Nice." The gold placard reading *General Manager, The Virology Lab of North Pangea, City of Seattle, FPNP.*

As the door swung in, the lights were already on revealing a very large oak desk with what appeared to be carvings of gargoyles located at each corner facing whoever would have been unfortunate enough to sit across from them. Historically, gargoyles were meant to ward off evil spirits but seemed to embody evil themselves or at least in the context of this setting. The desktop was neat and tidy. There were no random stacks of paper lying about or memos of phone calls to return. There was a faint waft of Hugo Boss still in the air. *Strange.*

Nick immediately went for the computer and jiggled the mouse. The blank computer screen came to life. "Yes!" he exclaimed, pumping a fist in the air. "No login. Whoever was on this computer didn't logout." He sat in the plush leather chair to get started but jumped up again like his pants were on fire.

"What is it?" Hazel asked worriedly.

"The chair is still warm. See for yourself."

She walked over and moved her hand along the seat. Sure enough, it was still faintly warm. Hazel looked up in alarm. Nick took two long strides over to the door; closed and locked it. He flicked the switch of the automatic lights to turn them off. The only light came from the computer screen and the early evening sunlight streaming in through the slats of the office window shades.

"Someone was just here," he whispered, ducking down.

"Yes, but where is he, or she, now?" she whispered back. He shrugged, not able to come up with a good answer. In the distance a chop-chop-chop sound of rotary wings sliced through the air. They both crept to the window and looked out across the backside of the building. Through a gap between two skyscrapers about a block away the unmistakable body of a black helicopter was lifting into the air. As it ascended the helicopter veered to the right giving them a clear view of its broadside. Flashing in bold, gold letters "N.P." reflected sunlight in a blaze and then vanished as the aircraft made its turn and headed off in the distance.

"Do you think…" Hazel began.

"Yes," was the answer. "Our suspect just flew away." *We weren't the only ones to have survived whatever happened last night at precisely 7:30pm.*

CHAPTER 4

"Well, let's get started. The sooner we find anything the sooner we can get out of here," Nick laced his fingers and stretched them out in front of him, cracking several knuckles, rolling his head from side to side in a 'let's do this' type of warm-up. Hazel had seen him do this exaggerated maneuver many times before when starting research for different papers in school. He sat down and scooted the chair up to the computer. The little arrow on the screen went for documents first.

After some time of letting Nick do his thing, Hazel finally asked, "Well, anything?"

"Moving on to his corporate email account if I can get in that is. All I've found so far are a few documents related to the ID2040-Alliance initiative which is what landed us and our parents in Anvac to begin with. Oh, yeah, and this dude's name is Christopher MacPherson. A pretty hoity-toity name if you ask me. He has degrees in, let's see, biochemical engineering, computer engineering, and finance. This guy must have been in school forever."

The ID2040-Alliance—the bane of existence for all those who lived in Anvac—was a world-wide initiative to document and identify all citizens, the result of The Great Wave. The Great Wave originally started as a localized MERS outbreak in Iraq, but scientists quickly discovered that what they thought was a MERS outbreak was actually a deadlier strain of the same virus that began sweeping the continents. The original virus had mutated to a much more serious strain, with higher infectious rates easily passing from person-to-person, animal-to-person, and from person-to-animal. Scientists were afraid because this new strain was prolific, and like the original MERS virus, with no known vaccines or treatments. The death rate had skyrocketed from a 30-40% mortality rate to a 60-70% mortality rate. In the end it killed about 75 million people around the world before it was contained.

Before scientists and governments knew what they were really dealing with, outbreaks were occurring around the world. Sadly, it hadn't been contained quickly enough by curtailing the frequency of international travel. The World Health Organization worked fast and furious with the best scientists around the world to create a vaccine that would alleviate the onslaught of the disease. They worked around the clock on a vaccine while doctors on the frontlines sought treatments to help patients who were already sick. A majority of those in Anvac had gotten sick and survived on a combination of treatments and sheer luck. The vaccine had been fast-tracked and met with high levels of success. All bureaucratic red tape had been removed for the widespread release of the vaccine. But those in charge decided to attach strings; to use the crisis as a prime opportunity to roll out another behind-closed-doors-conspiracy-level initiative. World governments agreed that in order for citizens to get the life-saving vaccine, citizens had to agree to the ID2040 Alliance terms. These terms stipulated that each individual receiving the vaccine must also receive a BioID in the form of a very tiny tattoo placed in the middle of the forehead or on the right hand. These tattoos could then be scanned to access all information relating to that individual. Depending on the purpose of the scan (DMV versus grocery store), one quick zap could immediately access that person's personal identification number, vaccination and health records, education level, employment history, criminal records, and how much money they had in the bank.

The BioID was promoted as a convenient way to keep one's personal information and money safe, eliminating the need for ID cards, birth certificates, or bank cards. Identity thieves would (and did) become a part of history. People liked the idea of making hands-free transactions at stores and knowing whether or not a fellow citizen was vaccinated simply by looking at their forehead or hand. To the general public, there didn't seem to be any downsides to the use of this new technology. The governments unleashed very effective ad campaigns, promoting the new vaccine and the new BioID. It was offered for free, making promotion and acceptance that much easier. The Great Wave—the name given to the pandemic—had created so much fear that people signed up in droves no questions asked. The drive to live outweighed most individuals' skepticism and desire for privacy. People were willing to trade in their freedom for a vaccine. Those who were opposed to either the vaccine or the BioID, or both were eventually the one's shipped off to places like Anvac.

At first individuals and families still had a choice. They could do business by choosing to wear a mask and gloves while out in public, but much like mask shaming when The Great Wave washed over the world, ID shaming became very commonplace. Walking down the street people would furtively glance at another's forehead or right hand and if they didn't find the telltale three miniscule little dots, it was fair game to call them out. Eventually it was no big deal to physically harm someone who hadn't complied. Businesses started using scanners to determine whether a person was allowed in. The public sentiment demanded that businesses reject those who hadn't gotten the vaccine as a precaution and so, in a move to ease tensions, governments gave into the demands of its citizens and unilaterally agreed that those without a BioID were a threat.

Governments, cities, and municipalities issued laws that citizens must get the vaccine and the BioID or they would be forcibly contained under the guise of protecting civilization. Eventually, those without a BioID were not allowed to do any business and were forced into ghetto-like communities to keep them away from the general public. Fear having won out over common sense. It wasn't until later that unsealed documents revealed that the strain of MERS had been unleashed on the world, either accidentally or purposefully, and had been genetically modified in a virology lab, location undisclosed. But by then, it was too late to combat popular sentiment and most people agreed that regardless of how The Great Wave started, the outcome was beneficial. Those in Anvac were forced to stay.

"Where did you find the info?" Hazel asked.

"On his Resume. He keeps a copy on his desktop. Sorry, just thinking about the ID2040-Alliance stuff. Remember?"

"Yeah, I remember. All of my friends dropped me because I didn't sport three dots. It was like the latest fad. I tried drawing them on my hand once so they would think I had gotten one, but someone called me out because they weren't exactly in the right place. One girl grabbed my hand, spit on it and wiped the dots off. I was actually glad when we first moved to Anvac. I was tired of getting bullied.

"So, about this guy," she turned back to the screen, "Pretty powerful. Right?"

"Yeah, I mean, he was running the place."

"Anything else?"

"Not yet," Nick returned to the screen and double-clicked an email server icon. "Yes!" Nick exclaimed, "Luck is on our side. He didn't logout of his email account. We're on the right track now. If there's anything, it's gonna be here." He turned his attention back to the screen.

"He didn't even care about logging out," Hazel surmised. "He must've thought he was all alone here."

"Or he just didn't care," Nick quipped.

"Yeah, or that, too. Do *you* think he knew we were here?"

"Maybe. My guess is, yes, but he didn't think we were worth his time."

Hazel started looking around the rest of the office while she waited. There weren't many pictures. Only a couple featuring a mid-40s looking man with dark brown hair and a too white, too perfect smile teeth almost too big set in a lightly tanned face. The tilt of his chin revealing an arrogance she attributed to wealth and power. In one picture he is seated with some high-powered senators or diplomats. Hazel couldn't quite place them or remember their names. In the other this same guy was on a boat with a very attractive, younger-looking blonde with legs for days in a skimpy hot pink swimsuit. Hazel looked away. It was hard to picture anyone having fun just after saying goodbye to her parents. She decided to take the photo with the official-looking people, so she grabbed the frame and slid the photo out. She turned it over. There was an inscription on the back, *To Chris, Here's to more power than the Hoover Dam.* The names were listed in a different hand from left to right *Senator Donnelly, Amber Silverton (CEO of Apple), me, Cal.* Hazel put the photo inside her journal for safe keeping. The printer came to life behind her and spit out several sheets of paper.

"What did you find?" she asked grabbing the pages and skimming the subject heading.

"Read for yourself," Nick indicated the printout. "We need that for evidence."

"Evidence?" Hazel looked surprised and then started reading.

VACCINE UPDATE

From: Calvin Hastings <Calvin.hastings.fpnp@pcn.gov>

To: Christopher MacPherson <Christopher.macpherson.fpnp@pcn.gov>

Chris,

Congratulations are in order! Vaccine 526 has been an outstanding success. I almost can't believe how successful. Scary accurate. At any rate, the shutdown code was first used in Africa. That whole continent with maybe a few savages here and there is now completely free of any invasive species know as human. I think it would be fun once we get settled to do a little hunting, if you know what I mean.

Since we used the shutdown code, our scientists have verified that bodies are immediately petrified. They look okay—translucent, a little blue, stiff, kind of like marble. The only thing that kind of freaks me out is how the veins turn black. Makes everyone look like they're covered in black spider webs, but they won't rot or smell. Beautiful! I think your idea to let nature takes it course is a great one and that this petrification will keep the diseases and smell to a minimum. Like I said, genius.

So now that our trials are completed, we are ready to do the main shut off. I've gotten confirmation from PCN to hit the "kill" switch—aww, bad turn of phrase, ha ha—tonight at 10:30pm Eastern time. That means it's lights out for you at 7:30. So don't be out after dark is all I'm saying.

PCN has arranged for a helicopter to come give you a lift tomorrow at 4:30. That should give you time to wrap things up there. We don't need any loose ends so dispose of the plebes in the lab anyway you want, just make sure they end up somewhere where the smell won't be an issue. Also, please make sure there isn't anything to tie all this back to the BioID. PCN is pretty insistent that we cover our tracks. There may be future need to reinstitute a BioID. One can't be too careful. Anvac needs to be cleaned up as well. Our resources are at your fingertips. The overall goal is population reduction so keep that in mind. PCN has no qualms about how you complete this task. Just make sure no one's left to breed. That's the whole point.

We've hired Sweepers to start there in Seattle and find anyone still around. They can either decide to send them to Denver to work or to dispose of them however they see fit. They will start there and then make their way to Denver doing a sweep of any town they come to.

I look forward to seeing you tomorrow early evening. I've heard that Denver is really nice this time of year. You going to bring that beautiful blonde I met?

Remember, the world is our oyster.

Cal
President
Federation of the Peoples of North Pangea
Pangea Confederation of Nations

P.S. You might want to delete this email.

When she was finished, Hazel handed the email back staring hard at a worn spot on the floor. "Well?" Nick asked, folding the paper and put it in his backpack. He sat back down at the computer to keep searching.

"Why didn't he delete the email?" Hazel looked at him, puzzled.

"Maybe he got sloppy or was in a rush.... He obviously didn't check our parents. My dad still had the note in his pocket."

"Yeah, or he wanted us to find it," Hazel finished.

"I highly doubt that. I think he just got cocky is all."

"You realize we're alive because our parents refused to let us get the vaccine, right? They're dead because they didn't," she sat in an empty chair on the opposite side of the desk. "Do you think they knew? About the vaccine I mean."

"No. Probably not about the vaccine. But I'm guessing that they learned something about the BioID stuff while they were here. My dad didn't want to get it because he said it was an invasion of privacy. What I'm thinking is that something in the BioID was used alongside the vaccine as a way to essentially turn people off, like a light switch. The vaccine and the chip worked in tandem."

"Wait. Chip? I thought it was just a tattoo."

"The tattoo is meant for the scanners to access the chip. Underneath the tattoo is a virus-sized microchip. It's where they store the data and how they track movement. Everything else is backed up on ginormous servers in..."

"Where, Nick?"

"In Colorado. Denver to be more exact," he finished.

"That's where this Christopher MacPherson guy is going to meet this other guy Cal. Hey, wait," Hazel took out the picture she had put in her journal, flipped it over to show Nick the name and then back to the picture. *Cal.* He looked about the same age as Christopher, but with longish dirty blonde hair in a messy bun on top of his head, a short close-cropped beard, and a fading sunburn that left white creases at his eyes.

"Do you think our parents were planning something? To stop it?" Hazel asked. "I mean, my dad kept quizzing me about what I would do if…"

"Yeah, maybe, hopefully but if they knew, why didn't they say anything?"

Hazel shrugged, "Maybe they didn't want to worry us until they had a plan. Maybe they didn't know when things were going to happen and just ran out of time." It was pointless to conjecture since the people who might have helped shed light on things were no longer around. Nick turned back to the computer to check a few more places before calling it quits. From Hazel's side of the desk, she saw the light on Nick's face change as he clicked on different folders and tried to access different programs. His face was grim, "Just a few more things to check. K? A lot of these programs are password protected. We were lucky to get into the email." His eyes reverted back to the screen. "Here we go!" he exclaimed as he moved in for a closer look. "Check this out. I'm looking at the server and here's a file named *HLewis.* Do you think this is your dad's?"

Hazel got up and peered over his shoulder, "Probably not. His first name is Scott. It's just a coincidence," Nick double-clicked it on a hunch and a pop-up screen appeared.

He turned to Hazel, "What would your dad choose for a password?"

Hazel thought for a moment, "Ummm, freedom?" Nick typed the word into the box. It jiggled from side to side indicating the wrong password and 2 of 3 attempts left displayed in the upper right corner.

"What else?" he asked, fingers poised over the keys.

"Uh, try anvac." Another jiggle and 1 of 3 attempts left in the upper right corner.

"Think," Nick encouraged.

"Oh, um, try Freedom20 with a capital 'F.'" Nervously Nick entered the word. The login screen disappeared; three documents showed up in the folder. The first document was labeled *Dear H*. Nick double-clicked it and a short letter opened.

Dear Hazel,

Don't forget to feed the cat. The food is in the closet.

Dad

Nick turned and looked at Hazel. "You don't have a cat."

"No, but I know what he's getting at," she whispered. "We have to go back to Anvac."

"What? Why?"

"He hid something in the closet. That's what I think at any rate."

"Okay. Need me to print this?" She shook her head. Nick closed the document and then double-clicked the second document. It simply read *Denver*. He closed it and then opened the last document. *I love you. Do what's right*. Nick printed this one and handed it to Hazel. "His last words, Hazel, thought you might want a copy."

"Thanks," she said taking the paper. She added it to the photo in her journal. "We should probably get going. It's almost dark and we have to go back to Anvac before they do something to it." Nick's heart skipped a beat. *Sweepers*. With a sense of urgency, he nodded, dragging the *HLewis* file to the trash, and got up from the computer.

CHAPTER 5

Ash had started fluttering down in a sick kind of snowfall giving a greyish appearance to the landscape. The light was waning fast; Hazel and Nick walked quickly down the street making as little noise as possible. They were now deeply aware of the fact that they were not the only ones wandering the streets and wanted to remain undetected. Several times Nick thought he saw shadows walking across distant intersections.

There wasn't enough ash, yet, to leave much of a trace, but it was only a matter of time. Some of the buildings they passed were still blazing brightly. Nick gave a wide berth to these infernos knowing they could collapse anytime just like the Twin Towers did so many years ago. He had watched enough video footage in history class to understand the devastation a falling building could cause. *That was the last time this country was truly united*, he thought sadly. Wars, riots, and endless strife had taken its toll. Hazel followed Nick's lead, lost in her own thoughts and anxious to get back to Anvac. She needed to find whatever her father had left in the closet. She didn't want to think about next steps beyond getting to the apartment. She figured they would decide those later.

It took longer for them to get back to Anvac than anticipated. Nick was still determined not to spend the night there, so he encouraged Hazel to be quick. He had spotted a relatively nice hotel not too far from Anvac that looked promising. At this point he didn't care that they wouldn't get there until after dark. It was probably a better idea to walk after sunset anyway.

They reached the wide-open front gates of Anvac about an hour after dark. Nick and Hazel stepped through on high alert watching for anything out of the ordinary or at least nothing more suspicious than frozen people. Nick looked into the two guard shacks. Both guards were pale, marble-like statues. He speculated that a brave kid had found the gate keys and opened the gates. There weren't any kids around that they could see. Anvac looked like the rest of the city—empty. When they reached Hazel's apartment, they noticed the door hanging by one hinge. Nick stuck his arm out to block Hazel from entering, making a motion for her to wait. He wandered through both rooms looking for signs of life and finding none, let Hazel enter.

"Who do you think was here?" she asked.

"Maybe some kids looking for stuff," he tried to be reassuring, but by the looks of things whoever had been here wasn't just looking for rations. Papers were scattered throughout the rooms, furniture moved, broken lamps on their sides, the couch cushions had been slashed and the stuffing ripped out haphazardly, clothing was strewn about and both beds had been thoroughly destroyed.

"Let's just hope they didn't find what they were looking for," Hazel said as she picked her way across the room to the closet. The closet door had been completely ripped off its hinges and was lying on its side next her parents' bed. She started looking through the closet's contents and found a bag of cat food that had been knocked over, some kibble spilling onto the floor. She laughed, "It really is cat food! I wonder where my dad found it." Turning the bag upside down, she dumped the rest of the food onto the floor, sitting now on top was a sandwich-sized Ziplock baggie the contents obscured by the grease from the food, "It's like finding the prize in the cereal box. My dad even made this part kind of fun." She smiled sadly and dumped the contents on the kitchen table, washing her hands before sorting through the small pile of items. Hazel systematically examined the small cache. One silver PNY 512GB USB 3.0 flash drive and ten 1-ounce Gold American Eagle coins still in white cardboard packaging with clear cellophane windows on each side.

Hazel picked up the flash drive and held it out to Nick, "Any idea what might be on this?"

"Nope, but I'm hoping it has some answers. Five hundred and twelve gigabytes is a lot of storage," he said taking the flash drive from her. What me to hang onto this?" He asked. She concurred and he buried it deep in his pocket. "We need to find a computer and soon."

Hazel looked up, "Why soon?"

"I mean, other than wanting answers? Well, because I don't think the power is going to be on much longer."

"Why do you say that?"

"Well, think about it, the government of whatever Pangea just wiped out most of humanity. There won't be anyone to maintain the grid."

"Oh, I didn't think about that. Good point. How long do you think we have? I mean, before the power goes out?"

"I think we'd be pushing our luck if it lasted more than a couple of days. We should check my place, grab anything else we might want and get out of here. I feel like a hot meal and a hot shower before bed. You?"

"Sounds like a good plan." She put the gold coins inside an inner pocket of her backpack, looked once more around the disheveled apartment. Who would ransack it? What were they looking for? Hazel noticed a family photo on the kitchen counter and grabbed it. "I almost forgot this," she said tracing her fingers along her parents' faces. It was one of their last family photos taken in Maui just before the plague hit. They were all in their bathing suits, hamming it up on the beach. Palm trees, sand, and the beautiful ocean behind them. She remembered being embarrassed when her dad asked a random stranger to take their picture. She added this to her growing collection in her journal.

Nick's apartment looked similar to hers. Maybe he was right about kids just looking for stuff. He grabbed a couple of photos of he and his dad. His favorite photo of his dad was when he was young. He'd been a hitchhiking hippie back in the day. He was turned to the side to show off his giant backpack, grinning at the camera with a long mustache and long brown hair under a leather pageboy hat. Nick donned this hat now, putting his trucker hat in his backpack, looking very much like his father in the picture at almost the same age. He smiled and recited in his best Bilbo voice the famous line from *The Fellowship of the Ring*, "'It's a dangerous business, Frodo, going out your door. You step onto the road, and if you don't keep your feet, there's no knowing where you might be swept off to.'" And with that, he turned and closed the door to his apartment for the last time.

"Alright hobbit," Hazel chuckled looking up at him, "Let's get to that hotel you were thinking of." She smiled and tugged at his sleeve.

Nick half skipped, half ran, down the street as they neared the gates. They were officially leaving Anvac! The ash was still falling, casting the city in a wintery dirty snow covering; the smoke was thick making breathing more painful. "I'm dreaming of a whi..greeyyy Christmas," he sang arms overhead and spinning like a little kid in winter's first snow. He was walking backwards watching Hazel get covered in the stuff and suddenly stopped singing and grabbed Hazel pulling her to the sidewalk. He pointed back the way they had come. Several ghostly apparitions at the gates of Anvac were barely visible in the smoke. As Nick and Hazel watched, they heard the metallic clang of the gate shutting. The figures hopped into a large black SUV that was already covered in a fine layer of ash and started to make tracks headed toward Nick and Hazel.

"What are they doing?" Hazel whispered, then quickly ducked down as the headlights flicked on illuminating the street, the beams turning a reddish yellow through the haze. The SUV was picking up speed. Luckily, Nick and Hazel were standing next to a large black dumpster and were partially screened from view. They slid in behind it just as the vehicle passed them. Nick scrutinized the vehicle trying to ascertain who these people were. The windows had dark tint, so it was impossible to see who was driving. He noticed a white government-issued license plate and committed the number to memory: 767 PNG.

"Sweepers," he whispered.

"You sure?"

"Yeah, pretty sure."

"We should probably get to our hotel as soon as we can," Hazel said as she extracted herself from their hiding place. "Do you think they saw us?"

"No, otherwise they would have stopped," Nick responded still clutching Hazel's arm. They started walking again, the ash dampened the sound of their feet on the road, but left footprints now that the ash had accumulated. "Can't sneak away like this," Nick commented.

"Do you think we should wipe out our footprints?"

"Naw. Too hard, we'd just leave a smeared path instead of footprints. Whoever they were, they're gone now. I haven't seen a single living person other than you and them" he pointed the direction the SUV had gone.

"And the guy in the helicopter," she reminded him.

And the shadows in the ash, he thought, then said, "Try not to worry. The bigwig has already left town. The Sweepers were probably just locking up the gates to keep us in until they round up anyone else out here." As he said this an earsplitting rumble ripped through the stillness followed by a dark grey cloud mushrooming over Anvac. They both ducked in automatic response. Hazel turned around to look, then squinted back at Nick. He was watching from between his forearms, "Or they're just going to blow everything up and move on down the road. I don't think Anvac exists anymore." Their clothes and hair rustled as the wave of heat whooshed over them, swirls of ash enveloping them for a few moments. "Let's walk quicker while the ash is moving. It will hide our footprints better," Nick grabbed Hazel's hand as they jogged toward the hotel.

"I guess we just need to hope that they won't come back this direction looking for survivors," Nick said as he opened a gold-gilt framed door with the words *Royalton Hotel* scrawled across them. "Here we are," he made a sweeping gesture. "Welcome to the poshest hotel on this side of Seattle." They entered the lobby. It was cool and the air was fresher. There were little table lamps set between oversized dark brown leather armchairs scattered throughout the lobby. Some of them were occupied by more frozen people. Unfinished cocktails still sitting on the small tables. One drink was permanently grasped in an older gentleman's hand. His petrification had been so quick that he hadn't even dropped his drink, his dark navy suit jacket was open revealing a crisp white button-down dress shirt with one little light golden stain from his whiskey. His light and dark blue striped necktie draped neatly across the armchair. The mouth was slightly opened as if he were in the middle of saying something to his partner—another gentleman frozen in time, a shot glass at his lips. Vacant eyes staring past his companion and across the lobby.

"This is kind of creepy," said Hazel as she took in the few patrons scattered around the lobby. "We aren't sleeping down here, are we?"

"Of course not," Nick reassured her. "I wouldn't bring the only girl I know to the nicest hotel within walking distance and not get a nice room for her to stay in."

"Two rooms, right?" Hazel raised her eyebrows. "Two rooms. One for you and one for me."

"Yes, I hadn't gotten that far," Nick blushed. "You're my best friend. It wouldn't be very smooth to make any moves, yet," he grinned with a slight chuckle. "I mean, seriously, our parents, Anvac, these people," he indicated the room. "I'll make sure we have adjoining rooms, if that's okay," he finished.

He then asked, "Do you have a preference for which floor?"

"Second," she said. "I don't want to be too high up. If the power dies, I don't want to have to go down that many steps."

"Agreed."

"But first, I'm hungry. And want a shower."

"Good idea. Second floor rooms coming right up. I will consult with the general manager here and see what he has available." The lobby desk took up almost the full length of the wall opposite the entrance; the hotel name emblazoned across the front in large swirling gold letters. The ledge of the desk was shoulder-high with a smooth black quartz top. Hazel rested her hands on the cool surface. She could see glints of sparkles that caught in the light as she moved. Nick walked behind the desk. The manager was still standing at the desk, head cocked as if he were intently listening to instructions. "Ah, good," she heard Nick say, "Our good friend, the manager, here, says there's no problem with getting adjoining rooms on the floor of our choosing. He's directed us to the stairwell on our far left," Nick stood, indicating a door holding a master keycard in his right hand, "and now we may take showers and find something to eat before retiring for the evening." Hazel loved it when he was in these moods. He was funny and unassuming. She knew he was covering up his hurt, but it was the preferred until they could each be alone to process the day.

"And here we are, madam, room 206 connected by one door to room 208 where yours truly will be spending the night," Nick led Hazel into the room crossing to the window and drawing the blackout curtains to keep the light from escaping and then used the door between the rooms to let himself in next door. "Want me to close the door?"

"Maybe while we take showers. We can leave them open tonight if we want. Let's get ready for dinner. I'm starving."

"I'll race you to the kitchen," and with that, Nick closed the door.

Hazel stood under the shower in steaming hot water for a long time; sure, she was hungry, but the luxury of not running out of hot water *and* getting to stay in as long as she wanted was something she was going to enjoy while she could. Hazel eventually got out and used one of the very heavy, plush hotel towels to dry herself off. *Maybe I should take a set of these before we leave*, she thought. She wrapped her hair up in another towel and dressed in a clean pair of jeans and t-shirt. Then, before going down to join Nick for dinner, she scrubbed her ash-covered clothes in the sink and then hung them up to dry. She slid into a pair of thick white terry cloth hotel slippers with *RH* embroidered on the tip of each toe in gold thread, wrapped herself in an equally lush robe for extra warmth and then shuffled down to the first floor to find the kitchen.

Hazel found the kitchen through a side door next to the lobby desk. Nick had already found his way there and turned from the fridge to look at her, waving a drumstick in her general direction his mouth full of something he'd already found. He turned back to the task at hand and eventually dropped his treasures on the counter—a half-empty milk jug, more fried chicken, eggs, bacon, cottage cheese, and baked beans. Once unloaded, Nick turned his attention to searching the pantry for anything else that might tickle his taste buds.

"What exactly *are* you having for dinner?" Hazel laughed as Nick procured a chocolate cake from the pantry.

"A buffet. Smorgasbord. Anything and everything!" he moved to the next pantry in his excitement. "Do you know how long it's been since I've eaten good food? I mean, *good* food with enough to fill me up?"

"About as long as it's been for me," Hazel teased now seeing what else Nick had overlooked in the fridge, extracting a carton of orange juice, a sliced honey-glazed ham, and a block of cheddar cheese. She put these on the counter next to the foods Nick was still piling up. Looking in the pantry, Hazel found an unopened box of Life and decided she would take that for later. She started making a pile of foods to take and foods to eat for dinner. In the foods to take pile she added several boxes of instant oatmeal packets, beef jerky, and trail mix. For dinner she added a loaf of fresh dark rye bread setting a container of real butter next to it. She found a toaster in a cabinet and cut generous slices of the rye bread, popping them in. The coils glowed orange, Hazel rubbed her hands above the toaster to warm them, then bent down to inhale the rich scent of the toasting bread. While she waited on the bread, Hazel cut several large slices of cheese from the block and added several slices of ham. She heard the toaster ding and grabbed the bread spreading generous amounts of butter over each surface. Then sat down to join Nick in the biggest meal they'd eaten since moving to Anvac.

"That's all you're having?" Nick asked, scrutinizing her selections around bites of chicken.

"Phsaw! This is only the *first* course. I plan on overeating and then rolling into bed to sleep off the first well-earned food coma I've had since I quit going to school," she laughed, taking a large bite of bread.

"Okay. Phew! I thought I was going to be the only one to eat like a pig tonight," he said taking a large bite of chocolate cake. "Oh, man," he swooned, "This is sooooo good." He crammed the rest of the slice into his mouth. He dispensed with etiquette and, using his fork, dived into the rest of the cake. "Hope you didn't want any of this."

"I got my own. Thanks," Hazel said pointing with her fork to another chocolate cake.

"You better hurry up or I might just help myself to some of that, too."

"Try it, buddy," she narrowed her eyes. "I have the fastest fork in the west. Just ask my friend Sam who tried to eat off of my plate once. I left four neat puncture marks in his hand."

"I'll remember that the next time I decide to help myself," he backed away from her cake in mock horror. They both laughed and continued to eat in silence.

After a half hour they had eaten just about as much as they could handle. Hazel decided to take some provisions to her room for a midnight snack which was to include about three-quarters of the chocolate cake. She would pick up the to-go foods on their way out whenever they chose to actually leave. Nick gathered a few foods for his midnight snack. They stacked the dishes in the large dishwasher and headed back to their rooms. They made their way through the motionless, dark lobby avoiding looking too long at the few patrons frozen in time.

Once back in his room, Nick cracked the door separating his room from Hazel's. He needed some privacy and time to think. Falling back onto the down comforter, sinking a couple inches into the soft thickness, he lay still as the wave of grief descended on him. It was a palpable heaviness that pinned him in place. The tears started and he knew this was a hurt he would carry with him for the rest of his life. He knew it wouldn't feel this sharp and painful forever, but he would never be able to fill the hole his father's death had left.

He lay flat on his back for what seemed like hours, but when he wiped a fresh onslaught of tears from his eyes, he was surprised to see the little alarm clock read just after 10pm. The red numbers blurred as saltwater obscured his vision again. His mind took him back to the day when he was six years old. His dad was teaching him to ride a bike, the training wheels newly removed. He smiled remembering how scared he was and how much he wobbled. How his dad—daddy—held onto the seat, hand gently on his back for reassurance, running just behind him. Nick pedaled faster. Without noticing, his dad had let go. Nick remembered the moment he realized his father's hand was no longer guiding him. He'd looked behind him, his father smiling and yelling, "Don't look back! Look forward! You got this!" Nick had turned his head in time to avoid running onto the sidewalk. He'd swerved at the right moment and continued down the street. The wind whistling past his ears, the rush of excitement and the exhilarating first taste of freedom.

He said aloud to the darkness repeating his father's words, "Don't look back. Look forward. You got this." Then, "But, Daddy, do I? Do I got this?" He rolled over, released gulping sobs, into the pillow. With these final thoughts, Nick drifted off into a restless sleep, spending the next few hours dreaming—his brain attempting to make sense of the world around it.

Hazel was undergoing a similar experience in the other room. She was curled up in a tight ball on the right side of the bed, the side closest to the window. She watched the outside world, smoke ghost-like filling the quiet streets, as tears wended their way past her nose across her cheeks landing without much ado on the bunched-up pillow. What were her parents working on? What's on the flash drive? *Why didn't dad tell me what was happening? I could have prepared better.* And somewhere a thought came to her in her father's voice *Because if you knew ahead of time you would have tried to stop us and risked your own life. We didn't tell you to keep you safe.* She sighed. It was probably true and now it was time to take things into her own hands, show her parents that she was well prepared. To honor their memory by achieving her own success, whatever form it took. Hazel remembered the book she had grabbed first thing that morning *Living on the Earth.* For how long? Until the Sweepers find them? Until they could make whoever did this pay? It was probably a dangerous undertaking at a minimum and could cost them their lives at a maximum. But who cares? Right? Everyone they cared about was dead. *That's not true*, she thought, *Nick is sleeping in the next room. I care about him and there will possibly be others.* A small, sad smile flitted across her face as she drifted peacefully off to sleep. She did not dream.

CHAPTER 6

The sun was shining directly in Hazel's face as she languidly stretched and squinted through her dark eyelashes at the light. She stretched more as she rolled to her back and looked at the ceiling gathering her thoughts. For a moment she forgot where she was, but as sleep gave way to wakefulness the pieces started fitting together as she remembered where she was and how she had ended up in this very comfy bed. Reluctantly, Hazel pulled herself to from between the warm sheets and decided to take another luxuriously hot shower before breakfast.

Hazel walked into the kitchen, hair still wet, to find Nick already eating breakfast and working on a laptop. "Where'd you get that?" she asked eyeing the computer.

"Oh, this old thing?" he greeted her drawing out the words. "I've had it for years. Just kidding. I used my managerial privileges to search rooms for it. I found a couple others, but they were all password protected. This was the first one I found that didn't need one. I made sure it had a charger, too. I'm keeping it plugged in as long as I can."

"Smart," Hazel affirmed grabbing a bowl from the shelf and helping herself to a generous serving of Corn Flakes. She found a banana to add to the mix. Nick had made coffee and she filled the nearest mug, taking in the aromatic scents of the perfectly brewed dark roast. She sat down to eat and asked Nick what he was working on.

"The flash drive," he said, pouring himself another cup. "There is so much on this drive. It was almost completely full. Lots of background information on the ID2040-Alliance program and the BioIDs. Your dad also added some information on the vaccine and how it was created. He includes all the science behind it. A lot of it I don't really understand, though. I am definitely not up on my scientific jargon. There are scans of the scientists' notes, too, but the handwriting is hard to decipher. What I'm trying to figure out is how they were able to turn everyone into marble. And how our parents fit into all of it. Were they working for this MacPherson guy or were they test subjects? I *hate* that idea," he stopped, shivered and sipped his coffee. His eyebrows knit together in a moment of anger picturing their parents at the lab. He continued, "Just the idea that they were being used somehow gives me the creeps. There are some other files, but I haven't gotten to them. The names are all numbers, like 18.02-19.01. Maybe call numbers or something. I haven't looked at them yet. I also went online. The Wi-Fi is still working here so I thought I would check some news sources."

"Oh? Find anything? Any idea what's going on? How widespread?" Hazel jumped at the idea. Any form of news would be welcome.

"No. No updates on what's actually going on out there, but on one site—one where they used to keep track of all sorts of numbers including the population and the national debt—I checked it on a hunch. I remember the last number on each of those always moved faster than the eye, like a slot machine that kept spinning to infinity. Well, today there was only one number and it wasn't moving," he pulled it up spinning the laptop to show her. "10,500,000."

"What does that mean? It doesn't say what it's referencing."

"I'm not exactly sure, but..." he trailed off.

"But what?" she pursued.

"Well, by the look of things, that might be about how many people are left."

"Where? In the U.S.? I mean North Pangea."

"No. In the world," Nick scanned Hazel's face to see the effect of this statement. She stared at the far wall digesting this bit of information. He turned back to the computer screen, "That would be my guess. The Great Wave killed about 75 million people and by the look of things, that was nothing compared to what we've seen so far."

"You're serious, aren't you," Hazel stared at him, the gravity of the situation finally taking full effect. "But this might be just Seattle," she tried to sound upbeat.

"Doubtful. The email talked about Africa. Remember?"

She indicated she did.

"Sorry. I didn't mean to ruin your breakfast," he referenced the spoon that hung midway between bowl and mouth in Hazel's hand.

She put the spoon down, "I think you're right. So, who's left besides us who don't have a BioID?"

"No one. Or maybe a few who are useful. The way that Cal guy was talking in the email, I wouldn't be surprised if this kill switch only left certain types of people alive and a certain number. And those who didn't have the BioID. Don't forget about the Sweepers. They were hired to do a very specific 'clean-up' job across the country. Whoever's in charge thought things out."

"Have you checked any of the underground sites, like those run by other antivaxxers? What about them?"

"I did and they're all offline. A lot of those were taken down when we were forced into the Antivax corridors. Hazel," he continued, "We have to do something."

"What do you mean?"

"I mean, we have to do something to stop it."

"Stop what? Whatever it is has already been done."

"Well, then maybe..." he sighed, "I don't know. Maybe find those responsible and hold them accountable for their actions."

"How are two teenagers going to stop a one-world government?"

"I don't know. That is a great question, but maybe it's just a matter of getting some answers or doing *something*. Like, what did they do to our parents? Why did they eliminate almost the entire world population?"

"I know what you mean. We don't know, yet, if that number is about the population, but if it is, I know why they did it. We don't need to find someone to tell us that," Hazel ate a soggy bite of cereal, swallowed, then continued, "It's for the environment. My dad told me about the Georgia Guidestones and how it sets the world population at a certain limit."

"The Georgia Guidestones?"

"Yeah, these weird Stonehenge-type stones in Georgia. No one knows who put them there, but in the languages of the world it talks about the need for balance and to maintain a certain population. Maybe there's something on the flash drive my dad put there for us. There are ten guidelines. The first one is about keeping the population under 500 million to make sure it's in balance with nature. Another one addressed reproduction and how it should," she paused and looked up, searching for a phrase, then, "and I quote, 'guide reproduction wisely—improving fitness and diversity' whatever that means. The rest of the guides talk about government and unity."

"So, you solved one part of the equation..."

"Oh!" interjected Hazel, "and the last guide quoting again," she cleared her throat and held her right arm up, index finger pointed to the ceiling, "'Be not a cancer on Earth—leave room for nature—leave room for nature.' So weird."

"What's weirder is that you can quote them," Nick looked at Hazel with incredulity.

She shrugged, "One of my friends in school was memorizing them and I helped her study. It came in handy since my dad used to talk about them, too. Plus, it's awesome conspiracy theory stuff and it just kind of sticks with me. You know?"

Nick chuckled, "Okay you weirdo, but we need answers about the other stuff, too. What did they do to our parents? What are they planning next?"

"You don't think they're done?"

"Not in the least. Now that they—whoever *they* are—" he added air quotes around the word—

"Pangean Government."

"Yeah, them. Whoever the bigwigs are, I'm pretty sure this might've been only a phase one or two. How are they going to control those they didn't off?" He looked hard at her.

"That's a good point. And what were our parents doing in the lab?" Hazel added.

"And can we make those who killed the world pay for their crimes?" he let the question hang in the air.

"Revenge?"

"No, justice."

Hazel bobbed her head in slow agreement, then peered over his shoulder in the direction of the lobby. She whispered, "Did you hear that?" she set her spoon down and slowly got off the stool. Nick closed the laptop, slipping the flash drive in his pocket, having heard something, too. Again, a noise from the lobby put them on alert. It sounded like someone bumping into a side table and jarring a lamp, which they could see wobbling. Something hit the floor and rolled.

Nick got to the kitchen door and slowly swung it out, "Hello? Hello? We can hear you. Come out, we're armed." He lied.

"Uh, hello?" said an unfamiliar voice. "Coming out with my hands up. Please don't shoot." And from one of the dark brown chairs a tall boy with shock red hair stood up. Beside him a younger girl, tall with long hair, the same bright red, also stood up. Both turned to face Nick.

"Uh…you can put your hands down," Nick said apologetically, at once realizing these were kids. "I…I don't have a gun or anything. I just said that in case…uh…in case…"

"No worries," the stranger chuckled nervously his voice giving a small crack on the last word, lowering his arms slightly, "I understand. Would've done the same thing," he seemed embarrassed, dropping his head sheepishly and running a shaky hand through his short red hair making it stand up in even crazier tufts.

"I'm Nick. Webber," Nick said, "and this is Hazel Lewis," he pointed at her. "We're from Anvac. What're your names? Where are you from?"

"I'm…I'm Henry Durante and this…this is Alice," the boy indicated the girl. "She's my sister. We slept in the lobby last night. I couldn't find a key to any of the rooms. We didn't know anyone was here," he finished quickly.

"I smelled the coffee," Alice said shyly and looked at her brother.

"Come in!" Hazel beckoned in a friendly manner. Now that she saw them, she wasn't at all intimidated by them. Henry and Alice hesitantly approached the kitchen, but relaxed once they were in the light and could see that Hazel and Nick were not much older. Hazel grabbed two mugs and poured each of them a cup. "Cream or sugar?" she asked.

"Not for me, thanks," Henry replied. "Ahhh," he inhaled taking the cup from her, "I needed some caffeine." Alice shook her head 'no' to cream and sugar, too. They all sat down not quite knowing what to do with themselves.

"Ummm, want some cereal?" Nick prodded. "Anything? We just kind of helped ourselves last night and this morning. You can have whatever you want."

Alice decided she was hungry enough to overcome her shyness and, in the awkwardness of the situation, she found a large skillet and threw some slices of bacon in. Then found another skillet and began cracking eggs into it. She deftly added just the right amount of milk and stirred in some cheese. It wasn't long before the smell of frying bacon permeated the entire kitchen. Alice pulled four plates from a shelf and offered bacon and scrambled eggs to each of them in turn.

"Wow!" Hazel said. "Thank you! It's been a long time since I've had bacon and scrambled eggs." She took a big bite of eggs. "These are perfect!" she exclaimed, her taste buds reveling in the flavors.

Alice looked embarrassed, then said, "Well, I like to cook, and bacon and eggs are pretty easy. Helps me relax."

"It's how she tries to compensate for being so quiet," Henry added.

"We'll keep her," Nick joked. "So," he continued, "how old are you guys?"

"I'm 16. I'll be 17 in three weeks," Henry puffed with pride.

"I'm 16," said Hazel encouragingly. "But I won't be 17 for a couple of months."

"I just turned 15," said Alice, taking another bite of scrambled eggs.

"I'm 17 and will be 18 in two months," Nick added, asserting his position as the oldest of the group.

"So," started Henry, green eyes skipping from Nick to Hazel back to Nick, "how are you guys still alive?"

"We're antivaxxers," Nick stated. "Until yesterday we were cooped up in Anvac—the ghetto they forced us into."

"I've heard of it. I walked the perimeter once. I was going to write a paper on how Anvac was like the ghettos during World War II. But my teacher axed the topic. 'Too controversial' she told me," he rolled his eyes.

"What about you two?" Hazel scrutinized their foreheads and right hands. She noticed that Alice and Henry both had three perfect little dots in the middle of their foreheads. "You have the BioID," she frowned in confusion. "How…why…," she paused trying to articulate her thoughts. "How are you not dead?" she finished.

"Oh, yeah. That," Henry raised his hand to his forehead.

"Yeah that," Nick was catching on. "How do you have a BioID and are still breathing?"

"Um, well…," Henry hesitated.

"You should just tell them the truth, Henry," Alice said.

"Okay, so," Henry began slowly. "Our mom was an antivaxxer, too." Hazel and Nick exchanged puzzled looks. Henry continued, "And she didn't want the BioID. She didn't trust it. Mom was dating some sort of conspiracy theorist nut who said we shouldn't get the vaccine or the BioID either and since you couldn't do life without it, we were kind of up a creek, if you know what I mean."

"Yeah, he was right," Nick interrupted. Henry looked at him for an explanation. "We went to a virology lab yesterday looking for our parents because they didn't come home the night before. We found information that corroborates what your mom's boyfriend was thinking. The vaccine and the BioID were used as a way to shut people off. Just end their lives."

"You mean, all the bluish-purple super pale people with black veins?" Alice asked, her cornflower blue eyes narrowing in scrutiny.

"Exactly," Nick continued, "Somehow this dude named Christopher MacPherson was able to use the vaccine to, I don't know, maybe spread something throughout a person's body so it would allow them to be turned off…like a light switch…"

"Or used as an excuse to make everyone get a BioID," Hazel interjected.

"Like a replicating deadly virus!" Henry blurted out not catching Hazel's words.

"Well, yeah, maybe something like that. We're not quite sure," Nick went on.

"I love science mysteries like this! It would've had to been throughout the whole body. The petrifying process had to be universal in the body for it to work," Henry talked with his arms animatedly, emphasizing his words cutting Nick off again.

"Yes, well, *anyway*," Nick spoke louder, and Henry returned his attention to what was being said. "Well, anyway, somehow this vaccine either worked with the BioID as a kill switch or the vaccine was maybe just a way to get everyone to get the BioID. We still have some digging to do. Either way, the BioID was used to kill everyone who had it. They made it work so that it petrified the bodies so there wouldn't be any decay. I think that was smart, I mean, of course I don't like what they did, but we at least don't have to deal with the smell or the diseases that decaying bodies cause." He continued, "Then last night as we were leaving Anvac some guys showed up…"

"Sweepers," Hazel input.

"Yeah, Sweepers. And the next thing we knew the whole place blew up," Nick finished.

Henry looked surprised for a moment, "Sweepers!?! I think we maybe saw them last night. Big black SUV dark tinted windows? Government plates? Shady looking characters?" The more excited he got, the faster he talked.

"Yes. Yes. And yes," Hazel concurred.

"We need to find these guys and wipe them out!" he said excitedly. "I always wanted to go on an adventure."

"Slow down there, cowboy," Alice teased. "We don't even know who they are, where they are, or how many of them are out there."

"You're just talking about the Sweepers anyway," Hazel responded. "The ones we really need to go after are the ones who did this to begin with. Sweepers are just the cleanup crew. It's like getting the street dealer without getting the big guy higher up the food chain. The big guys are in Denver. All the world elite or at least those in North Pangea. There's probably too many to take on by ourselves," Hazel said. Then turned to Nick, "Show them the website. It's the only thing he could find online." Nick pulled the strange number up on the computer again and turned it to show Henry and Alice.

"Population reduction," Henry stated matter-of-factly shaking his head from side-to-side, left hand cupping his chin. "Denver, huh?"

"Henry," Alice stopped him, "tell them about our IDs." She sighed trying to get him back on track. It was obvious she was used to Henry's rabbit holes. "We can figure the rest of this stuff out later."

"Oh yeah," he picked up the story again, "Well, I guess mom's boyfriend was righter than Alice or I thought. So, anyway, our mom's solution to the issue was to get fake BioIDs," Henry reached up to his forehead and picked at an invisible edge with his fingernail. He found what he was looking for and peeled off the three little dots. In his hand was a sheer piece of silicon with three little dots perfectly placed in the middle. Henry held it out to Nick.

"Woah, this is good," Nick examined the silicon. He handed it gently back to Henry who replaced it, the silicon edges seamlessly disappearing again at the temples and into the hairline. "Who did this? Does it work? I mean, does it bypass the scanners?"

"Yeah, it bypasses the scanners. Our mom found a really good, *very* expensive computer hacker to create them for us. One for me, one for Alice, and one for her. Mom actually had to sell the house. But it was worth it; they work. This hacker, BioDie, that's his street handle, made them for us. Personally, I would have thought of something a little cooler for a secret identity if I could make technology like that, but whatever," he paused in mid-thought, snapped back to attention, "So, anyway the reason he's astronomically expensive is because, not only does he create the look alike, but he also creates fake files that pull up our names and information whenever it's scanned. Quite ingenious if you ask me. My mom asked BioDie to actually create our files using fake names, too, just in case we were on the records somewhere listed as antivaxxers, but he assured us that the new files overrode any information the government currently had on hand. Plus, the added expense would mean only one of us would have been able to get it. So, my mom trusted him and had him make one for each of us. But now I think my mom must've gotten the real deal because we found her yesterday morning the same as the others," he shuddered.

"Why would your mom get the real BioID and not tell you?" Hazel asked.

"Because I think she ran out of money," Alice said between sips of coffee. She was quiet and her eyes sparkled in the light.

"I think our mom ran out of money because she used some of it to pay for her boyfriend's fake ID and when it came to hers, she didn't have enough to cover it," Henry explained. "Our mom was always trying to take care of everyone else, but forgot to take care of herself," he pointed to his forehead, "her *boyfriend*..."

"Ralph," Alice interjected.

"Yes, Ralph," he said the name like a curse word, "was a freeloader. He was manipulative and preyed on our mom's fears if you know what I mean. So now Ralph is running around out there free as a bird. Our mom is dead and here we are," he finished.

"The only good thing about Ralph is that it turns out he was right after all. I just thought he was some sort of rightwing nut. I was mad at my mom for listening to him," Alice surmised. She sarcastically added to his memory, "Thanks, Ralph."

"Hey," Nick piped up, "Do you think this hacker is still here?"

"Yeah, pretty sure," Henry uttered.

Nick looked at Hazel, "Maybe we should get fake ones, too, just in case. I mean, we might need them when we get to Denver."

"Yes!" Henry jumped up excitedly.

"Wait a minute. We haven't decided that we're actually going," Alice said with a tinge of panic. "I mean, it's a possibility," she hastily added when she saw looks of disappointment on the others' faces. "Well, I do think maybe we should go. Eventually. I'd like to at least confront the people who did this. For answers if nothing else."

"Well, I mean, what else do we have to do?" Nick questioned.

"Ummm, let's see. Avoid Sweepers. Stay alive. Find a new place to live. They could all be viable options," Alice methodically ticked off on her fingers.

"Or we could get the bastards first and then find a place to live," Henry said from the other side of the counter, green eyes glinting over the rim of his coffee cup, excited at the prospect.

"I'm with Henry," Nick gave him a thumbs up. "We have to do something about our parents. It'd be easy to let it go, but how long before they come rounding us up?"

Alice caved, "Sounds like all your minds are made up already. But we have to be smart about this and I think you're right. If we're going to go to Denver, we need to be prepared. They may use scanners to let people into the city. But where are we going to come up with the money to pay this time?"

"Well, money seems to be obsolete right now, so maybe we just see what he wants instead. As long as it's a reasonable demand we may be in luck," Nick suggested.

They decided not to waste more time at the hotel. Hazel and Nick packed as much food as they could carry, one towel each, and cushy slippers—a lightweight luxury they didn't want to leave behind. Nick held onto the computer. Henry and Alice also had backpacks to which they added more food, towels, and slippers, too. They would wait to delve into the rest of the files on the flash drive after they located BioDie. With the possibility of losing power looming, Nick had decided it would be wise to get their fake IDs made before the lights went permanently out.

CHAPTER 7

With backpacks loaded Nick, Hazel, Henry, and Alice slipped through the gold-gilt doors of the hotel out into a silent grey city. The sky was overcast leeching color from the already ash laden streets. The smoke was stifling and all four covered their mouths with shirts. Henry led the way taking as many back alleys as they could, walking down main streets only when necessary. At one major intersection, Henry halted the group and went up to a police car that was sitting in traffic. He opened the door and started rifling around.

"What are you doing?" Nick asked looking around in each direction. Still no signs of life.

Henry finished and extracted himself from around the officer bringing with him a gun belt. "Extra protection?" he smiled and held it up. "It's a pretty handy tool belt if you ask me. Let's see here," he examined his find, "we have a very nice firearm," removing it from the belt and checking the sights. He examined the make and model. "Nice! It's a Glock."

"Hey, hey, make sure the safety's on," Nick reached out.

"It's on, see?" Henry turned the gun and showed him the safety.

"We've taken gun safety classes and learned to shoot when we were younger. Before they made it unlawful to own guns," Alice reassured them from the other side of the vehicle. She was digging in the glovebox. She pulled out four disposable masks and handed them around.

"Thanks," the group said collectively. The top half of their faces were already grimy with ash leaving upside down grey beards on their faces.

"What else have we here," Henry put the gun back in the holster, snapping it in place. "We have pepper spray. This could come in handy if we don't want to kill someone, which I personally hope to avoid and will be a last resort, or if we run into any wild animals. We have our baton, high mag flashlight with extra batteries, a taser, very cool, a nice pair of gloves, a Leatherman, handcuffs, two extra clips, and a window punch, just in case we need to break any windows," he wrapped up making sure all the pieces were back where they belonged then belted it around himself. "Oh, grab the shotgun, too," he turned to Nick.

Nick reached in and grabbed the shotgun, surprised at how heavy it was, and searched the vehicle finding two extra boxes of shells and put them in his backpack. "I haven't ever shot a gun," he admitted to the others.

"That's okay. Once we get out of the city, I can teach you," Henry said, "In the meantime, let's just hope we can leave before trouble starts."

"Which I hope never starts," Alice added under her breath.

"What about *that* gun?" Hazel asked pointing to a very military-looking gun in the back seat.

"Yes!" Henry reached in and pulled it out. "It's a semiautomatic rifle! Always wanted one. For hunting or target practice. That's all," he reassured the others. He sighed like a kid making his Christmas wish list as he took the gun from Hazel. He looked around, "Any extra magazines? Ah, here!" He pulled out two and put them in his bag then slung the strap across his back. "I look like a real vigilante now," he grinned. Alice could tell Henry was creating far-fetched imaginary scenarios in his mind where he would end up the hero, just like he had when playing make-believe as a kid.

"Henry, we are not going to become the Suicide Squad," Alice joked bringing him out of his revery. "You are still the same dorky brother I had three days ago. Of course, you do look a little cooler now," she gave him a friendly once over and punched his shoulder.

"This is more like cosplay," Nick quipped, "but with real guns. So be careful. Just sayin.'"

"I always wanted to be Aela the Huntress from Skyrim," Alice said grinning. "Now we need to find a bow or a sword." She started looking around as if she would magically find what she needed.

"Aela. Alice. I see the resemblance," he smiled at her. Then sighed, "I used to play that game, too, until they took away all our electronics."

"So, you think there'll be trouble?" Hazel asked bringing them back to reality.

"Well, I wouldn't be surprised. I mean, from what I can gather the only people left running around are these sweeper weirdos slash military types, a bunch of kids, and antivaxxers smart enough to have a fake BioID. I mean what can go wrong, right?" Henry chuckled weakly.

"There's another cop car," Nick pointed down the street. They walked over hastily to see if they could find more gear. There were two officers in the car with equally impressive belts like the one Henry had found and another shotgun. Alice and Hazel took these. Another block further and they found a belt for Nick. By the time they reached the alley that led to BioDie's hideout, they each had a police belt, three shotguns, two rifles and police vests for each of them, having gone back to get these from the officers they had pillaged already; they'd been lucky that the officers were in positions where getting the vests were relatively easy. "Might as well," Nick had said. "They won't be needing them anymore and we can't be too careful."

"Okay guys. This way," Henry turned down a very dark, damp alley. They hesitated and looked left and right before heading toward the dead end. It terminated at the back of an old three-story brick building that had been converted into small one- and two-bedroom apartments. The bricks were green from damp, dripping water from the light rain that had begun to fall. There were two old plywood doors almost parallel to the ground that led to the basement access. Henry walked over and lifted one of the heavy doors, exerting and calling on all the muscles he had to get it open. Once the door reached its apex, Henry lost his hold and the door fell slamming open, the sound reverberated off the walls of the surrounding buildings.

"Smooth move, Henry," Alice chided.

"At least the door's open," he retorted, releasing the flashlight from his belt and flicking it on. "Now, everyone, keep quiet and let me do the talking." They followed him down a long dank hallway. The floor was compacted dirt, and the walls were grey cinderblock, clammy to the touch. Henry made several sharp turns around corners and then stopped outside an unremarkable door. He knocked twice in quick succession, followed by three more taps. They heard some shuffling and then a voice asked in a high-pitched falsetto, "What is the airspeed velocity of an unladen swallow?"

Henry smirked and looked over his shoulder at the others, "What do you mean, an African or a European swallow?" He winked at the others and with that, they heard several locks being turned. The door opened a crack, the door chain still stretched across the opening.

"Ah, Henry! It is you. Come in! Come in!" the door closed, the chain was pulled back and the door swung open. "Quickly now," a late thirty-something obese man who smelled slightly of mildew ushered them in. He stuck his head out into the hallway looking both ways to make sure no one else was there and then locked the door behind them when he was satisfied that they had arrived alone. He secured three dead bolts and the chain before turning his attention to the group.

"What was that at the door?" Nick whispered to Henry out of the side of his mouth.

"Monty Python and the Holy Grail," he grinned. "It was a system I set up with BioDie when my mom was getting our IDs done."

"So, you kind of know him pretty well, then?"

"Not really. We connected with the movie, that's about it. And I like computers," Henry faced BioDie. "BioDie, this is Nick Webber and Hazel Lewis. You remember Alice," introducing them. "Guys this is the genius known as BioDie." They all tilted their heads in greeting. Handshaking had become a thing of the past when the Great Wave swept the nations.

"And to what do I owe the pleasure?" BioDie scrutinized Hazel and Nick as they walked deeper into his apartment, or lair, as Hazel thought of it, the loose boards wobbling underfoot.

"They need BioIDs," he stated. "We're going to Denver to get the bastards who just destroyed everything."

"What are you talking about?" BioDie asked raising an eyebrow. By way of explanation, he added, "All I know is that there hasn't been any news on the Internet for about two days and no one is returning my texts. I haven't been outside in about four months." Nick was surprised at first, but then figured that people like BioDie tended to keep very low profiles when making things that were highly illegal.

Henry communicated to BioDie all they knew about the current situation, describing how people had instantaneously become statues and what they looked like. He conferred with Nick for permission talk about the possible connections between the vaccine and the BioID. Nick approved; no reason to keep this from BioDie since he was obviously opposed to what the government had been doing.

BioDie sat back when Henry had finished. He inquired, "So you're saying my friends and I were right? And now you want me to help because you're going to go and get these creeps? That about sum it up?"

"Yes," Nick answered before Henry could. Then continued, "We know that you charge a lot for these IDs and I'm pretty sure we could easily scrounge up the money to pay and…" he stopped as BioDie held up his hand.

"If what you're telling me is true…"

"It is," Henry couldn't help himself.

"If it's true, then money's useless now," he finished touching on Nick's thoughts from earlier. "I'll tell you what. I'll make IDs for you and Hazel. All you have to do is find me one thing."

"What's that?" Nick was worried about this agreement and swallowed gearing up for the worst.

"I want a Karmann Ghia," he smiled and sat back.

"A what?"

"A Karmann Ghia. It's a very old, *verrryy* cool Volkswagen. It's a sports car they made from 1957-1974," BioDie smiled thinking about it with relish.

"Exactly where would we find one?" Nick looked perplexed. "I don't even know what they look like."

"Not to worry. Here," he reached for something behind him and handed it to Nick. "This one's for sale. It's a fully restored Maya blue 1968 Karmann Ghia. Here's the address," he pointed to the bottom of the page. "My guess is, it's still there based on what you've told me. Bring this and I'll have your IDs for you."

"O-kay," Nick said slowly, clutching the printout. "This is probably going to take a while. The streets are clogged."

"It's going to take a while to make your IDs. I figure you'll get back here about the same time I get done."

Nick asked, "And when we get back where do you want us to park it?"

"Just outside the door you used to come down here," was the answer.

"Umm, excuse me Mr. BioDie," said Hazel.

"Just BioDie."

"Okay. BioDie. Do you think we could get a few extra IDs?" Everyone looked at her wondering what she was getting at. "Well, you see, there might be more kids like us who have lost parents and decide they want to bring down the government and if they go with us, they won't have an ID and that could cause us to run into trouble. You see?" She finished with a small smile. All eyes reverted to BioDie.

He drew in a long breath and then puffed out his cheeks, exhaled a waft of putrid garlic breath several days old. Hazel swayed in the draft trying to breathe and not offend him at the same time. He acquiesced and said, "Yeah. I can do that. I'll make four extras. I'll give you all the info when you get back. I wouldn't normally do this—I'd be asking for a lot more in return, but if there's any chance you can bring down North Pangea, I'm all for the revolution—it would at least be one domino in the stack," he looked determinedly in the distance at the thought.

"We should probably get going if we're going to do this," Henry said jumping up from the low chair he had taken, eyes watering from the lingering smell of BioDie's breath. He grabbed the paper with the details on the Karmann Ghia from Nick. He looked at the address and grinned, "I know exactly where this is!" And with that they headed back outside.

The rain had increased while they'd been down in the bowels of the building. Murky grey rivulets of water were coursing down the street. It was a relief to be outside in the fresh air. They all took gulps of it to cleanse their lungs. They seriously appreciated the rain. Not only was it washing away some of the smell from BioDie's lair, the heavier rain was slowing the spread of building fires and simultaneously clearing the city of smoke. Hazel raised the hood of her sweatshirt and Nick pulled out his rain jacket.

"Okay, smarty," Nick said turning to Henry, "lead the way."

Henry puffed up with importance and took off at a good trot feeling pretty good about his successes so far that day. In his excitement, he paid no attention to the rain. He had his belt, had gotten a guarantee for new IDs, *and* he knew exactly where they were headed. "We're going near Pike Place Market," he said over his shoulder. "There's a car lot there that specializes in classic cars. It's a long walk, but we can probably get there before dark if we hurry. I don't think we'll be able to make it back until tomorrow." They tightened their straps and picked up the pace.

Henry had been right. It was a long walk. They were tense the entire way constantly glancing around, checking side streets, approaching large, crowded intersections with caution, looking for any movement. Nick or Henry would scout ahead to check for warning signs. They spotted a few kids running around in small packs, but they always darted away when noticed. Nick was pretty sure they were from Anvac. It was a relief knowing they had gotten out before the explosion.

The four of them eventually made it the Pike Place area. It was eerily deserted. Whenever any of them had visited before it was always bustling with activity. Vendors selling homemade crafts, fish flying through the air, kids visiting the disgusting gum wall. The first Starbucks always had a super long line. Hazel often wanted to get coffee there just for bragging rights but avoided it because she hated to wait. There was another café around the corner always with a much shorter line and with better coffee anyway.

They kept to the far side of the street, away from the pavilion area. The storefronts and stalls were empty and dark. A good place for people to hide. They didn't talk and doggedly followed Henry without question. Eventually they started to relax as they moved on from the market. Henry turned the corner and Pike Place was no longer visible. Half a block further and they were at the car lot. Henry stepped over a low chain to enter the premises.

Nick looked around dreamily at all the cars sitting there. They were streaked with grey, but were beautiful, nonetheless. He wiped the hood of a cherry red Porsche Boxer with his forearm and whistled softly through his teeth, "Now that's a gorgeous car."

"Yeah, not bad," Henry agreed. "What about that one there?" He pointed and knowledgably recited, "It's a classic 1967 sleek navy-blue Stingray Corvette."

"Whoowhee! That's nice," Nick concurred and cupped his eyes at the passenger window to look inside it. "I think I'm drooling. I take it you've been here before?"

"Yeah, a couple a years ago when my dad was going through his mid-life crisis. Unfortunately, he chose a blue 1980 Mustang. Totally uncool and then he ran away with a hot new girlfriend. Classic."

"I'm sorry."

"For what? Him choosing a crappy car or for walking out on me, my sister and my mom?"

"Both. I guess. My mom left us, too. My dad and me," Nick told him.

"I'm sorry to hear that, but don't worry about me. I don't miss him," Henry shrugged.

"Sure you do. You just don't want to say it. It hurts too much."

"Thanks Dr. Phil, but no. I don't miss him. Now let's find this Karmann Ghia and make plans to get out of here," he abruptly redirected the subject.

"Over here," Alice beckoned. "It's in the showroom. See." She pointed through the glass lightly tapping on it. She walked to the building door and tried it, "Locked."

"Here let me," Henry walked over detaching his window breaker from his belt. In no time, he had broken through the glass and reached in to unlock the door. "Think there's an alarm?"

"If it is, it's silent," said Nick cocking his head to listen. "Well, we should set up for the night and then figure out how to get this baby back to BioDie tomorrow. It's almost dark, it's raining and it's going to be a big job finding a route back to his place." The others agreed. There were two well-worn couches. Each girl took one apiece leaving the ancient low-to-the-ground, orange burlap chairs for the guys. Nick sat down and sunk so low that his knees reached his chest, "I don't think this is going to work." He stretched his arm out to Henry who hoisted him up. Nick turned and ripped the cushions from the frame laying them on the floor, then pulled out his hotel towel to use as a blanket.

They sat around in the growing dusk eating some of the provisions they brought with them. Hazel bit into another Snickers bar, concentrating on all the flavors flooding her mouth. She knew it wasn't the best dinner, but she had some catching up to do. Nick ate some cheese while Alice and Henry shared the leftover bacon from breakfast. They were quiet and satisfied. When it was completely dark, they all laid down on their makeshift beds to try and get some sleep. All of them exhausted from the day's walk.

CHAPTER 8

Sometime in the night Nick was awakened by movement flitting past the showroom windows. He sat up trying not to disturb the others and quietly moved to the nearest window to see what was going on. Henry was already at there, crouched down watching. Nick sidled up next to him. "Hey," he said to Henry. "What's going on?"

"I'm not sure," he replied quietly, "There's lots of people out there. Running down the street. Not making a lot of noise, though."

"Are they kids? Can you tell?" Nick was thinking about the kids in Anvac.

Henry squinted, "Dunno. I can't see very well." They both watched the street. Several small groups of people ran by their feet slapping the pavement in quick bursts. Nick hoped he could find faces from Anvac in the fleeting glimpses. Then headlights appeared at the top of the hill, illuminating the damp street, the vehicle then slowly made its way down toward Pike Place. There was a spotlight on the driver's side that swept from side to side. As it pulled up alongside the car dealership, the light swung brightly into the showroom. Nick and Henry ducked down barely escaping the light as it skimmed the windowsill where they'd been watching the runners. Nick was afraid the Sweepers would spot the broken glass where Henry'd let them in. His heart was beating hard and he could feel the rush of blood in his ears. Then, as if by some luck the light panned to another spot down the street and stopped. Nick and Henry slowly raised their heads to watch. They saw three kids illuminated in the light, hands up trying to shield their eyes. Two men got out of the vehicle and threw the three kids into the back of it using more force than necessary since none of the kids were putting up a fight. Nick could now see clearly that it was a black SUV with dark tinted windows, white license plate reflecting street-light as the vehicle resumed its forward progress. "That's the same vehicle or one like it that Hazel and I saw just before Anvac exploded," he relayed to Henry in a soft whisper.

"Gotta be those Sweepers. It looks like they're rounding up anyone who isn't dead, yet. It's like they're herding them toward the market," Henry whispered back.

"I got the same impression."

"Should we go after them?"

"Can't."

"Why not?"

"We can't go after the little fish when we want the big fish to fry. Get it? If they know we're alive or what we intend to do, we'll never get the chance. Besides, they have a job to do and we don't want them to decide we aren't useful. Let's just avoid them for now."

"I guess you're right," Henry whispered back. "I just don't like seeing what I'm seeing."

"If it makes you feel better, neither do I. You want to save people, Henry. That's a good quality. But let's start at the top. You can save more people that way," Nick encouraged him.

"I just hope we can get this stupid car back to BioDie's place before we're spotted," Henry turned away from the window and slunk back to his makeshift bed. He tried to sleep some more but couldn't. Every time he closed his eyes, those three faces kept showing up, begging him to help.

As night was making way for day, Henry roused the rest of the group, "Listen up, ladies and gentleman, we're in for a long day and the sooner we get started the sooner it's over. The smoke has cleared which means we are going to be much more visible should creepers come creeping or sweepers come sweeping. Eat something quick and let's be on our way." He cheered everyone on to full wakefulness like a ring master at the circus and then searched the main showroom windows for a way to get the Karmann Ghia onto the road. Eventually he found a mechanism that allowed the largest window to roll up like a garage door. Once the exit was clear, he searched for the keys. He couldn't find them, "Uh, guys, a little help here, please. I can't find the keys." Nick, Hazel, and Alice started searching the spare keys hanging up in the manager's office. After a while Alice decided she was going to take a break to pack her bag and, walking past the car, started laughing. The keys were in the ignition.

"Well, then," said Nick, "How very obvious. Anyone know how to drive?" he turned to the others.

"I have my permit," Henry stated proudly. "But…" he wavered, "I haven't had much practice."

"You have more experience than any of the rest of us," Hazel pointed out. "Nick and I were locked up in Anvac before we were able to test and then they made it illegal for us to get a license anyway."

"O-kay, then, I guess I'm up," Henry laughed nervously. "I have a feeling that clutch is going to be an issue."

They got ready to go, suited up in their bullet proof vests and buckled their well-equipped police belts around their waists. Everyone piled their bags into the passenger seat of the vehicle and Henry sat poised behind the wheel. "Here goes," he said and turned the key in the ignition. Nothing. He tried again. Nothing.

Nick, Hazel, and Alice were all staring at him. Henry started to blush, then remembered the clutch. Of course! The clutch. He depressed the clutch, his left leg wobbling, right foot on the brake and turned the key. The engine roared to life and everyone cheered. Then the car died. Groans.

Then Henry started it again. "I let up on the clutch," he shrugged, beet red by now. He moved his right foot to the gas and started to let up on the clutch giving the car as much gas as he thought it needed, like he had been shown when his dad was test driving the Mustang. The Karmann Ghia started to move forward slowly, then lurched and rocked back and forth. "Oops." Was all they heard. The car started again, and this time Henry was able to get the car to move several feet before killing it again.

"This is going to take some time," Alice shook her head. "We might as well start walking ahead and seeing what needs to be moved out of the way." The others agreed and Nick explained to Henry what they were going to do. Thankfully there weren't any cars in the way from the lot to the top of the first hill on the left-hand side. The few vehicles on the road were in the right-hand lane. Drivers sat immobile feet still firmly pressed on brake pedals, engines out of gas. Any vehicle from the left lane was now entangled with others at the bottom of the hill. Nick ran ahead and double checked that the intersection at the top was clear. It wasn't. Alice and Hazel were spaced out some ways down the hill and he ran back down to tell them to signal Henry to wait. The hills were going to be the toughest part of this trip. They surmised that it was going to be best if Henry could get a running start and make it all the way up to the first flat intersection without stopping.

Hazel joined Nick and they began the process of clearing vehicles from the intersection. Although neither of them had a learner's permit, they weren't completely inexperienced. They had secretly had opportunities before the Great Wave to learn the basics in empty parking lots with their parents. Every car in the intersection was out of gas, so had to be moved manually, one person steering and pushing from the door, the other pushing from behind. The first two cars were easy to move as they were lightweight compact models. The larger vehicles took more work, but once the intersection was cleared Henry was given the okay to head up. From the bottom of the hill the engine revved. The car started to lurch forward then the motion became smoother as Henry picked up speed. The engine was emitting a high whine by the time he reached the intersection. When the car leveled out, Henry applied the brake, sending the Karmann Ghia pitching forward, rocking a couple of times before stopping completely.

"Um, next time maybe take it out of first gear," Nick suggested.

"Yes, but how?" Henry asked.

"Never mind. Good job getting the car to the top of the hill, now don't let it run back down." Henry stomped his foot on the brake and held it there as tightly as he could turning a little pale at the thought of rolling the wrong direction. "You can relax," Nick reassured him. Henry set the emergency brake before killing the engine and getting out. His legs were wobbly from the excursion. "Your next job is to get the car from this intersection to that one," Nick pointed to the left. There didn't seem to be that many cars in the way and it was a relief to see that this street was on a flat plane. If he remembered right, there were only two more steep hills to go and then it would be smoother sailing back to BioDie's.

They spent the entire morning moving the car going systematically from one intersection to the next. Getting the drivers out of vehicles presented the biggest challenge. The drivers whose hands were completely wrapped around steering wheels were the hardest to move since the hands had to be broken off. Nick figured out that the window breaker came in handy for this, but still turned a slight shade of green every time he had to use it. Once a driver could be moved, Nick and Hazel worked together to lift the driver out and set them on the edge of the sidewalk. Sometimes a driver would tip over and break, a head popping off here or an arm there. It was awkward work and highly unpleasant when a driver had to be dismantled and piled up in pieces on the sidewalk as happened a few times during the day, but as they continued, they devised a system that made the job faster, not necessarily easier.

Once an intersection or lane was cleared, Henry would drive up to the next traffic jam and then help the others in clearing vehicles. The best they could do was to create a one-lane wide path down the middle of the streets. Some of the streets were already cleared and they could see evidence of where the Sweepers' SUV had been in the night. It looked as if large bulldozers had simply blazed a path for the Sweepers. It was messy, but efficient.

At last, Henry was cruising the final block delighted that the end was in sight. The others were trailing behind. He pulled into the narrow alley and very nearly collided with a blue dumpster that was a little too far from the side of a building. He stepped on the brake and turned around to see if anyone had seen his near miss and was really glad that he had been without witnesses. He pulled to the back of BioDie's building, turned off the ignition and set the emergency brake. Henry slowly uncurled his hands from the steering wheel and stretched them back into shape. His hands had been glued to it and hurt from the pressure. He got out and breathed a sigh of relief and then punched the air in excitement. He drove! And got the car there in one piece, not a scratch on it! *Barely* he reminded himself. By this time the others caught up and got their bags from the passenger seat. Henry pocketed the keys. They'd made it and it was only 2pm. Time to spare.

The four of them repeated the scene from the day before outside BioDie's door. He admitted them quickly and quietly and relocked the three locks and chain behind them. They had prepared for the stench of BioDie's abode by chewing peppermint gum picked up at a convenience store along the way, but when they entered, they realized that BioDie had cleaned house and taken a shower during their absence. "I love what you've done with the place," Henry complimented him.

"Yeah, well," BioDie looked down, embarrassed. "Keys?" Henry dropped them into his waiting palm. "I'll be right back." He left them standing there. Hazel and Alice had already chosen spots to drop their bags and take seats. Nick joined them as Henry looked around the space. There were model cars on six shelves that took up one entire wall. He inspected these close up. Every classic car one could imagine was sitting there. He picked one up, appreciating the attention to detail, BioDie walked in and

Henry quickly set the model back on the shelf. He walked over and moved the car half an inch to the left.

"Nice job, kids," BioDie said. "It's beautiful and not a scratch on it. Thank you."

"What are you going to do with it?" Alice asked.

"The car? Nothing, really. I just wanted to add it to my collection," he indicated the cars where Henry was standing. "It's not like I'll be driving anywhere, but if I wanted to, it's there. I might just spend time sitting in it. Is there a tarp?"

"Yeah, it's behind the driver's seat," Henry told him. "We can put it on when we leave. So, what do you have for us?" he joined the others and sat on the edge of a dark purple corduroy couch. There was a frayed rip on the arm and the fabric was a lighter shade of purple on the seat cushions, faded after decades of use.

"I've got more than you asked for," BioDie grinned. He walked to a bedroom-turned-office with computers from floor to ceiling and brought back a small cardboard box brimming with manila envelopes. "These," he handed eight envelopes to Henry, "are six fake BioIDs and the files that go with them, plus two hard copy files for you and Alice. You already have the BioID." Henry looked in one envelope and withdrew a shiny black zippered pouch and a file. "The pouches are fireproof," BioDie continued. I have two extra pouches for you and Alice. Store your IDs in there until you need them. Keep 'em safe. No need to take a chance right now. Go ahead, do it." He proffered the two empty pouches to them. Alice took the pouch and removed her fake BioID placing it inside. Henry did likewise.

"Good," BioDie went on. "The files, like Henry and Alice's, will show you the information I programmed onto it that could show up if the IDs are scanned. Don't get them mixed up. Bad idea." Henry grabbed a file from the box and looked in and saw that he was holding Hazel's and handed it to her. He flipped through the other envelopes, found Nick's and handed it over. The other envelopes all had different first initials and last names.

BioDie grabbed something from behind him and held up his own fake BioID, "I need to show you how to put these on. Nick and Hazel, go ahead and get your IDs out." They did. "Now, usually it works best when you put your finger right on top of the three dots and then press that to the middle of your forehead," they mimicked his movements. "Yeah, just like that. Good. Then follow the edge keeping it at your hairline," they followed his example, "Yep, yep. That's right, then finish by smoothing it out and getting rid of any air bubbles." Hazel and Nick turned to each other. They were surprised at the invisibility of the silicon and marveled at the three little dots in the middle of their foreheads. BioDie grabbed a scanner just like the ones used by the government and zapped Nick's dots. He turned the screen to show Nick the information that popped up: Nick M. Webber, FPNPID#3781209, Vaccination Records: Current. The screen flashed green and reset to the default screen, flashing "ready for scan" on the display. Nick looked at BioDie, "That's amazing! Thank you." BioDie bowed.

"Okay," he turned to Hazel, "Your turn." She stepped up and he scanned her dots, showing her the screen: Hazel S. Lewis, FPNPID#9573479, Vaccination Records: Current. Another green flash and another reset.

"Thanks," she said and peeled the ID from her forehead, gingerly placing it back in the pouch. She added it to the envelope and walked over to find a safe spot for it in her backpack.

"Now," BioDie turned his attention to the envelopes left in Henry's hands, "These IDs are all ready to go. I decided to give gender neutral names to the other four. That way they can be used for anyone. Did you notice that sex isn't listed on the scan? That was part of the Gender Equalities Act of 2022 where sex and gender were removed from any form of identification. Makes my job a lot easier," he grinned. "Now, for the last part," he got up and removed something from a nearby filing cabinet. "This," he handed Henry a small blue flash drive, "is a part of the bargain that I didn't tell you about."

Henry took the drive and turned it over in his hands, "What is it?" he asked, not quite sure what to do with it.

“That, there,” BioDie pointed, “Is Operation Covax.”

“Operation Covax?” Nick perked up.

“You’ve heard of it?”

“No, but it’s the name of a file on this flash drive,” he dug in his pocket for Hazel’s flash drive.

BioDie took it from his hands, “Where did you get this?” he held it up.

“It was my dad’s,” Hazel interjected. “We found a note on a computer at the Virology Lab from my dad that said I needed to feed the cat. And when I went to see what the clue meant at my apartment in Anvac, we found that. We don’t have a cat. See?”

“I was briefly looking at it yesterday morning,” Nick took up the story, “And one of the files is called Operation Covax. What it is?”

“Wait, Lewis, right?” BioDie ignored Nick’s last question looking at Hazel.

“Yes, Lewis, that’s right.”

“As in Scott Lewis, by any chance?”

Hazel indicated the affirmative.

BioDie sat back organizing his thoughts, “Okay, it’s like this. I knew him. Scott. We worked together in the real world at Microsoft just up the road. We didn’t like the direction things were going so we were going to venture out on our own. Then the Great Wave hit, and we had to go underground. I hid out here and made fake IDs, but never knew where Scott ended up and didn’t know how to contact him. I searched on all the back channels the dark web had to offer and couldn’t find a trace of him. So, he was in Anvac? And worked at the Seattle Virology Lab?” he looked again at Hazel.

“Yes, he was in Anvac. We’ve been there for the last 18 months,” she replied. “They took away all of our electronics that’s why you couldn’t find him, and it was probably too dangerous to find you when they were at work. I still don’t know what they were working on. My parents were working at the lab along with Nick's dad, but they never told us what they did. They might've been test subjects," she ended sadly.

"They weren't test subjects. I guarantee that, but you don't want to really know what they were doing. Let's just leave it at that. But what you should know is that when your dad and I saw things going the wrong direction, we created a program. One that could essentially undo what the government was trying to do with these BioIDs. I guess your dad was a little late," he smiled ruefully, "but, we have another chance, or I mean, you have another chance, to undo things."

"You mean we can unfreeze everyone!" Henry got excited. Nick shivered at the thought—all those dismembered people. He turned slightly green again.

"Afraid not," BioDie shook his head. "Unfortunately, that was permanent. What I mean is, you can stop them from controlling the population in the future. Get rid of the BioID system. This flash drive," he looked at the one in Henry's hand, "contains a virus. A computer virus that will infect the mainframe where they keep all the BioID data and wipe it clean. Gone. No more ID tracking, null and voiding them. It's a kill switch."

Henry smiled and firmly gripped the flash drive, "So this means we can take them down!"

"But will this kill everyone who has the real BioID like it did the other day?" Nick interjected. "I mean, I don't want to be responsible for more deaths."

"No, it shouldn't. We didn't have a chance to try it out, but it's designed for you to unleash the virus and wipeout the BioID system only, not hurt those who have it," he looked earnestly at Nick. "There's minimal risk."

"Is there a way to make it so we *do* freeze them?" Henry asked tentatively, "We need to end the cycle. Look what they just did to about 7 billion plus people. They wiped them out without a second thought and now their goons are cruising the city looking for leftovers, like us. Either way, it's a risk I'm willing to take. Who's with me?"

Hazel raised her hand, thinking of her parents still in the lab, and Nick's dad, and all the kids in the cars who were sitting there in a permanent state of marbled stiffness. So, what if it cost a few more lives? Henry was right, the risk was worth it. Besides, her dad was one of the architects for this project. She looked up and scrutinized BioDie's face again, "Wait...," she paused, thinking, "You're William Jensen, aren't you?" BioDie sighed and nodded. "*You* were the genius behind the BioID technology." He nodded again. "I recognize you. I think you came to our house once, but a long time ago. That's why it took me awhile to place your face. So, tell me, this computer virus can you alter it like Henry suggested?"

"I can," BioDie held out his hand for the flash drive. He walked over to a laptop, fired it up, inserted the flash drive. The others watched the screen as code appeared. It made no sense to them, but BioDie knew exactly where he was and what he was doing. In a few minutes, he ejected the flash drive and handed it to Henry, "Now, it's an actual kill switch, just like the one they used three days ago."

"But what if we don't want to use it?" Nick asked, a little concerned at the thought of more people ending up like statues.

Hazel interjected, "Then we can use the one on my dad's drive, right?" She looked at BioDie, "It must be the same program."

"Yes," BioDie agreed, "Now you have a choice."

"I will not hesitate. Who's with me?" Henry stood and looked around.

"I'll go to Denver," Nick put in, "but I want to see what they're doing before I commit to using it. Fair?" The others agreed.

"Can I take a look at what's on your flash drive, Hazel?" asked BioDie. She handed it to him, and he inserted it into the laptop and waited. It took a few seconds for the computer to recognize the device. There were lots of files listed. Not many of them seemed to pique BioDie's interest, until he got to a secondary file labeled "Denver Servers" and double-clicked on it.

"Ahhh, here we are," BioDie drew their attention to the document. "These are the blueprints of the warehouse where they store all the servers. You're going to need this if you want to find the mainframe." He went up to

File and selected Print. In the other room they could hear a printer spitting out pages. Henry went to retrieve them and found an empty folder to put them in.

"Anything else on there?" Hazel asked after a while.

"Yes, but not so much as relating to Denver."

"Besides Operation Covax, what else is so important?"

"Well, some of the other files will give you the background information on the BioID program and the ID2040 Alliance. How it works. The vaccine was able to help cells reproduce at a fast rate in the body and so when they activated the kill switch, it petrified every cell in the body and not just individual parts. That's how it works."

"I was right!" Henry yelled in their ears.

BioDie continued, sticking his finger in his ear, "The rest of these files are a record. They're for you to preserve. It's our history. See these files," he pointed to several files Nick originally thought were call numbers, "These are all historical dates and I'm guessing there are documents in the folders that correspond to the dates. Look," and he double-clicked the first one. "And there they are. Scans and PDFs; e-versions of history books that relate to each time period. I'm guessing you'll find the same thing in the rest of the files. Your dad was curating a comprehensive archive of the history of us. Of the world. They started trying to erase history ala *1984* and then really ramped up when the powers that be decided it was time to enact their initiative. Whatever you do, Hazel, don't lose this flash drive. It contains things that you will never have access to again in our world. They destroyed it all."

"I thought those were call numbers," Nick admitted.

"Disguised to look like that, I'm sure," BioDie reassured him. He continued looking at folders, "Ah, and here," he selected a folder named Operation Covax, "Is your copy of the kill switch, now it's the one that will simply wipe out the system, not shut everyone down," he concluded ejecting the flash drive and handing it back to Hazel. "I noticed that he scanned all your family photos in, too." She gave the flash drive a tight squeeze and handed it back to Nick.

"Thank you, William," she said. "We will definitely guard this with our lives."

"So, what does 'Covax' stand for?" asked Alice.

"'Covax' stands for Counteractive Vaccine. Operation Covax was designed to undo the technology used for the ID2040-Alliance by eliminating the government's ability to do what they did three days ago. We were just too late."

Henry looked at an old animated Betty Boop clock on the wall, eyes going from one side to the other, "Guys, it's 4:30. Think we should get a move on?" He packed up the manila folders, zipping them securely in his backpack.

"Yeah, we probably should," Nick stood and stretched. He held out his hand to BioDie. BioDie grasped it in both of his and shook it. "Thank you so much, William, you've really helped us out. I really hope we make the right decision when it's time. Just because I lost my dad, I'm still not sure if I want to use the kill switch on your flash drive. But I'll make sure the right thing is done. I promise. I really want to ask them first why they did this."

"Oh, that's easy. It relates back to the Georgia Guidestones where they suggest that the world population stay below a certain number—I forget what that is specifically and the Internet is down—the idea is to keep everything in balance, but somehow I think they went to the extreme and will eventually find that their foolhardy ideas will bring them more trouble than they thought," BioDie said.

"I was right!" Hazel interjected. "I was telling Nick about them last night. All about population control and saving the environment."

"I know it's probably a crazy answer and nothing will be satisfactory enough to justify the killing off of almost the entire population. But I think you're right in tracking down those in charge. Hopefully they can provide a more thorough answer. Sure you guys can't stay here tonight?" he offered.

"Thanks, but I think we need to keep moving and start making concrete plans," Nick returned. He stepped over and gave BioDie a big hug, a gesture that had gone by the wayside during the Great Wave. "Maybe you should go back to using your old name now. I think I like William a lot better."

"Yeah, I suppose so. The whole moniker is kind of overdone and pointless now that everyone is dead and there's no need for my skills or won't be very soon," said William sadly. "Come back and see me if you can." He started walking them to the door.

"We will, promise," said Alice. "What are you going to do for light when the power goes out?"

"Don't worry about me, I have a generator. And perhaps I can evict some tenants from some of the nicer apartments in the building. They have more windows. I can always come back down here and work. If I'm not here when you get back, I won't be far," and with that, he closed the door behind them.

CHAPTER 9

Once back outside, Henry went over to the Karmann Ghia one last time, taking out the cover and locking the door. "Thanks for the ride," he whispered softly as he looked at the car, having grown emotionally attached to it during the day. He flung the cover over the top of the car, making sure it would keep off the rain and any prying eyes, then he tightened his backpack straps and joined the others who were waiting for him at the end of the alley.

"Where are we headed?" he asked cheerily as he caught up.

"I'm not sure yet," said Nick. "Let's just start walking. We can talk about our next moves."

"I know," Alice piped up. They all looked at her. "We need to go to REI."

"REI?" Henry repeated.

"Yeah! We can stock up on things for our trip. They will have most of what we need," she reasoned.

"That's actually a really good idea," Hazel agreed. "And besides, I heard they're having a killer sale right now. Oops, bad word choice," she laughed and jogged a little ahead, always ready to go shopping. Her thoughts were now consumed with the thrill of getting to shop without a budget. It drew her focus away from her parents where her mind had been wandering. It was a welcome distraction.

"There's one only a couple of blocks from here," Henry retook the lead and started trucking.

"He's like a living, breathing map of the city," Nick whispered to Hazel.

"Yes, and it's very convenient, too. And, much more pleasant that our old TomTom."

"Much," they both laughed as they followed Henry's lead.

The store was closer than they anticipated, and it didn't take long to get there. It was located in a popular outdoor shopping center with lots of other stores that could also be useful in preparing for the trip. The parking lot was still full of cars, some cars had silent drivers sitting behind the wheel heads turned looking over their shoulders as if they were getting ready to pull out, shopping bags resting in the backseat. Some customers were seen dotting the landscape having solidified where they stood. As they made their way cautiously weaving through cars, they found more people on the ground broken, having fallen over in mid-step. As the four of them walked, they constantly kept an eye out for Sweepers. They approached the outer double doors of the store and Henry whipped out his window breaker from the police belt. He was ready to get to work when the doors swished open. Henry looked a little embarrassed, having forgotten that the store would have still been open at 7:30. They proceeded, Nick grabbed the large ice axe shaped handle of one of the inside double doors and held it while everyone entered the store.

The store was eerily quiet. Customers were still standing at the registers, their transactions frozen in time, employees in the process of bagging items. Henry grabbed a CLIF bar at the counter, unwrapped it, and stood there eating. "Well," he said around his bite, "we might as well go ahead and shop." He started to head off toward the clothing department, Alice stopped him.

"What exactly do we need?" she asked looking around a little bewildered. There were several tents set up near the entrance complete with small campfire chairs. She walked over, dropped her backpack on the floor and sat down. "We should probably figure out the logistics before we start grabbing a whole bunch of stuff. Are we sure we're going to Denver?"

Nick spoke up, "I think we kind of already decided that. Right?" He turned to the others. They showed their agreement. "One thing I want to make clear is that I'm still not sure about using the code, but we have time to decide that later when we know what we're actually dealing with. Everyone okay with that? I know some of you are eager to use William's flash drive, but I think it would be wiser going in wanting more info before we make a very permanent decision." They concurred again. "So, since we *are* going to Denver, we need to figure out our mode of transportation. Hazel and I kind of know how to drive. Our parents did teach us a few things before we were sent to Anvac. Henry now knows more and had great practice today."

"But what about the roads?" Alice asked. "They're going to be a lot like the streets we had to deal with when getting the Karmann Ghia to BioDie's—William's—apartment. The freeways are going to be a mess. Wouldn't it be easier to use bikes?"

"No way!" Henry said. "We should definitely drive. It's quicker."

"I'm not so sure," Nick stepped in. "I think Alice is making a good point. Even though riding bikes will definitely take longer, I think driving would maybe be even harder. I mean, look how long it took us to move one car about five miles."

"I still say we use cars," Henry held firm.

"Hey," Alice responded, another idea coming to mind, "we can start with bikes, that way we will be able to get through cities and towns easier. Avoid traffic jams that type of thing. When we get out onto the open road maybe we can find a truck or something to haul our gear as far as the tank of gas will take us or until we run into another traffic jam. Either way, we can make decent time. Plus, there's no hurry really."

"That's a good idea," Hazel said, supporting Alice. "So, with that in mind, what shall we shop for? I'm itching to get started."

"Well," Nick replied, "we should probably find a couple of tents. Maybe one for the girls and one for the boys or however we want to sleep."

"Or just one for all of us. Less to haul," Hazel suggested.

"Speaking of which. Exactly how are we going to haul whatever we choose to take? I can't carry much on my back if I'm riding a bike," Alice stated.

"I got it!" Henry snapped his fingers. "We'll each choose one of those," he pointed excitedly toward the back of the store.

"That's smart," Alice followed with her eyes. They were looking at a row of yellow canvas bike trailers. "We can each choose a bike and use a trailer to haul stuff."

"Good find," Nick approved. He was already eyeing a matte black GHOST FRAMR 6.7 bike. He looked at the price tag and whistled through his teeth. "Wow, that's expensive. I think my new credit limit will easily cover it, though," he smiled and straddled the bike, finding the sweet spot on the seat. He kicked the kickstand up and took it for a short jaunt around the store, weaving through customers whose REI shopping experiences had been extended indefinitely. Nick rode to the front of the store and parked the bike in front of the display tent. "This is the one for me," he grinned. "It's like Christmas!"

Henry pulled up next to him on an army green bike. "It's a Mukluk Carbon NX Eagle Fat Bike!" he exclaimed. I was saving up for this before the Great Wave." He whooped gleefully reflecting the smile on Nick's face. "I think this is *better* than Christmas! Did you ever watch those shows on Nickelodeon where a kid would get five minutes to run around Toys R Us and fill up as many shopping carts as they could with anything and everything they wanted?"

"Yeah, I remember those shows," Nick uttered, a wistful look in his eye. It had been every kid's dream to get those five minutes.

"This is exactly how I thought it would feel getting to do something like that. And you know what?"

"What?"

"We don't have to rush!" and with that he took off again on the green bike doing a victory lap through the store. When he made it around again, he finally parked the bike and stood back, eyes running along the body frame, appreciating the fine craftsmanship. "Hey ladies," he yelled across the store, "Make sure to get a good bike for riding on the roads." A couple of minutes later, Alice and Hazel rolled over on two identical Cannondale Habit AL 2s in reddish copper. Both looking very pleased with their bikes. Henry gave an appraising nod as they got off, flipping the kickstands down.

Nick was hauling a trailer toward them, "Okay, guys, you each need to go get one of these and bring it over here. I'll go ahead and start attaching the hardware." He stopped at his bike and plopped down with a set of tools he'd picked up in the bike shop at the back of the store. He also found a rack attachment for the trailer in his search which would add more available space for hauling their gear. The others went back to the bike section and picked out three more trailers and accompanying rack attachments, bringing them over to Nick.

While Nick was busy getting their bikes ready for the road, Henry grabbed an FPNP Road Atlas from a rack and sat down to start mapping out their route. "We should probably see which way we are going before we choose our supplies," he suggested, flipping to Washington State and finding Seattle. Even though the United States had been incorporated into the larger Pangea Confederation of Nations and renamed The Federation of the Peoples of North Pangea or FPNP for short, the individual state names had stayed the same, this being too big of an undertaking with the side effect of causing a lot more confusion and pushback. Henry's fingernail scratched across the mileage chart as he located the intersecting box showing mileage between Seattle and Denver, "Here it says that it's one thousand three hundred and twenty-nine miles to Denver." He looked up, "That's going to take at least two and a half weeks if we can cruise a hundred miles a day."

"That would be pushing it, don't you think?" Hazel sat down next to Henry with her own copy of the atlas. I would think an average of 50 miles per day barring any major obstacles would be much easier. Plus, I don't see a reason to have to rush. What's been done is done."

"True," joined Nick, "and we should prepare for a longer trip to be on the safe side. We'll get there when we get there. I'd rather take my time and enjoy the trip a little if we can. It's been a long time since I've had the freedom to do what I want."

"Well," continued Henry, "if that's the case it's, let's see, September now…hmmm… that puts us there late October. If things get really screwy maybe November. Colorado. Mountains… Maybe we should just wait 'til spring. We could just camp out here." He said this last statement tongue in cheek. Everyone knew he didn't want to wait. And wouldn't.

"Har, har," Nick volleyed. "We'll leave first thing tomorrow and then get there when we get there. Like Hazel said, what's done is done. We can't bring these people back to life. I'm sure NP won't be making any major moves for a while until the dust settles. At least that's my guess," he finished attaching the trailer to the bike and moved to Henry's. "What we do know is that we need to prepare for cold temperatures regardless. And to have a good time," he smiled and turned back to his work.

"So, do you have a preference for which states we go through?" Henry asked turning back to the atlas. He turned to the page showing all of North Pangea. His face was close to the map tracing potential routes with his finger. "We could go south a ways and head through Oregon and over to Idaho or we could cut across Washington directly into Idaho and down to Utah from there or head over to Wyoming or cut across to Montana and then Wyoming and on to Colorado or…"

"Any way to avoid big cities?" Alice asked peering over his shoulder. It was a practical question, and the more often big cities could be bypassed the better.

Nick gave this question some thought, agreeing it was a good idea. He got up from his work, taking another atlas from the rack. He turned to the Washington State map, "I think that we should really consider going south sooner since it *is* already mid-September and it's only going to get colder from here on." He scrutinized the first possible leg of the trip, "It looks like heading to Boise would be the best route. We can use the back roads in order to avoid any of the bigger cities, especially Boise." He pointed with his fingers and traced the route, the others followed along, "So from here, we take 90 to 84…"

"Wait," Alice cut him off, flipping to the state map in another atlas. "If we're going to avoid big cities maybe we should avoid the freeways, too. They're probably more crowded and the Sweepers will be using them. They'll be moving slower if they have to get out and move a lot of cars. If we started out here on highway 410," she pointed and traced the route, "we could follow it all the way across the state. See here," she showed them, "it merges with 12 before heading through Yakima. We can't avoid the freeway completely, but we can avoid it most of the time. Highway 12 goes all the way to the Idaho border here," she pointed to a town called Lewiston. The name was in bold font which meant it was a sizable city right on the state line. She continued, "Once we get there, we can figure out the next leg of the trip. I think we'll have a better idea of what we're doing by then and whether or not we need to go certain ways to avoid Sweepers and anyone else who might pose a threat. Remember that Sweepers are the main danger, but most likely not the only danger. We need to give ourselves time to adjust. And be flexible," she concluded eyeing the others.

Hazel looked at Nick and shook her head, adding, "I think that's smart. I've been through a lot of the places along that route. My grandparents lived here," she pointed to a little town called Clarkston, right next to Lewiston. "It's on the Washington side," she offered. "It's kind of hard to tell."

"What do you know about the towns and stuff?" Henry asked.

"Well," Hazel started recalling to memory, "it's a lot of farm country. There are small towns every so often, but with the exception of Yakima here," she indicated, "we probably won't see a whole lot of people and I doubt if the Sweepers will want to take the back roads. According to the email, they're just supposed to take the most direct route to Denver which means they may or may not even consider going through Yakima. They might head south earlier than that. It's a gamble, but I think Alice is right about staying away from freeways as much as possible."

"I think that settles it, then," Henry got up and tucked the atlas into his trailer. "Lewiston here we come. Nice work, Alice," he commended her. "I think that we should start shopping and get things we will need for both now and later when the weather turns cold. Don't forget we need food, bedding, a tent or two, and anything else we might need. If we're not going to go through large towns our options might be pretty limited at times." Nick was just finishing the third bike when the rest scattered throughout the store to begin stock piling essentials.

Alice and Hazel started in the women's clothing section first. Both of them were giddy with excitement at being able to get whatever they wanted without having to consider the price. As they shopped, they agreed with the boys that it was like that show on Nickelodeon, but way better. The time limit thing always caused Alice some anxiety for the kid with the cart. She would secretly try to get the kids to turn this way or that with telekinesis through the TV. She was hoping they would grab the same toys she would. Once she even applied to be on the show and was disappointed to never hear from the network. But now, here she was with a similar opportunity, but way better she decided.

It wasn't long before their arms were full. They walked back to the staging area by the bikes and sorted through their new wardrobe. Hazel and Alice had teamed up to get similar items so they could share. Each of them discovered they had the same taste in things, starting with the bikes. The essentials for each of them included a pair of them of very sturdy canvas pants, convertible pants that could be unzipped to make shorts, 7/8 leggings for comfort and eventual use as a second layer, a thermal top and bottom base layer for cold weather, snow pants and matching ski jacket with a grey print resembling camouflage, an extra-large REI Co-op fleece sweatshirt, a down vest for added warmth, ten pairs of underwear, two bras, and six pairs of thick winter socks. They also had new sneakers, flip-flops, and winter boots. Both of them had also changed into new outfits leaving their old clothes on the floors of the changing rooms. Hazel was wearing a steel blue pair of hiking pants and matching green and blue striped tee. Alice wore grey hiking pants and a light purple tee. Both of them were wearing identical turquoise raincoats. The look was finished off with new waterproof hiking boots.

"What are you two? Twins?" Henry looked over, dumping an armload of similar items by his bike.

"Well," Alice grinned, "We are basically the same size, we like the same style and we figured that we could swap outfits or borrow items if we need to."

"Yeah," Hazel answered. "Kind of like a two-for-one deal." She turned back to start folding clothes.

"Too bad that won't work for me and Nick," Henry looked across the store where Nick was now selecting his own items, having finished with the trailers. Nick stood a few inches taller than Henry. Both of them were tall and lanky, but it was surprising how quickly Nick's muscles were making a comeback after only a few days of eating better. Henry was a little jealous since no matter how hard he tried, he couldn't gain weight and muscle definition of any kind eluded him, even when weightlifting on a regular basis.

Once Nick rejoined them, they realized they needed to decide on the fundamental community items necessary for a trip of the magnitude on which they were about to embark. They agreed on two Big Agnes 2-person tents. The tents were lightweight and could be erected with a vestibule, an area that was perfect for keeping the bikes under cover during the night. The tents were bright orange which would make hiding a little more difficult, though, but there was hope that the route that they'd decided to take would be enough to keep them from being detected. Along with the tents they gathered four identical lime green mummy-style sleeping bags; four dark blue self-inflating sleeping pads; four sets of collapsible bowls and cups; one small two-burner stove with six extra canisters; Life Straws for each of them; large canteens for water; tarps; four mess kits; biodegradable laundry detergent, soap, and shampoo; and more waterproof matches just for Nick. Alice added a couple extra blankets and Henry gathered all the food they could find.

After making sure they had everything they could anticipate needing, the four of them spent the next hour or so distributing the weight between the four trailers. Alice and Hazel were going to be responsible for hauling most of the food and canteens for easy access. Henry and Nick would haul everything else. Each of them was responsible for their own clothing, bedding, and anything else outside of the shared goods. Hazel decided to select larger hiking backpacks for them, too, to replace their original backpacks just in case they ended up not being able to ride their bikes. They each tucked their original backpacks inside of these. In the morning they would be strapped to the trailer racks with bungie cords Henry had found.

By the time the planning, mapping, and shopping spree were completed, the sun was nearly set outside. The sky was painted with red and darker blues mixed with splashes of purple. Henry broke the silence of hard work, "I'm going to find where the light switches are and at least dim the lights so it's not as easy to see in." Their minds all immediately reverted back to the danger of the Sweepers; in their excitement they had blissfully, if momentarily, forgotten about them. Now Sweepers were again crawling through their thoughts.

Henry had no trouble finding the dimmer switch and set the lights to just barely on. They were exhausted from the day's work and figured getting to bed early would help them shove off quicker in the morning. They each grabbed sleeping bags and pads identical to the ones they already packed. There was no reason to take the packed ones out yet since there were plenty more available. Alice thought it nice to be able to try out some of their new gear before leaving the store just in case they wanted to make an "exchange".

There were two tents on display, so Alice and Hazel set up in one while Nick and Henry unfurled their sleeping bags in the other. The tent openings were facing each other at little more than a right angle. A fake campfire sat between the two tents. The girls laid on their bags facing out toward the boys. Hazel was eating the last of her Snickers bars. The box of Cap'n Crunch next to her.

"You know, Hazel," Nick said, taking a huge bite of Twinkie, "We're going to have to eat a little better than this."

"Yeah, but our diets can start tomorrow. To new friends and new adventures," she toasted, holding the remaining bite of chocolate bar in the air. Alice grabbed a handful of cereal, held it up in salute before downing the whole lot at once.

"To new friends and new adventures," the other three echoed.

CHAPTER 10

They were settling in for the night, looking up through the skylight of the tents to the dim lights above when a spotlight lit up the storefront in an eye-bruising blaze. The four were on instant high alert and held their breaths. Nick and Henry looked across at Alice and Hazel, then all four turned toward the front door of the store. Someone was coming in. Loud voices were heard, one distinctive voice, nasally with an accent, British maybe, yelled above the rest, "Anybody in here?" A flashlight swept the store, pausing at different points of interest. The bodies of the last customers cast long shadows on the bookshelf containing state maps and National Forest booklets. The four in the tents willed themselves lower, not daring to breath even a little. Again, the light cast shadows across the tent walls. Nick and Henry turned their head so as to hide their eyes, their tent door giving them a better view of the front door. The man who had spoken took several steps further into the store. He was wearing military fatigues, khaki colored; the cut reminiscent of Nazi uniforms from WWII, he was only missing the hat and the mustache. *Please don't see the bikes, please don't see the bikes, please don't see the bikes* Nick thought as he waited for the Sweeper to spot him. Just as the light was about to hit the first trailer, a noise in the far corner of the store diverted the man's attention. He swiftly moved in the direction of the fitting rooms.

There was a scream and a scuffle. Several racks of clothing had been jarred. "By order of the Federation of the Peoples of North Pangea, you are under arrest," the man with the accent yelled. Several more Sweepers, noticing the commotion joined the fray.

"Get away from me," a raspy tenor screamed, "Get your hands off of me! You have no right!" Then, "Ahhhhhhhh, my shoulder! Stop it!!!!" A final wail of pain echoed through the empty store. There was more movement and then the four Sweepers, including the man with the accent, were frog marching a teenage boy with dark shaggy hair and a very obviously dislocated shoulder, to the front doors. The men and the boy exited the store. A few doors slammed outside, and a vehicle moved slowly away.

Nick was the first to speak, "We haven't been the only ones in here all day," fear making his voice barely audible. "I think we were really lucky that whoever that was didn't give us away. Did anybody see him?" They all shook their heads in the negative.

Henry asked, "What are we going to do? He saved our lives."

"What can we do? We don't know where they're taking him and other than having black hair and now a dislocated shoulder, I don't know who he is."

"Well, maybe we can look for him tomorrow before we leave," Hazel sat up, breathing a little easier. "It's the least we can do. He knew we were here and didn't say anything."

"How do we even start to figure out where they're taking him? What would we do if we actually found him?" Alice asked.

"I don't know," Nick said sadly. "I really don't, but we owe him our lives. I think he made that noise on purpose. Did you see that man's flashlight was almost to the trailers? If he'd seen those we would have been caught."

"You mean Hitler in the funny uniform? Yeah, that was too close. But why would this kid risk his life for ours?" Henry questioned. "It doesn't make any sense. None."

"Not much we can do about it tonight," Nick pointed out.

"Oh, yeah?" Henry jumped up. "It's nighttime, the Sweepers are easier to find at night. Their headlights are a dead giveaway." He was pulling on his shoes, "If we go now, we can probably find them. Pretty sure they're not too far from here." He stared at them. None of them moved. "Come on guys, if we're going to do this we have to go now. We can come back for our stuff later." He was about ready to go out the door when Nick joined him.

"Stay here," Nick said to Alice and Hazel. "The fewer of us out there the better."

"But," Hazel started.

"Please, Hazel, stay here and guard our stuff. We'll be back soon."

"And if you aren't?"

"Then rearrange the supplies and head out. Go to Denver. Figure out what to do from there," Nick dug in his jeans pocket and pulled out Hazel's flash drive handing it to her. "Hang onto this."

"If Denver is so important, then why are you going out there now?"

"It's the right thing to do. It's a life. There aren't many of those left," and with that he and Henry slipped through the doors.

The night air was cool. The earlier rain having dissipated all the smoke and cleaned the streets. Nick was tightening his bullet proof vest and police belt when he joined Henry at the corner of the building. Henry pointed down the sidewalk. A black SUV was parked several store fronts down from where they stood. The man with the flashlight was checking the store like he had theirs. He was opening the door to go in, the others were standing outside waiting for orders.

"I have an idea," Nick whispered. "They're checking each store. If I can go around back and let myself in through an employee entrance, I can create a distraction. Then you can get the kid out of the SUV and get back inside REI before they know he's gone." Henry approved the plan. It was a good.

"It looks like they're headed to the next one already so go down a little further," Henry breathed. He surveyed the remaining stores. REI was located at one end of the complex and the Sweepers still had several to go before reaching the end. "Uh, there," he pointed, "Go over to the American Eagle. I'll try and get as close as I can and wait."

Nick took off at a fast jog and rounded the corner out of sight. Meanwhile, Henry made his way toward the American Eagle, keeping one eye on the SUV and one on the men walking to the door. The brake lights glowed; white lights flashed as the driver put the vehicle in drive. The SUV slowly moved to the next store loose rocks grinding under the tires. *One to go*, thought Henry, *Hurry up Nick*. Henry stayed low, moving from behind one parked car to the next. By the time he caught up with the SUV at the American Eagle, he was less than a car length away. He watched the driver put the vehicle in park and get out, leaving the door wide open.

The man with the flashlight was just looking into the storefront windows when the lights inside lit up. Nick had tripped the automatic lights. *Way to go, Nick!* Henry silently cheered him on. The men started to run, drawing their holstered pistols, as they swarmed through the doors. This was Henry's cue. He ran to the open driver's side door and jumped in. This hadn't been part of the plan, but a stroke of genius struck while waiting for the chance to run.

"Hi! I'm Henry," he cheerily said as he slammed the door and threw the vehicle in drive. *Whew! Thank God it's an automatic*, he thought as he stepped on the gas. He was halfway past the next store when he tooted the horn. The next thing he knew, every Sweeper was running after the SUV. A perfect diversion! Henry looked in the rearview mirror to see the dark-haired boy staring wide-eyed at him. He accidentally hit a bump causing his passenger to fly up and hit his head. Henry looked at the mirror again and realized it hadn't been a speed bump. He swallowed the horror and turned onto the four-lane street picking up speed. A couple of times he hit the brake hard and swerved to miss stalled cars. "Sorry!" he said, grinning from ear to ear as the boy in the back swayed from side to side before righting himself again. About two blocks later, he turned right, saying, "Get ready to bolt. We'll lose them first and then head back to REI if that sounds okay to you?" The boy in the mirror indicated agreement, a grunt of pain exiting his lips, his dislocated shoulder visible through this t-shirt. "You wearing cuffs?" Henry asked. The boy nodded.

"But the key's in the cupholder," came the same raspy voice Henry recognized from before.

"Awesome," Henry looked down, then swerved to miss another car. "I'm Henry, by the way, of Henry and Nick's Awesome Rescue Service. I'd shake your hand but I'm driving."

"And mine're cuffed and you already told me your name," he pointed out. "I'm Jackson. Jackson Clayburn. How much will I owe you for your services?" he smirked.

"First rescue is on the house," Henry grinned again pleased with the success of the mission so far. "Okay, I think it's about time for us to boogie. They know we turned here, and we are nice and close to a couple of side streets." He reached down and grabbed the handcuff keys, looping them around his index finger. He put the SUV in park, jumped out, and assisted Jackson out of the back of the car. Henry immediately directed them down a very dark side street, pulling Jackson in behind a large dumpster about halfway down. "Here, let me see those," he grabbed Jackson's hands. The absence of light made it a little trickier, but in no time, Jackson's hands were free and the two of them were moving again. They turned down another side street, essentially doubling back the way they had come. In the distance they could hear the rev of an engine. They walked another block then ducked hastily behind another dumpster as a large spotlight zoomed down the avenue. Once the light vanished, they were on their way again, furtively checking their surroundings.

It took a while to get back to REI, but both breathed a sigh of relief when they rounded the corner of the building and saw that no black SUVs were awaiting their arrival. Apparently, the Sweepers were done for the night or at least in this neighborhood. Nick gave Henry two thumbs up by way of greeting as they walked through the doors.

"This is Jackson Clayburn," Henry introduced the dark-haired teen. "That's Nick, he set the lights off in American Eagle, that's Hazel, Nick's best friend, but quickly becoming Alice's twin—she's my sister," he pointed at Alice. Each of them bobbed their heads in turn.

Hazel walked up to Jackson and started prodding his shoulder. "That's going to have to go back in," she stated business-like.

"Hazel thinks she' a doctor," Nick said.

"Actually," she rolled her eyes, "My mom was a physician's assistant and she taught me a couple of things." She looked at Nick, "My dad had a dislocated shoulder after we move to Anvac. She showed me how to pop it back in to save us a trip to the ER, which would have taken a couple of days because of the bureaucratic red tape. May I?" She turned to Jackson. He consented, his already pale features losing more color. "Okay," she continued, "you're going to need to lie down on the floor." Jackson complied. Hazel knelt down next to him, grabbed his arm and pulled it about forty-five degrees from his body. Next, she grabbed his hand, pulling it toward her. When nothing happened, she placed her left foot into Jackson's rib cage just under the shoulder and pulled again. The shoulder slipped back into place. "There, all done," she stood and helped Jackson sit up.

The rest of them crowded around Jackson, taking seats close to him. "Were you in here all day?" Nick asked.

Jackson stated, "Yeah, I got here just before you did."

"Why didn't you tell us you were in here?" Henry looked confused.

"I don't know. I guess I was just scared. This whole thing is totally weird. I recognize you," he looked at Nick. "I lived in Anvac, too, but you know how it is, we kind of all kept to ourselves. I never came out to meet my mom at the buses until they didn't show the other day. That's why you probably don't recognize me."

"Makes sense," Nick said. "So why didn't you give us away when the Sweepers came in here? And thanks for creating the distraction, though, seriously."

"Sweepers? Is that what you call those jerks? Kind of a fitting name for them. Well, I couldn't see letting them take all of you. I mean, I don't know where they were going to take me, nowhere good, that's for sure, but you all seemed to be having so much fun getting ready for this trip that I didn't want anything to mess it up. He almost saw your bikes," he indicated the yellow-topped trailers. "I had to do something."

"Thank you so much," Nick said again. "I'm relieved we were able to get you out of there. Henry, that was genius taking their SUV. Crazy, but it worked!"

Hazel looked over at Alice who gave her a knowing look; a silent agreement between them. Hazel turned to Jackson, "So, do you want to come with us?" Everyone shook their heads "yes" eyeing Jackson.

"I would, but I'm going to head north. Listening to you all make your plans today gave me the idea to do what you're doing but go find my older sister and her two kids instead. They live, or lived, depending on what I find, in Vancouver, B.C. They were in a place called Novax. Another place just like Anvac, but they had a little bit more freedom. They at least were allowed to watch the news and stuff. Still, they couldn't have any personal contact with people. My sister sent my mom a letter before they made it illegal to write to people. Speaking of which, do you know what happened to her? My mom, I mean?" he turned to Hazel and Nick.

Nick's head drooped. He was about to explain when Jackson said, "You don't need to tell me. She's dead, right?" Nick's look told him the truth. "I figured. When none of them came home the other night and then when these Sweeper dudes blew up Anvac, I knew that she wasn't going to be coming home. Ever. They died at the lab, didn't they?"

"Wait. You knew about the lab?" Hazel looked, puzzled.

"Yeah. I know they were sworn to secrecy, but my mom told me. She said that if she didn't come home one day that they had probably offed her or something."

Hazel asked, "What did she do there? We couldn't figure out what any of them actually did."

"My mom was a computer software engineer before everything, you know. She worked with Chris before the Great Wave."

"Chris? As in…Christopher MacPherson?" Nick asked.

"Yep. One and the same. Chris asked my mom if she could help with the technology they were developing in the lab. When she said 'no thank you' he got the government or whoever to force her to do the work. I think the same went for all of the parents in Anvac. There was a lot of brain power in the group. You realize there's another Anvac on the other side of the city, right?" Hazel and Nick looked at each other, surprised. This was news to them. Jackson continued, "When they created the communities, they sorted out the residents putting the smartest ones in the Anvac we lived in. Ours was actually designated Anvac West. The other Anvac, Anvac East, was about three times bigger. Didn't you see the explosion the other night on the other side of town?" None of them had. "Think about it, Hazel, your mom was a PA, my mom was a software engineer. What did your dad do?"

"He was an IT specialist," she said quietly.

"My dad didn't have any credentials like that," Nick pointed out.

"Who was your dad?"

"Alex Webber."

"Then you never knew what he really did, did you?"

"What?"

"He was one of the creators of MERSV-5 vaccine which Chris used to create the final version—MERSV-6," Jackson stopped, opening a bottle of water that Alice handed him.

Nick looked at him, shifted in his seat, stunned, "But my dad always worked in real factories making things like parts for machines and stuff."

"That's what he told you. This vaccine stuff was top secret. I mean, come on, the MERS virus was genetically modified by the government in order to get everyone to take this vaccine. I still don't know exactly why, but it was something very few people knew about. My mom being one of them."

"We know why," Hazel said.

"You do?"

"Yeah," she pointed to the customers at the checkout counter.

It dawned on Jackson, "A petriclysm."

"A what?"

"Petriclysm. Cataclysmic petrification. Petriclysm. They used the vaccine to wipeout humanity."

"Excellent term. Describes it perfectly. Yeah, it worked with the BioID," said Nick. "People had to have both in order for it to work. So, wait, you're saying our parents are partially responsible for all of this?" he looked horrified.

"Not voluntarily," Jackson reassured him. "They probably used us kids as leverage. As long as they played along there wouldn't be any problems."

"That's why they never told us what they were doing," Hazel said to Nick. "It makes sense now. This really does mean we need to get to Denver and use the kill switch on them."

"I'm still not sure if it justifies killing everyone else," Nick put in.

"Wait, you have a kill switch?" Jackson sat up.

"Two of them just to be safe," Henry joined the conversation. He'd been itching to get involved but hadn't been able to add anything to the conversation, yet. "This guy, BioDie, gave us one and modified it so that if we use it, we can wipe out everyone else with a BioID just like they did to the rest of humanity and then we found out that Hazel's dad also had one on a flash drive he hid for Hazel, but that one will only knock out the technology without affecting the person. It's called Operation Covax. Very cool stuff."

"BioDie and Operation Covax?" Jackson laughed to himself.

"AKA William Jenson," Hazel pitched in.

"No kidding! William? I met him when I was younger. He worked with my mom and this other guy, Scott Lewis…"

"That's my dad!" Hazel interjected.

"Woah, small world," he gazed off across the store. "Where's he living now?" he turned back to her, he cringed at the look on her face. "William, I mean. Sorry." Henry filled him in on the details, writing the address and directions down on a piece of paper he found by the registers. "Thanks," Jackson said taking the paper from him, "I think I'll go see him before I leave town. We have some catching up to do."

"You sure you won't come with us?" Nick prodded, now really wanting Jackson to join them. He'd be a real asset and Nick was sure Jackson could give him more intel on his father.

"I'm sure. Thanks," Jackson assured him. "If I didn't have my sister and nieces to find, I'd be happy to help, but until I know they're safe, I just can't. Hey, it won't take me as long to get to Vancouver and find out if they're okay as it will for you guys to get to Denver. I overheard your plans for the first part of your trip. Once I know anything, I can come after you guys. Catch up maybe."

"Hey, that'd be great!" Henry said.

"When you get to Lewiston, find someplace to leave me a note as to which way you're headed next."

"How will you find our note?" Henry asked puzzled.

"You'll figure it out. I promise," he said. "Now, I need something to eat." He stood and walked toward the dressing rooms where he had been caught earlier. He came back with a well-used hiking backpack and brought out a container with leftovers from somewhere. It looked like chicken pot pie. "I raided a Marie Calendars on my way here," he said by way of explanation. He sat down to eat. They all thought this a marvelous idea and grabbed food from their backpacks to join him.

Nick and Henry grabbed a sleeping bag and pad for Jackson and scooched over to give him room in their tent. It had been a long day and an even longer, too eventful, evening. It wasn't long before all of them were sound asleep.

CHAPTER 11

The five of them slept later than they planned. Henry was the first one to get up and start fixing breakfast, trying out a small two-burner stove identical to the one they had packed. He boiled some water and made coffee for them. The girls got up next, the smell of coffee giving them the incentive they needed to get moving. Nick and Jackson came out of the tent a little after that. Henry was busy making the second pot of coffee; the first pot already gone.

"We should probably add a chair for each of us," Henry looked at them, offering to top off their cups.

"Only if we have room," Nick held up an empty cup.

"I'm sure you can find room," Jackson held up his own cup for Henry to fill. "You will be glad you have them later. And if they get too heavy, you can always leave 'em behind somewhere down the road."

"See," Hazel said, blowing on her coffee, "He's smart."

"Are you sure you can't come with us?" Alice looked at him, batting her big light blue eyes and flashing her winningest smile.

"I would, but first Vancouver. I ride bikes a lot, so it won't take but maybe a couple of days there and back."

"Now you sound like a hobbit," Hazel giggled.

"Don't pay any attention to her," Nick looked at her.

"At any rate," Jackson continued, "I just need to check on my sister. As long as I know she's alright, I won't stay. She's pretty self-sufficient. Lived in a hippie commune for a while. The commune is completely off-grid and if there aren't any Sweepers up there, she and her friends will probably go back to their homes as soon as they think to."

"I look forward to you joining us, then, in the next couple of days," Nick smiled.

While they got around to leave, Jackson started gathering his own supplies. He grabbed a bike like Nick's, having always wanted one, too. Nick helped him out by getting the trailer hooked to the bike and the rack attached to the top. Jackson grabbed a small one-person backpack tent. "I already have one, but it's pretty old," he explained. He grabbed a couple of solar-powered camp lights and a battery pack. Henry thought this was a good idea and grabbed a couple, too, stowing them in his trailer.

Henry grabbed another protein bar from their stash and was munching it while watching Jackson pack. "Hey," Jackson started, indicating the food in Henry's hand, "you might want to reconsider eating the food that you packed. It's mostly freeze-dried and all of it is packaged tight. It's going to last a lot longer than most of the food in grocery stores, restaurants and so on. Raid those places first. That food," he looked at Henry's hand again, "should be eaten only in emergencies." Henry swallowed slowly, not wanting to finish the bar now, a guilty look spread across his face. "You might as well finish it now," Jackson laughed.

Henry ate the rest and then said, "I didn't even think about that. You and I, we'd make a good team. You think about things I don't." The others were learning that, even though he had really good ideas, Henry wasn't so cocky that he couldn't take suggestions or help. They all appreciated his enthusiasm and his willingness to learn and let others lead, too.

By the time all was ready, Jackson was close to finishing his own packing. The others gathered round to go over their route with him again. Nick found Jackson a copy of the same atlas they were using and highlighted in green the optional routes they might take after getting to Lewiston. No matter what, the end of the line took them to Denver. Jackson assured them he would meet up there if nothing else. He held the door for the others as they started wheeling their bikes and trailers outside.

Henry and Nick surveyed the parking lot for any suspicious SUVs but didn't spot any and waved the others through the doors and out into the coolness of morning. Henry and Nick surmised that the Sweepers figured whoever had been in American Eagle was long gone now and that this area was clear.

Nick, Hazel, Henry, and Alice said their "goodbyes" and "hope to see you soons" and "be safes" and were off. As they left the parking lot, all four of them turned and waved to Jackson who was watching them from the sidewalk outside the store. Once they rounded the corner, he went back inside to finish getting ready for his trip north.

It was a beautiful day to start a long bike ride. The sun was warming things up and burning off the early morning fog; only a trace was left by the time they reached the freeway. The sun was emitting a pleasant fall-day warmth, shining through light clouds that were high in the sky, the musty scent of fallen leaves enveloping them as they rode. Henry took the lead. He knew his way around the city pretty well. Before the Great Wave he had taken to riding his bike, walking, or riding public transit all over the city and with the ability to memorize routes and to map out destinations in his head, he knew the easiest way to get to the I-5 freeway where they would later intersect highway 410. They wove through stalled cars and silently played follow the leader; when Henry swerved, they swerved. When he took an exit, they all took the exit in succession.

There wasn't much talking during this first part of the trip. They were keen on getting the heck out of Seattle and really on their way before being spotted by Sweepers. It didn't take them long to get to the freeway. It was necessary to take use it until they could exit and pick up 410 via route 164 to Enumclaw. Henry was confident they could get to Enumclaw by the end of the day beings that it was only about 40 miles from where they started. He'd memorized the route and rode on without needing to stop to consult the atlas. The first leg was approximately 26 miles. Henry deftly led them toward an I-5 south on ramp but bypassed it and took an exit from I-5 north.

"What are you doing?" asked Nick from behind.

"We're going south on the north side," he called over his shoulder like this should have been obvious. "The Sweepers will take the other lanes if they take I-5, which I'm sure they will. This way, they'll be on the wrong side of the freeway, buying us some time in case we need it." He grinned and turned to focus on finding a way through the crowded lanes.

It was slow going at first. Alice had definitely been right that the bikes were a much better form of transportation. There were several pile ups that required them to walk their bikes around, up, and over. At one point, Nick and Henry had to lift the bike trailers and carry them one at a time quite a way before it was clear again. The jam on the freeway looked like it contained a couple thousand different vehicles. When the Petriclysm happened, the vehicles on the freeway had continued on their forward trajectory until they were involuntarily stopped primarily by this pile up. While the guys worked on the trailers, Alice and Hazel worked together getting the bikes across. One pile up was so bad that the four of them had to double back, look for an exit and use unknown side streets to get around the vehicles on the freeway. Once they made their way to the other side of the massive pile up the freeway was essentially clear of vehicles with only the occasional one scattered here and there having veered into the concrete barriers.

They were starting to feel more comfortable as they put some distance between them and Seattle. The city was still too close behind them to relax much, but each time one of them turned around to look at the mass of buildings, they were smaller, fading eventually to model-sized versions as the distance grew.

They were now all riding side by side, crowded more to the middle of the four-lane freeway, occasionally swerving to avoid random vehicles. For the first time since the Royalton, Hazel and Nick found themselves next to each other and somewhat alone.

"So," Hazel looked at him, his side profile to her left, "How're you doing?"

"I'm fine," Nick glanced over at her as they parted to go around a blue Honda Accord that had crash-landed on its side, the driver had partially landed half out the driver's side window and now resting on the asphalt, the head having been thrown some yards into the median. Only a nose was distinguishable from the shattered pieces.

When they rejoined each other, she said, "No, really. How are you? What are you thinking about?"

"I'm fine, really. I'm just thinking about my dad. That's all," he paused. "It's just been a lot to take in," he admitted. "I mean, one, he's dead, and then to find out he was working with viruses and vaccines? He was some sort of scientist or something? I mean he was my best friend and now after what Jackson said, I am so confused. I thought he told me everything. It's like, if he couldn't tell me what he was really doing, did I know him at all?" He shook his head.

"You knew your dad," Hazel tried to reassure him. "I mean, yeah, he didn't tell you everything. But do those closest to us know everything about us? No. So then, what makes you think we know everything about them?"

"But this is about his job! You would think he could talk to me about his job. It would be a pretty big part of anyone's life. Why would he lie to me and tell me that he worked in a factory making things?"

"Well, a factory isn't that much different from a research lab. Maybe he didn't tell you because he couldn't. I mean, our parents weren't allowed to tell us where they went every day when they left Anvac. Jackson was clear on the fact that he knew only because his mom broke the rules. Maybe our parents thought they had broken enough rules already and didn't want to push it. Or they were doing everything they could to protect us. Sometimes the less one knows the better. What about that?"

"Even so, if he wasn't supposed to tell me I still think he should have. It makes me feel like he just didn't trust me."

"I really don't think it was a matter of trusting you. He was probably trying to protect you. Like my parents were trying to protect me. I mean, what would have happened if you'd let something slip?"

"But I wouldn't have. I know I wouldn't have said anything."

"Really? Even if you knew that what they were doing was going to wipe out the rest of humanity? Even then?"

"I see your point," his chin dropped to his chest.

"But *you* knew what they did for a living," he tried to continue the argument.

"Yeah, before we moved to Anvac," she pointed out. "Because their jobs didn't require secrecy before. Maybe your dad's job has always been top secret. He might've worked for the government. A lot of those jobs are high-level security and those who have them have to sign contracts stating they won't say anything about what they do."

Nick readjusted his grip on the handlebars, he looked over at her as they swerved apart again, this time around a tractor-trailer with the trailer on its side having been drug some ways down the freeway before stopping. "I still wish he would have told me," he said when they reconnected. Then, "How do you feel about going to Denver?"

"Fine. I like the idea that we're going to do something about all this," she looked around at all the cars and drivers. "I mean, if there is anything we can do about it. Otherwise, I'm just glad to be out of Anvac and doing something like this. Even though it's super weird to have the freedom to do whatever we want, it's also kind of fun. I have to admit."

"I agree. This is a taste of freedom that I don't think we've ever really experienced even before the Great Wave."

"Yeah. My mom always used to warn me that they were already taking our freedoms and that the masses simply didn't care."

"I miss my dad more than anything, but are we really going to use the permanent kill switch?"

"I'm still thinking about it. I mean, they just wiped out almost all of humanity."

"Well, what kind of outcome do we want after the immediate petriclyzing of everyone else? Who's left and what's the goal? Go off and live out the rest of our days trying to find enough food to eat? Repopulate? Can you live with the knowledge you were responsible for taking another life or lives, in this case?"

She pondered this, "I think I can live with myself. Or at least I hope I could. I hadn't really thought of what happens *after* Denver."

"Maybe we should before we do something we regret. If the goal is to repopulate, don't you think the more people we start with, the sooner we get the job done?"

"Why is it so important to repopulate?"

"I guess it feels kind of lonely, if you know what I mean. There are still people out there, ones who didn't make the horrific decision to petriclyze most of the world's population. What if some of them still have a BioID? Surely the elite saved some people to work, keep things running."

"Probably. But remember Cal's email where he thought they might go hunting in Africa? He wasn't referencing the animals there. He was talking about people. We'd be saving them. So, in my mind, I don't think using the kill switch on the people who didn't think of humanity as human are the kind of people I would want left the repopulate the earth. I want people like you and Henry and Alice. And Jackson and his sister. You know, people who can think for themselves and who care about others. Plus, there's more power in making one's own decisions than making a life-altering or, in the case of the petriclysm, a life-ending decision for others."

"But wouldn't you be acting just like them?"

"Not really. I'd be the one eliminating the ones who wiped everyone else out. Retribution. Eye for an eye. That sort of thing."

"I see your point. But right now, we can't isolate certain people. If we could isolate those who are responsible without killing the others, I would consider it. But right now, it's one kill switch or the other. It's kind of an all or nothing. Even knocking out the BioID system would go a long way to taking these people down a peg. I think I'm leaning toward simply wiping out the system. I do want justice for those who died, but I'm not ready to waste more lives if I don't have to." He turned and earnestly looked at her.

By this time Nick and Hazel had fallen a little behind. They looked up and noticed that Henry and Alice had stopped and were waiting for them. Henry peered over his shoulder to see if they were coming. His eyes widened, then yelled, "Sweepers!! Headed this way." He turned back around and started pedaling as fast as he could. The others stepped on it, too, going as fast as they could weaving through the traffic on their side of the freeway. Nick took a quick look over his shoulder and could see three black SUVS hightailing it down the road. The four of them approached an on/exit ramp and left the freeway. Henry led them to the bottom of the ramp and quickly ducked under the overpass, hiding in the shadows. They tucked their bikes out of view of the freeway as best they could and climbed to the top of the steep concrete incline that led to a ledge just under the lanes above it. There was a shelf where they could sit and drop behind a short wall to hide if they needed to. Henry released his gun from his belt just in case. Then they waited.

It wasn't long before the first SUV passed overhead. The vehicle was still going along at a pretty good clip, still not catching up to the pending giant pileup that stopped the southbound traffic. They waited for the second vehicle to pass, muscles tensing for a possible confrontation. Some seconds after the first vehicle, the second went whooshing by. Now, for the third and final one. They waited. Nothing. Then, a slow-moving vehicle came to a stop just above them. Nick could see the driver get out of the vehicle and give a cursory scan across the landscape. The blood came rushing to his ears. *They spotted us. It's gotta be the yellow trailers. Oh God, please let them leave.* As he refocused, a thin golden stream came over the side of the overpass, pooling in a mound of soft dirt between the two sides of the freeway. The liquid began running down the hill as they heard the driver get back in the vehicle and speed off.

It took some time for the group to breathe again and thank the powers that be that they hadn't been spotted. They slid down the concrete incline and returned to their bikes. That had been way too close.

"I think we need to wait for a while," Nick regained his composure first. He took a deep breath and exhaled.

"I think that tractor-trailer kept them from seeing us," Henry said.

"That and I don't think they were necessarily looking for people. They must be done with Seattle and are headed to the next big city or something. That'd be Portland," he replied. "What happened to all the people they found? I thought they were supposed to keep some of them."

"I don't know," Henry grabbed the handlebars of his bike and started walking. "Maybe they didn't find anyone to keep."

"I'm really glad we went after Jackson."

"Me, too," Henry agreed. "Hey, let's go over there." He pointed to a Home Depot they hadn't noticed in their panic. They started looking around to realize their exit had been another shopping center on the outskirts of Auburn. They wheeled their bikes over to the store and walked through the automatic double-doors. They didn't see the green bus trundle across the freeway overpass behind them.

"What are we looking for?" Hazel asked, putting the kickstand down.

"Paint," was the reply.

"Paint?" she questioned.

"Yeah, that was a close call and we got lucky. I don't want to risk being a sitting duck again," he pointed to the bright yellow covers of their trailers. "Help me find some spray paint in brown, olive green, and black. We're going to camouflage our trailers."

"Sounds like a good plan," they all agreed. The spray paint was locked in cages and it took a while to find the right key. They raided the orange vests of random employees and tried each one. They were about to give up when Alice decided to rummage around the paint mixing station and found the key there. They selected several cans in various colors, unhooked and unpacked the trailers. All four of them wheeled the trailers to a wide aisle and began the task of painting over the cheerful yellow. It was kind of sad to get rid of the original color, but this way it was much safer for them. They wanted to remain invisible unlike normal bike riders where standing out was key. When they were done, they bagged the rest of the paint to do the same to the tents that night and left the trailers to dry while going to the outdoor area for some fresh air.

Nick brought up the conversation he and Hazel had about using the kill switch BioDie had given Henry. "So," Nick started, "I think Hazel and I are in agreement that we want to use the code on her dad's flash drive to wipe out the system."

"Why?" Henry interjected. "Why not just get rid of all the rest of the people with BioIDs? I mean, they're the ones in power."

"Not all of them," Nick countered. "Think about it. How many people in menial jobs like janitors, garbage collectors, and those who run the sewage plants would be needed to keep a large city like Denver operating?"

"I don't know. Probably a lot," Henry mused, his eyes staring intently at empty pots on a nearby shelf.

"Right," Nick continued. "Those in charge would have been smart enough to keep those types of people around to keep things running. They aren't going to be the ones to get their hands dirty."

"So, they basically have slaves," was the reply.

"Right. And all of them have the BioID, too."

Hazel spoke up, "I think Nick is right about not using the program that will kill off everyone else. I think he's also right about leaving people to repopulate if for no other reason than we don't want to be the last humans on earth or close to it."

"What if we could only use the kill switch on those in power?" Henry asked.

"We thought about that, too," Nick looked at him, "but we have no way of changing the code."

"I see the dilemma," Henry rested his chin on his hand. "I guess you're right and we should just plan on using the one to wipeout the technology and hope we get the chance to deal with the powers that be in some other way."

Nick looked relieved, "Thank you for understanding. I hate, and I do mean, hate what they did, but I'm not willing to sacrifice the many for the few."

"So, do we keep going?" Henry asked, worried that the trip might get called off.

"Of course," Hazel piped up. "We can still figure out a way to take down the big bosses. Plus, we need to use the kill switch my dad gave me to destroy the BioID system. Remember? The servers are in Denver."

"Oh, yeah! That's right," Henry looked excited again. "Duh, I was so focused on the one that I forgot about the other. Yeah, let's do it!" All four of them looked more relaxed with the knowledge that they weren't bent on killing more people. It had been weighing on each of their minds after the excitement of the previous day had worn off. Each in turn looked forward to the trip with enthusiasm minus the dread of the end goal looming ahead.

By this time the paint was dry, and they were all ready to go soon after, although they were a little hesitant to continue for fear that the Sweepers weren't too far ahead. Henry had a great idea to raid the McDonald's across the street. He assured them that they could have anything on the menu they wanted as he had once had a very short stint working in a McDonald's. His mom made him quit after the toxic combination of teenage funk and old grease became too much to handle. She had upped his allowance at that point as long as he promised to never work fast food again while he lived under her roof. Needless to say, it had been a win-win for both of them.

They parked their bikes outside to let the trailers air off some more while Henry took orders and began cooking. To everyone's delight, the food tasted just as expected. Henry cooked up another 20 cheeseburgers and apple pies for them to take with them, heeding Jackson's advice to use up the food they could find before using their rations.

"Why not take fries?" Nick asked.

"Burgers and pies are okay if they're cold, but cold French fries? No thank you. And even if we find a way to reheat them, fries are never the same," Henry shook his head sadly. "So, eat up. We can do this again and again until the power goes out. But only McDonald's. It's all I know."

Alice took out a plastic garbage bag from a box she'd picked up in Home Depot to put the food in. "No need to have everything smelling like fast food," she gave before being asked.

Once they'd eaten their fill, they consulted the atlas again. Auburn had been their starting point for highway 410, but they were about two exits or so away. They were leery about getting back on the freeway and decided to find a way to their route taking the side streets that ran adjacent to it. They continued to walk their bikes in order to allow the Sweepers even more time to get ahead of them. It took almost an hour for them to find the highway, but were excited that, at least for a while, they wouldn't have to worry about being followed.

Once they were through Auburn, they remounted their bikes and headed toward Enumclaw, their final destination for the day, was fifteen miles down the road. The sun was already well past its zenith and they wanted to set up camp before nightfall. They wended their way through more rush hour traffic frozen in time. It was getting toward dark by the time they reached the outskirts of town. Instead of setting up their tents for the night, Nick suggested finding a hotel where they could spend the night in more safety, take hot showers (desperately needed), and raid the kitchen like they had at the Royalton. They had seen no signs of life since the overpass.

CHAPTER 12

Early the next morning they discovered that the kitchen in the hotel definitely wasn't as well stocked as the Royalton had been. However, on the bright side, it was well stocked with Starbucks coffee and everything needed for a filling continental breakfast. Alice made waffles, scrambled eggs, bacon, and hash browns for them. She cooked up all the bacon she could find and made as many waffles as she could figuring that these could be eaten cold along the way. Unfortunately, eggs weren't as portable, so she used them all and made sure that they ate those first, finishing them off completely.

Before they shoved off for the second day of their trek, they laid out the tents on the wide lawn in front of the hotel and painted these to match the trailers. The tents were left to dry and air out to be repacked just before leaving. The four were not as eager to begin as they had been the day before, each of them so seat sore that walking was a challenge. Their glutes and lower backs all feeling the ride and dreading the upcoming one. Hazel disappeared across the street into the drugstore. She came back with several first aid kits, an economy size bottle of acetaminophen for headaches and general pain, extra bandages, other medical supplies just in case, and boxes of patches for muscle pain. She instructed each of the others to put one on each cheek while she took two for herself and went to the bathroom. Hazel surmised that it was necessary to combat their seat soreness if they were going to keep moving. She reassured them that they would eventually get used to riding and wouldn't be in so much pain. They all thanked her and took patches for themselves.

Alice ducked out as the others were getting ready and making last minute preparations. "Where are you going?" Henry hollered at her.

"I'll be right back," she yelled over her shoulder.

Several minutes later she came back carrying a very large paper sack. "What in the world?" Henry asked. She tipped the bag to show him all the pastries from Starbucks. She'd raided the display case plus the shelves in the backroom.

"They're going to go bad if no one eats them," she shrugged. "I mean, some of them are already a little stale, but if I have to say goodbye to one of my favorite places for the rest of my life, I'm going to enjoy as much of it as I can before then. I also picked up a couple pounds of coffee and ground them, too. Oh, yeah, and a French press. We can have fresh coffee when we want."

"What happens when we can't grind it?" he asked.

"Well, then we should be on the lookout for an antique shop and pick up a manual grinder," she answered. "Until then, we have pre-ground coffee." Henry took off at a trot back to the Starbucks. Twenty minutes later he emerged with another full sack. This time, full of pounds of ground coffee. He started shoving the coffee in any spare space he could find. Alice looked at him quizzically.

"What?" he looked back at her. "No reason to need to go searching for a grinder, yet."

"Just as long as you're willing to haul that yourself," Nick came up behind them, watching Henry pack coffee.

"Wait!" Henry yelled and ran off again. This time he headed in the direction of the grocery story. Another ten minutes later, he reemerged carrying a Styrofoam cooler. He had filled this with bags of ice and cans of Coke, Dr. Pepper, and other types of cold soda. He started unstrapping his backpack to put the cooler underneath it. Nick looked at him quizzically. "Hey, if Alice is right about not having certain things again in a long time, then I'm going to enjoy ice cold sodas while I can," and with that he finished re-strapping his things to the top of the trailer rack. He looked up to say he was ready and saw Nick and Hazel jogging across the parking lot to the grocery store only to emerge another 10 minutes later carrying their own coolers.

"He makes a good point," Nick smiled while adding his own cooler to the trailer. "I'm willing to haul it."

"What did you get?" Henry inquired.

"Gatorade and Jones Soda," he grinned.

"I approve. Maybe we can do a swap when we stop for the night," he pondered. Nick shook his head in the negative.

"No way, my man. You can go back and get more if you want." And with that Henry took off a third time and came back with several of his own Gatorades and root beers to add to his mix.

"What did you get?" Henry asked Hazel as he was cramming the new beverages into the cooler. He didn't quite have enough room for all of them and had to store a few warm ones in his backpack.

"Uh, let's see. I got iced coffee, diet Coke, Fiji water—a personal favorite—and ginger ale, just in case someone gets sick."

Finally, with the tents repacked, coolers filled and strapped down, coffee and various foods evenly distributed and packed, they were ready. "All set!" Henry shoved off with one foot. The others following suit.

It was a beautiful fall morning. Some of the trees were already yellowing and dropping their leaves at the hint of cooler air. The sun was shining again. Something that every Seattle native was thankful for and enjoyed as much as possible. They started the day at full speed ahead, although a little slower with more cargo in tow, trying to put as much distance between themselves and Seattle and the Sweepers as possible. They were quiet as they pedaled. The sound of their tires on asphalt was the only noise they added to the sounds around them. Overhead, birds were already flying in Vee formations as they prepared to migrate south for the winter. The highway took them through tall, dark fir trees that overhung the road. Light playing hide and seek between gaps in the trees; the deciduous trees adding flashes of light green, red, and yellow as sun peeked between shadows.

They started to climb steadily and after about 15 miles, Henry pulled into a campground that was to the right. Some late season campers were still there. Tents and trailers just as they had been on the night of the Petriclysm. Thankfully the campfires had all burned down and been snuffed most likely from the rain that came later. The stillness was heavy. Here there hadn't been many people to begin with and now the emptiness was amplified by the sheer stillness around them. A few birds flitted here and there, but nothing else moved.

Henry got off his bike, resting the handlebar against a tree to keep it upright. He dug in his trailer and pulled out the atlas. Sunlight was peeking through a couple of trees, making Henry's hair look like it was on fire, flames rippling as he moved. He flipped it open to the map and traced with his fingers to find their route.

"Uh, guys, we have a problem," he said while the others watched. They parked their bikes and joined him. "Um, you see here," he pointed, "This is a very high mountain pass. I think we might have accidentally overlooked it."

"Chinook Pass," Nick read. "Have you ever been up and over it?"

"No," Henry shook his head.

"It's usually the last pass to open in the spring and so we usually went a different way," Hazel said, looking over Henry's shoulder, "It's high. We have about thirty miles to go from here to get to the top. And then we have to go down."

"Well, what are you waiting for?" Nick asked. "The sooner we get started the sooner we get to the top."

"I'm…Do you think we should go a different way? Maybe go an easier route?" Henry suggested hopefully, putting the atlas back.

"Wait, are you afraid of heights?" Nick looked at him.

"Uh, maybe just a smidge," he held up his thumb and forefinger to demonstrate, looking a little embarrassed.

"If you stay in the middle of the road, you should be just fine, Henry," Hazel coached, coming up beside them. "I'm sure a lot of the road has guardrails and there probably weren't a whole lot of people on the road when the you-know-what hit the fan," she smiled trying to reassure him.

"What about driving up and over?" Henry mumbled.

"Probably won't work," he said. "Even though there probably won't be a lot of cars on the road, it might be a little too dangerous."

"Uh, we could at least try," Henry's voice trembled. He breathed out through his nostrils and slowly grabbed his bike.

"Well, maybe. Uh, sure. We can try," Nick surmised looking around the campground at what vehicles might be available, nervous at possibly having to drive. "There's a nice quad cab over there," he pointed to a cherry red, four-door truck. It even had an extended bed which would make hauling their gear easier. "Okay, then. Henry, can you drive?" he asked optimistically.

"No," was the immediate response. "Sorry, it's going to have to be you or Hazel." Nick had figured as much. He walked over to the campsite and searched the family, looking for keys. He found them, then hopped behind the steering wheel and gave the engine a try. It roared to life. He tested the brakes, then slowly, painfully drove over to where he had left his bike.

It took some time to load the bikes and trailers. The trailers, though relatively small, were now pretty weighed down. Once everything was adjusted and double-checked to make sure they wouldn't lose anything, they clambered in and buckled up, Nick behind the wheel. No one said anything for several miles as Nick adjusted to the feel and size of the truck. It was hard for him to keep the truck in one lane but figured driving down the middle of the road wasn't going to be too dangerous—no oncoming traffic so to speak.

The first vehicle in the roadway was easy to maneuver around, being mostly in the left-hand lane. As they continued, they found that it was rare to see any vehicles on the road. However, there were plenty of places where it was obvious vehicles had gone off the road and over the embankments. Henry kept his eyes closed for most of the trip, peeking only every so often to check their progress.

Halfway to the top of the pass they stopped at the outhouses located in a parking lot on the left. There were only two other cars in the lot, 7:30pm on a Thursday in late September not a high traffic time. Nick and the others got out to stretch their legs. Even though they hadn't gone but maybe ten miles, it felt like they'd been on the road for an extremely long time. Nick had driven so slowly and cautiously that, in one sense, a long time *had* elapsed, and, even though it was definitely more expedient than riding their bikes would have been, the tension made the trip feel that much longer. They all would breathe easier once safely down the other side of the pass. Henry still far preferred the slow climb in a truck than on his bike, though.

Henry went to use the rest room but came quickly came out of the first door and checked the second and came right back out. "They're both in use," he relayed. "I'm just going to go over there." He pointed to a rather large clump of bushes. He hid behind them easily. Hazel grabbed some toilet paper from the first outhouse and tried to avoid looking at the person sitting on the toilet seat. It was hard to avoid seeing the look of concentration on the marbled face, pants down around the ankles. *What a way to go*, she thought to herself. *Please don't let that happen to me.*

While they were stopped, Alice pulled out the two-burner stove, a small pot in which she put water, the French press and some freshly ground coffee from the wide variety they now had on hand and made coffee for everyone. She figured that everyone needed a pick-me-up and could use a longer break. They'd already saved countless hours by using the truck. The air was cooler than it had been further down the mountain and the warmth from the coffee was welcomed. Each of them had a piece of coffee cake to round out their repast. Once they were ready, they hit the road again, Nick feeling a little more comfortable driving, but still wouldn't push the speed above twenty, which felt like racing on the sharp turns—he only took those at approximately 5mph.

As they neared the top, rounding the final corner, Nick slammed on the brakes coming to a sudden stop. Henry kept his eyes closed and started shaking, mumbling to himself that they were all going to die. Finally, he decided to sneak a glimpse as Nick got out of the truck. There were about four vehicles blocking the road, one of which was a large RV, leaning precariously toward the edge of the road, a smaller vehicle wedged underneath it, keeping it from sliding down the mountainside. Two larger sedans had crumpled into the end of the RV, sitting at odd angles that completely obstructed the path of the truck. Nick got out to survey the scene. Henry sat still in his seat, crossing his fingers and toes that there would be a way to get the truck around the mess. He could see Nick walking around the white sedan on the left and disappear to the other side of the wreck. A moment later he came back around shaking his head. End of the line, there being only room for about two people to walk abreast between the end of the sedan and the sheer rock wall beside it. Nick beckoned to the others to help start unloading their bikes and trailers.

Henry slowly got out, his legs shaking, but admitted that it felt a little better on solid ground. He didn't dare look toward the RV and beyond. They were only about a mile from the top of the pass. The tops of two hundred-foot trees were eye level. Distant ridges seemed to draw closer and then swim back as he looked out. He got dizzy and walked over to the rock wall and sat down.

The others let him be and began unpacking the trailers and bikes. One at a time, they wheeled the bikes to the other side of the wreckage. Once they were set, Nick went to talk to Henry and help him get up and get going.

"Hey," Nick said, as he approached and sat down next to Henry. "How you doing?"

Henry peered out from behind his hands, "Oh, I've been better," he said slowly. "I think I'm going to be sick."

"You're fine, Henry. We only have a mile to go to the top and then we can go down. If we hurry, we can be completely off this mountain before we stop for the night. Plus, we saved a whole heck of a lot of time driving this far. Good call. I'm sorry we couldn't go all the way, but, hey, the sooner we reach the top, the sooner we're down."

"I'm so scared I'm going to accidentally go off the edge. Or my bike brakes will quit working. Or I'll go too fast to stop and," he whistled and threw his thumb over his shoulder, "down I go. Aren't you afraid of anything? I am so embarrassed, but I just can't help it. I didn't know I was afraid of heights until we visited the Grand Canyon. I just cried and cried and cried and my dad made fun of me and then took my arm and pretended he was going to throw me over the edge."

"I am so sorry that your dad did that to you. Of course, I'm afraid of things. I'm terrified of drowning. I hate the idea that I wouldn't be able to breath. So, I learned to swim really well instead. I'm still afraid of drowning, but I also learned to like being in the water."

"Yeah, but how am I supposed to get over being afraid of heights?"

"Maybe start paying attention to just how amazingly beautiful it is up here instead of how high up we are. Maybe enjoy the fact that we may be the only people on earth who will enjoy this view ever again."

Henry looked up and looked around. He saw the tops of the trees lightly swaying in a cool breeze that brushed his cheek. He turned to the right and gasped. There in front of him in all her snow-capped glory was Mt. Rainier. His favorite mountain and one he often didn't get a chance to see living in a city that was too rainy most of the time for much visibility. He took a deep, steadying breath. Nick helped him to his feet.

"She really is beautiful, isn't she," he turned to Nick. "Thanks." They got up slowly and joined the others. They erred on the side of caution and decided to simply walk their bikes, enjoy the scenery as Nick had encouraged Henry. When they reached the top, they stood facing the mountain peak, so close it felt like they could reach out and touch it. There was a quiet lake that had made its home in front of the mountain, its water rippling, saying "Here I am, picture perfect" to any passersby. They stood still, taking in the view, allowing their eyes to lock the idyllic images firmly in their memories.

Then they started their descent. Nick and Hazel leading the way while Henry and Alice hung back. Henry still didn't feel much like riding, so they all walked the steep decline. It was so steep that they had to point their toes to keep from letting their legs runaway with them. It was really a good thing they'd chosen to walk their bikes instead of ride. Henry stayed as close to the inside of the road as possible. It was a long afternoon and took almost six hours for them to reach the bottom of the pass. Their leg muscles were sore from having had to keep them at such an odd angle for so long. As it was close to dark, they looked for a place to camp and were happy to find a campground nearby.

The tents still smelled strongly of spray paint, but with enough time between setting up the tents and using them to sleep, the hope was that the tents would seep off the aerosol smell and be ready for sleeping in. Hazel helped Nick and Henry gather firewood while Alice found enough rocks to ring a fire pit. While she waited for the others to bring the firewood, she found the four small chairs that Jackson had encouraged them to bring and arranged them neatly in a semi-circle. It wasn't long before the fire was blazing. After the trek they'd had that day, having covered nearly 65 miles between riding, riding, and walking they were exhausted.

"I know this is only the second day since we left, but what do you think about staying here all of tomorrow and resting?" asked Alice finishing a cheeseburger and grabbing a second one.

"I like the idea," Henry assented, now on his third. "Besides, it would give Jackson a chance to catch up a little bit. Think he's made it to Vancouver, yet?"

"I hope so," said Alice dreamily, nibbling on an apple pie. Henry eyed her suspiciously. She caught his look. "I really hope he can find his sister and his nieces and not get caught by Sweepers. That's all," she looked at Henry, giving him one of her most innocent looks she could muster, eyes wide and doll-like. She got up and rifled through the Starbucks bag. "Anybody for pumpkin loaf?" she held it up.

They brought out more cheeseburgers and pies, saving the waffles and bacon for the morning. There was no limit to how much they were allowed to eat now. Nick and Hazel especially took advantage of this fact. Nick had already regained most of the muscle mass he had lost while in Anvac. Hazel's ribs were starting to disappear again, which was such a relief to her. When she had picked out her clothes two days before, she'd counted on the fact that she would return to her old size and had selected sizes based on that. She was happy she'd had such foresight.

The evening got darker and colder. They threw their wrappers into the fire and silently watched them shrivel to nothing. It was enjoyable to watch the flames dance, soaking in the heat while letting their bodies unwind and rest from the stresses of the day. They let the fire die down and doused the remaining coals with water from the nearby stream before turning in for the night. Once everyone was comfortably in their sleeping bags, Henry flicked the solar light off and watched the stars twinkle far away overhead, ringed by a shadow of amazingly tall pine trees, the crisp scent washing over them all as they fell asleep.

CHAPTER 13

The next morning dawned bright, sun cascaded through the trees surrounding the two tents. The paint kept the tents darker on the inside than they would have if still bright orange. No one stirred for quite a while. The four lingered in their warm sleeping bags, snoozing on and off until the need for coffee and bladder relief overtook their need for more sleep. They were still stiff from the first two days on the road, so moving was limited from sleeping bag to outhouse—conveniently located across the way from their campsite—to chair by the fire, to gathering more firewood, resumed sitting, back to sleeping bag, and so on. The cycle repeated itself in variations throughout the day.

To officially begin the day, Henry used the French press and made several pots of coffee in succession, not able to keep the cups filled for long. Nick and Hazel gathered enough firewood for their first fire and then sat in their respective chairs, absorbing the heat from the various sources—sun, fire, coffee. It was a wonderful way to spend the day. There wasn't much talking, lots of napping, a little bit of leg stretching, and general relaxation, enjoying the slowness of the day. A much-needed respite after the week they'd already had. Nick calculated that it had been exactly a week since the Petriclysm.

Alice wandered off on her own, heeding the warnings from Henry not to wander too far. Nick and Henry chatted about what sports they'd played in high school. Nick, a shoe in, had played varsity basketball, starting his sophomore year. He didn't really like sports all that much, but being as tall as he was, it was expected of him. Henry, on the other hand, hadn't been very interested in team sports. "Yeah, I was more into gaming," he could be overheard saying to Nick.

"What kind of games? I played a lot of PS4 myself."

"PS4? No way, dude. I'm actually a PC gamer. Before the Great Wave, I was saving up to build my own gaming computer. I was captain of our eSports team. Oh, and I also ran long distance."

"eSports? Do you really consider it a sport? I mean, really?"

"Well, for those of us who aren't necessarily that athletic or don't like the jock culture, it was a great outlet for us. Plus, I had a lot of good friends on the team," he said sadly, thinking that the Petriclysm had most likely gotten them, too. "We were held to the same standards as your typical sports team member," he added for legitimacy.

"I see your point," Nick understood. "But I am surprised you weren't on some sort of sports team. You seem to be athletic. I mean, you're in great shape and you rode your bike a lot before this."

"True, I do like to run long distance and ride my bike, but I'm not so keen on the team sports aspect of football or basketball. You see this," he flexed his arm to show Nick. "No muscle. I tried everything. Protein shakes, weightlifting. Nothing. I'm just kind of scrawny."

"But you have endurance."

"True. I do have that. Speaking of which, do you want to go for a little walk? We should stretch out our sore muscles a little if we're going to be ready for tomorrow."

"Sure," Nick stood and yawned. "Hey, Hazel, want to go for a walk?" He bent down to look into the tent where Hazel was writing.

"No thanks," she shook her head and returned her attention to the journal in front of her.

September 30

Seems like forever since I had the chance to write but looking at the date it's only been seven day. Seven. Days. Really? Only a week since the Petriclysm? That's what we've dubbed it. Definition: "the cataclysmic petrification of almost 8 billion people". I think it could be a winner for new word of the year. Eight billion people? I can't really wrap my head around that. I mean, I see the evidence whenever I walk into a store or cruise down the highway, but that's not even a drop in the bucket compared the enormity of what humanity suffered one week ago. It's more like a drop in the ocean.

We took today off to rest. I'm really glad that Alice suggested we stay here an extra day. I know we've only been on the road for two days, but it's been a lifetime, it seems, since everything went down last week. I think we are all still weary from grief. All of us lost at least one parent. We've been on the go since everything happened.

So many times, in the last couple of days I wanted to ask my dad what he thought of this or that, what decision I should make; is it going to be the right decision? What did I forget to consider when deciding? I'm at such a loss and no matter what choice I make, I still feel like I am forgetting something important. I mean, like when Nick said he doesn't want to use the kill switch that William modified because he believes there are still innocent people with the BioID out there. I agree and he convinced all of us to use the other one. I hadn't even thought about that. I'm glad Nick is a voice of reason.

I will say that the best part of this whole situation, if there's anything good about it and I'm trying to find it, has been the freedom. We decided to go to Denver. If one can separate out why we're going and what we left behind, what we've lost, I'd say that this trip has been a lot of fun—well, the shopping part and the eating part and riding bikes as far as we want with people we like. It's been a long time since I've been in the forest or gotten to go camping. I love having fresh air to breath. It's nice not to be afraid of guards at gates or wondering if I'm going to have enough to eat. Of course, we worry about Sweepers, but right now, we haven't seen anyone on the road and it's highly doubtful that Sweepers would come this way. Alice was very smart in suggesting we take backroads and lesser used highways. I'm so glad to be surrounded by such smart individuals. It's a relief to share this strange time with others. It already feels like I've known Alice and Henry as long as I've known Nick. I'm so thankful they didn't turn out to be jerks. That would make this so much less enjoyable. I'm really enjoying the comradery of traveling together, helping each other, setting up camp, raiding stores for supplies and not having to pay. I like those parts. And we're still so far from Denver that we have plenty of time to enjoy these things before having to do what we've set out to do.

We haven't run into anyone else, yet. I know there are others out there like us who were either in a hellhole like Anvac or who had fake BioIDs like Alice and Henry, but we haven't seen them. The only other people we've seen besides each other, and this other kid named Jackson, are the Sweepers. They scare the crap out of me. Sometimes I think I see their black SUVs in the distance, but it's my mind playing tricks on me. Thankfully.

I think Alice and Henry have the right idea about enjoying all the conveniences of Starbucks and McDonald's as long as we can before they vanish completely. I never realized how much I did miss them until now. And I'll miss them all over again soon.

I don't think it's so much missing the actual food or anything, but the way of life it represented. The sad thing is the easy-to-get convenience of certain things in our lives is probably what led to our current predicament. Think about it, as a nation, we became pretty complacent, and when some of our rights were slowly being snatched up by those in charge, we didn't respond. We simply demanded more fast food and more entertainment. As long as the immediate desires were being fulfilled, we didn't care about much else. When the Great Wave hit, the majority of people were willingly throwing away their freedoms, almost hurling them at the government, demanding new laws that would make them feel safe. Some were compelled to act when people started touting that it was the "patriotic" thing to do, so even those who tended toward freedom jumped on the bandwagon in a last-ditch effort to show loyalty to all things USA. I also think people went along with things because they didn't want to get picked on for having "wrong thoughts". It's all the lemmings going the same direction even if it's wrong.

My dad was right when he used to tell me that there was more risk with freedom. I guess I wasn't really old enough, yet, to appreciate his wisdom. I see his point, though. Even better now that I am experiencing freedom again for the first time in over two years. It feels so good to be able to make certain decisions without having to think about whether or not I'm breaking a law or if I'm going to get in trouble or bullied. It feels really good to not be lying awake at night starving, praying that there would maybe be more food the next day. It still feels really strange walking into any store and simply taking what I need and sometimes taking something just because I want it. But I like it. No lie. Since there's no money and no people it's not technically stealing—although it still feels weird not paying. With most of humanity frozen solid, there's more than plenty for the taking. Sometimes the options are a bit overwhelming. Unfortunately, some stores are already starting to smell from rotting food. Mostly vegetables at this point. As far as I know, the power is still on. Nick says it won't be long now, though.

The freedom we—me, Nick, Henry, Alice, and Jackson—have is a lot scarier. There are no rules. Well, one rule. Stay away from the Sweepers. They're crazy scary and almost drove away with Jackson. I don't like to think about what could have happened to him if Nick and Henry hadn't gone after him. I guess another rule is that we do the right thing even when no one is looking. I still try to remember that I am a reflection of my parents and want to honor their lives—

The high whine of a distant motor caught everyone's ear. It was moving fast coming from the top of the pass. Hazel rushed out of the tent where she had been journaling, Nick and Henry returned from their walk around the campground. They looked frantically around for Alice who wasn't there. "Alice!" Henry loudly whispered, panic building. They saw some bushes moving and then Alice burst through them, running at full speed.

"What do we do?" she asked, winded.

"Hide," was all Nick could say. He picked up a canteen and doused the fire, sending up a plume of grey smoke. He sucked in his teeth realizing he had given whoever was out there a better idea that they were here than if he had just let the fire burn. "Crap," he muttered.

"Can't do anything about it now," Henry surmised. "They either take our stuff or they don't. It sounds like a motorcycle." Then, "we need to get behind those boulders," he pointed, "and be ready to shoot if necessary." They quickly grabbed their police belts parked inside each tent and scrambled behind the boulders. The engine sound drew nearer at a high whine as they positioned themselves behind the rocks.

Nick was crossing his fingers that the person or persons would simply drive on by, but as the vehicle neared, they could hear the high whine of the engine shift to a lower gear. Whoever was out there was slowing down. They heard gravel grinding under tires as the vehicle left the road and turned into the campground. The engine idled not far from where they'd left their tents and, after a pause, the engine came to a rumbling halt altogether, more gravel shifted as though underfoot. Whoever it was walked around their campfire.

They heard a whistle—"Bob White!" It sounded two more times "Bob White! Bob White!" Henry smiled and jumped up from behind the rocks before the others could grab him. "Jackson!" he yelled with a smile and ran over, grabbing Jackson's hand and pulling him into an embrace, using his other hand to slap his back while Jackson did likewise. To their amazement, there Jackson stood between the tents, releasing Henry's hand. He grinned at them as Nick, Hazel, and Alice came out from behind the boulder. Their attention was draw to a glossy black motorcycle with a sidecar parked near where they'd left the bikes.

"You rode that?!" Henry grinned in excitement pointing at the bike.

"Yeah, I thought it would save some time," Jackson smiled back, "but I brought my bike and everything else." He indicated the sidecar. It had a large blue tarp battened down around the top of it.

"Brilliant!" Henry surveyed. "Hey, we should all ride bikes. What do you think?"

"Probably not," Jackson responded, watching the gleam in Henry's eyes fade. "It was safe enough to get here because the Sweepers were going the other direction, but since we're headed practically the same way ourselves, the motors could give us away. It's just as easy to ride. 'Sides, I like a good, long bike ride with new friends."

"I suppose so," Henry kicked some rocks with his right foot in disappointment but agreed. The sound of Jackson's motor being a good case-in-point. He perked up, "Did you make it to Vancouver?"

Jackson smiled and gave two thumbs up. "I have a lot to tell you," he looked at them, "But first, I'm starving." He went and undid a couple of the straps that held down the tarp. He lifted a flap and extracted a small camp chair similar to the ones he had encouraged the others to bring. He unfolded it, setting it beside Alice's chair, unbeknownst to him. Then went back and scrounged around until he found a tinfoil to go container.

"Olive Garden," he said as he peeled back the cover to reveal cold cheese ravioli with plenty of marinara sauce. "Oh, yeah," he snapped his fingers, set down the dish and went back to the sidecar. He came back with a sizable foil bag, reached in and brought out a garlic bread stick. He waved it over the fire Nick had gotten going again, to warm it up, then bit into it. With his mouth full he asked, "Anybody else?" as he proffered the bag to the others. They all helped themselves and followed his example by running the bread over the fire and sat munching, the salty garlic dancing across their taste buds. After a couple of days of lots of sweets, the savory breadsticks were a welcome departure. "I have more if anybody wants," he set the bag down on a nearby rock.

"So," Henry mumbled between bites of breadstick, "How did you catch up to us so fast. I mean, other than riding that awesome looking bike and all." He dreamily let his eyes rest on the motorcycle again.

"Vancouver's only about 150 miles or so from Seattle. I waited around long enough to make sure the Sweepers left town, then went looking for a motorcycle. The sidecar was a stroke of luck, so instead of having to go back to REI for my bike and supplies and then catch up on bicycle, I was able to take it all with me. After I found my sister—more on that in a sec—I took different backroads and picked up your route in Enumclaw. I figured you couldn't be too far this side of the pass in only two days. I saw the outline of your tents in paint on the grass. Good thinking on camouflaging your tents. That orange would give you away in a heartbeat. It was luck that Nick threw water on your fire, too," Nick having told him already, "otherwise I would have passed you. I was planning on slowing down to look for you and if I couldn't find you, I would have waited in Lewiston, knowing that I would have beat you there."

"So, you were planning on riding your motorcycle all the way to Lewiston?" Henry eyeballed him suspiciously, trying to find a reason they could all ride one of those instead.

"No, I was going to ditch it just before Yakima. I wasn't going to risk drawing people out of their holes," he took a couple of big bites of ravioli and scarfed another breadstick before continuing. "Man, Vancouver was a mess. There were a lot more people there. No one tried anything, which was good, but still, it's total chaos."

"Any Sweepers?" Nick asked.

"Well, kinda. They were there and all, but they joined the antivaxxers in a kind of rebellion. They didn't trust those running North Pangea to follow through on their promises once they were done following orders. Also, they were pretty pissed at what NP had done. A lot of them lost people they know. So instead, they met with the leaders of Novax and they're setting up their own rogue government. My sister's the vice president!" he smiled proudly.

"And your nieces?" Hazel prompted.

"They're doing great! They're only 7 and 9, so they're happy to have the chance to go back to school once they set it up and very, very happy to have lots of food. I don't think they stopped eating the whole time I was there. Granted, I only stayed overnight and about half a day.

"I told them that I had to go and meet friends. That you were planning on a bike tour of the country and that I wanted to go with you so I wouldn't be staying. I didn't tell them you were headed to Denver or why. Even though the Sweepers weren't doing their job and I don't think they were intending on ever reporting back to the president, I didn't want to jeopardize our mission in anyway." They were really glad to hear that Jackson hadn't said anything. It was wise to be overly careful now. "They did ask me if I wanted to go back and help them set up the government when I was done with my vacation. You're welcome to go, too. I think they may have some bigger plans to actually go after the Pangean government, too. They all lost people they know and are itching for a little revenge or payback something like that. I didn't promise anything, but we have someplace to go if we want. Just throwing it out there," he took another bite of breadstick, salt sticking to the corners of his mouth.

"Did you see BioDie?" Alice asked.

"William? Yeah, I stopped by. He gave me a fake BioID like yours. Apparently after you left, he decided to make as many as he could before the lights went out. Have them on hand just in case, you know. And that reminds me, bad news, the power *is* officially out. It went out while I was going through Enumclaw. Good thing William already had quite a few of the BioIDs made. He also started to relocate his apartment to one above ground just after you were there. While I was there, I helped carry out a couple of bodies from the apartment he chose. It's weird trying to move them. I was afraid I'd drop one of them and break 'em. Gives me the creeps. But you'll be glad to know that the apartment he chose is very nicely furnished, clean, and modern. Oh," he paused, got up to grab something from the sidecar, and came back, handing a black shopping bag to Henry, "here, he asked me to give that to you."

Henry took the bag and felt that there was something pretty solid inside it. He unwound the plastic and untied the double-knots in the handles. He reached in and extracted a perfect replica of the Karmann Ghia he helped deliver five days before. It was even the right shade of blue. Henry turned it over in his hands, inspecting every detail. He smiled and looked at Jackson for an explanation

"William knew that you'd fallen in love with his car and figured you needed your own. I don't know how he knew that he'd be able to get one into your hands or anything, but he made that one for you," he said by way of explanation.

"I told him we'd try and come back if we were successful in Denver," Henry said cradling the model in his lap. "It's an exact replica. I wonder how he even found a model so soon?" he said more to himself.

"Oh, that's easy," Jackson answered, "He has a whole section of his bedroom full of new models in the box. He's storing them to do when he gets bored and with the lights off, I'm sure he's going to have a lot of extra time."

"Well, at any rate, he did a great job on this one. Hey look," he opened the tiny driver's side door and reached in. He extracted a piece of paper wrapped around an oblong object. He uncurled the paper and a small red SanDisk 512G flash drive fell into his palm. The six-inch scrap of paper was a note. It read in big block letters firmly pressed into the paper, "Everything you need to know about them." He looked up, confused. Nick read the note over his shoulder and went to find the laptop in his trailer. Once the laptop came to life, Henry slipped the flash drive into a port and waited for the device to be recognized. He double-clicked on the icon that appeared on the screen. The flash drive was full of files all named for different individuals. He recognized Christopher MacPherson's name, alongside Calvin Hastings, and several others from reading the news. He clicked on MacPherson's file. A long list of documents appeared. Jackson was looking over his shoulder now.

"Holy crap," Jackson said, "those are all of his personal records." He pointed to a couple of them, "See 'Vaccine records.' And there 'DMV records.'"

"BioDie, I mean, William, gave us all the personal records of all of these people?"

"Not just any people," Jackson looked wild eyed. "These are all the elites. Everyone who got to live. They're the ones who decided who lived and who died."

"Demigods," Alice whispered.

"Why would he give this to us?" Henry panicked.

"To you, Henry, he gave it specifically to you. I'm not sure what William intended, yet, but I'm guessing it's going to play a big part when we get to Denver. Find a really good place to store that. And whatever you do, don't lose it," Jackson admonished.

Henry bowed his head, the gravity of what he was holding taking effect. He reversed his earlier actions wrapping the flash drive in the note, sliding it through the driver's side door of the model Karmann Ghia, rewrapping the model back in the plastic bag. He walked it over to his bike trailer, burying it in a corner at the bottom, making sure to wind it up in his old sweatshirt for extra protection.

CHAPTER 14

They drew their chairs closer to the fire, a stack of firewood was ready for the long evening chat. It was starting to get dark and the shadows were descending on them. Henry offered sodas around, but Nick and Hazel declined, getting their own before the ice completely melted. Jackson thanked Henry and popped the tab, took a long sip and then started with the last part of his story.

"So, you remember the green buses, right?" he looked at Nick and Hazel, a shiver running down both their spines. The last time they saw the buses, they'd been parked in front of the virology lab. They indicated they did. "Well," Jackson continued, "I saw a couple of them. The Sweepers are using them." The dark night seemed heavier at his words. Black SUVs skimming down the freeway flashed in their minds.

"What?" Nick and Hazel let out, shifting to the edge of their seats.

"Yeah. They requisitioned the buses to haul away the people they choose to take with them. They rolled out a couple of hours after you left. Before I went anywhere, I went to see if I could find where they were keeping the people they rounded up. I was curious as to what kind of fate you saved me from."

"And?" Henry encouraged.

"And it's not good. If you had any reservations about using the Covax shutdown code, I wouldn't now." Nick and Hazel exchanged looks, they would have to tell Jackson their decision when they could. "So, here's how it went. I walked about half a mile back toward Pike Place Market. After what you told me about them kind of herding kids that direction it made sense to check there. I snuck through one of the buildings that face the market and went up a couple of stories to see if I could see better. There was a lot going on. There were three black SUVS and two green buses parked outside the main market entrance. I didn't have a great view from where I was, but in the distance, I could see the top of a guillotine. Like the one they used to roll into Anvac on occasion. Who knows, it might have been the same one. There was a long line of people that spilled out onto the street. I couldn't see what they were waiting for, but what I could see was the blade of the guillotine reaching the top and then falling. I am really, really glad I didn't have to see the final result," he winced at the memory. "I saw enough of that in Anvac. It made me sick. I stayed there and watched the line get shorter and shorter. Armed guards were all around, ready to shoot anyone who tried to run away. One did and headed for the building I was in. A little boy. Probably no more than 10. He didn't get very far before I heard the report of a gun. Again. I was glad I couldn't see anything," he studied his hands for a few, the face of the little boy fresh on his mind. Anger registering on his features as he replayed the memory.

After a pause he continued, "Once the line disappeared into the building, I was going to leave, but then another group made up of almost all kids with a few adults were marched out from the market and put on a bus. Of all the people I saw going into the market, the number that were put on the bus didn't even fill half of one of them." He shook his head sadly, then looked at each of them in turn, "Two of my best friends from high school are on that bus. Ivy and Felix. They must've been in East Anvac. I wanted to go after them, get them off that bus, but I just couldn't figure out how," frustrated, he crumpled the foil sack the breadsticks had been in and threw it into the fire, it burned in a bright flash of flame. "And then," he continued, "the buses started up and followed the SUVS up the hill and to the right. I had no time to act. But I'm pretty sure they were headed for I-5 South."

"We saw the SUVs," Nick confirmed, "But we didn't see the buses."

"Maybe they passed while we were in Home Depot or something," Alice volunteered.

"Maybe," Nick turned back to Jackson, "Do you think the buses would have been that far behind the SUVs?"

"Maybe a little way behind. I think the drivers of the SUVs like to go fast, but those old buses probably can only top 55 at best," Jackson reasoned. "Besides, it's not like they need the buses right away. They're for when the sweeping job is done."

"What kind of people were on the buses?" Alice asked.

"Well," Jackson thought for a sec, "If I had to give a general description of them, I would say healthy. Probably able to work. A lot. None of them looked sick and very few of them were female, that, I remember sticking out to me. Ivy and Felix, for example, are both very athletic. They still looked very fit when I saw them getting on the bus."

"What do you think they're going to do with the people?" Nick asked.

"Use them," Alice broke in. "It's as simple as that. From what Jackson described, they're only keeping the healthiest and then shipping them off to Denver. Why else would they need people?"

"Soooo, Nick was right. They're keeping people to work. Like slaves," Henry balked at the idea.

"Yes," Jackson jumped in. "Alice is right. Who else is going to grow the food and make sure the lights stay on? You think the elite are going to do the menial tasks? They won't give up their luxuries by any means, they'll just make sure they keep enough serfs around to run things."

"How do they keep them from revolting? These people they're capturing," Henry asked.

"That's easy," Hazel spoke up. "They threaten you. Hence the guillotine."

Henry looked confused. "I don't think I would want to be a slave or anything. I'd rather be gone."

"For some," Hazel cut in, "life is worth more than just being comfortable. It's not the quality of life, but life itself that's important. Besides, until death, there's always hope for something better."

"Very true," Jackson agreed. "So maybe it's our job to make sure those who are being forced to work are afforded the same opportunities we now have. We have freedom, we can choose where we go, what we eat, and eventually whenever the dust settles—if it does—where we live. I wish we could find a way to get my friends off that bus, but there's no way of knowing where they are."

"They're headed to Denver, at least for now," Nick spoke up trying to reassure Jackson. "Maybe we can intercept the buses in Denver or find them once we're done with our other business."

"That sounds like a really good plan, Nick. Yeah," Jackson stared into the fire. "I really want to get Felix and Ivy away from those people. Take them back to Vancouver with me."

"I'm going to free them all," Nick spoke up. "Give them the same opportunities I have now. Like you said. Oh, and before I forget, we've decided to use the Operation Covax version that Hazel's dad left behind. There are most likely still innocent people out there with the BioID. And who's to say they won't ID those they round up."

"As much as I want to get them, I understand where you're coming from," Jackson replied. "Taking out the system will cause a lot more damage to the elite. Give them a taste of their own medicine," he laughed, "They'll wish we'd used the other when all is said and done. They can't live without their luxuries." The way he put it made the others grin. It was more perfect than they had originally thought.

They were all quiet for a few minutes mulling things over, their gazes mesmerized by the licking flames. Nick got up to throw more wood on the fire. He stopped, a branch still in his hands. The others were instantly on high alert, turning to follow Nick's line of sight. Not far from their fire, tucked into the trees was a blue neon glow, floating about eye level. The light pulsated, glowing brightly, then fading from sight, only to grow bright again. Then, the light disappeared. Nick stood frozen.

"There it is again," Jackson whispered, pointing a different direction. The blue light had moved from the trees to spot a little to the right, closer to the water. Henry silently moved to the tent and unholstered his gun, keeping it at his side, coming to stand beside Nick and Jackson. Without a word, the three of them advanced to where this new light was pulsating, brighter, dimmer, brighter. They drew near to the place where'd they seen the first light. Standing in the trees, hidden from the tents was a person, frozen in time, backpack riding high on the back. The man looked like he'd been whistling when the Petriclysm took him by surprise. Henry raised his gun as they approached the light—it flashed and went out. They tracked the other light. It was another person, this time a woman, standing firmly on both feet, walking stick in hand, eyes looking down. Her face illuminated by the blue light emanating from the middle of her forehead. Nick stepped closer to examine this woman. "Look," he pointed. The beacon glowed brighter again, throwing a faint shadow of the boys behind them. "It's coming from the BioID." While he was staring at the three little dots, the woman's eyelids fluttered up in a mechanical motion, the pupils that hadn't been visible before focused on Nick's face. "Ahhhhh," Nick jumped back. "Did you see that?" he pointed at her eyes. "They moved! The eyes moved!"

"That's impossible," Jackson stepped closer.

"I'm telling you, they moved!" was the adamant reply.

"It's just the light. It has to be. They're dead. All of them. Turned to stone!"

"Look!" Nick contended. Jackson got closer. The woman's eyes shifted, focusing on him. The light now radiating so brightly that it lit up each of their faces. Then, the eyelids resumed their original position, and the light went out leaving them in utter darkness, trying to make sense of what they'd just witnessed. They were blind and waited until their eyes readjusted to the night, refocusing on the fire as they walked away. None of them said a word.

They came through the clearing where the fire had burned down. Hazel and Alice approached, recoiling at the looks of panic etched across the boys' faces. "What happened?" Hazel asked. Nick explained the best he could what they'd seen. Hazel followed up, "Wait, the woman was alive?"

"No," Nick shook his head. "No. The BioID was glowing blue and then her eyelids opened up."

"And her pupils focused on us," Henry put in. "Well, on you and Jackson. I don't think she knew I was there."

"She didn't know any of us were there," Jackson derided. "Some fluke with the BioID or something. Nothing more."

"I want to see this woman," Hazel stated. Alice shook her head in agreement. Nick sighed, not really wanting to see the hikers again in the dark. Henry was more amenable and went to the tent for a flashlight. He flicked it on to check the batteries, then motioned for all of them to follow him. He had a hard time remembering which direction they had gone to begin with, having been more focused on the light. Henry swept the flashlight from side to side. Trees shifting in the light, casting long dark shadows that moved in step with Henry's gait. Finally, Henry found the first hiker. The man was now to their right and they approached the statue from the side. Henry gave the girls a long look at this man. There was nothing remarkable. As far as he could remember, this man was exactly the same as before. Henry then started looking for the woman whose eyes had moved. He swept the light in wide arcs searching the surrounding area. Nick helped Henry and headed in the general direction they'd gone after seeing the first hiker, but the woman eluded them. They couldn't find her. Nick, Henry, and Jackson fanned out further, double-checking the area and the trees and still they could not find the woman who had stood not more than twenty feet from the man.

"She's got to be here somewhere," Henry mumbled to himself.

"Maybe you just forgot where she was," Alice tried to help. "How about we go back to the fire and try to find her in the morning. We'll be able to see a lot better then."

"No," Henry replied. "You have to see her. I know she's here."

"I'm sure she hasn't moved and won't by the morning," Nick reassured Henry. "Let's just get back to the tents. I would feel much better closer to camp. These woods are starting to play tricks on us." He grabbed Henry's arm and gently led him back to the fire.

Nick threw more wood on the hot coals, now restless and alert. He kicked his legs out in front of him. "You know what I want?" he said trying to lighten the mood, bringing the others out of their reveries. "I want a s'more. Next time we have the chance to do a little shopping, let's pick up the fixings." They all smiled and agreed that it was a fine idea. The fire slowly died; the mystery of the woman would have to wait until morning. Eventually they got up one by one to turn in for the night. It was going to be an early start the following day.

CHAPTER 15

The sun didn't come out the next day; it lay hidden behind a thick layer of dark cloud. Henry was up first. The others found him desperately searching the woods for signs of the female hiker they'd seen the night before. The man was still where they had left him, but of the woman they saw no sign.

"Maybe she was never there," Nick tried to help explain her away.

"Then why did all three of us see her?" Henry wanted to know.

"I'm not sure. Maybe we were just tired or scared or something. Maybe we ate something that made us hallucinate."

"All three of us? All seeing the same thing? I don't buy it," Henry walked off.

To be expedient, they didn't start a fire and instead used the gas stove to boil water for coffee. Once everyone had enough caffeine to get them partially energized, they set about breaking down camp and repacking the trailers. Jackson unloaded his sidecar and tucked the tarp into his own trailer. Then he walked the motorcycle to the boulders the others had hidden behind the evening before. He used extra brush to hide the motorcycle the best he could. He wanted to use the tarp to cover the bike for protection—hoping to come back and ride it again in the future, but knew the tarp was more valuable with him. There would be more motorcycles to come.

"Where's Henry?" Alice asked.

"Henry!" Jackson yelled. "It's time to go!"

No response.

"Henry!" Jackson yelled again. "It's time to go! Nick, check the outhouse. I'll check the stream." Jackson was walking along the water's edge when Nick caught up to him. Shaking his head. Henry wasn't in the outhouse. "Maybe we should check where we might've seen that woman last night. One more time. I'll bet you anything, he's looking for her again." They headed off in the direction. A few minutes later they found Henry, rooted to a spot in front of the woman hiker. She was much further away from the male hiker now.

"I found her," Henry stated as they approached. "We were looking in the wrong spot. Or she moved. She moved I know it." The three of them looked at her. Eyelids still half-closed, walking stick still in the right hand. She looked just as they remembered after the blue lights had gone out.

"Well," Nick said, putting his arm around Henry, hoping to head him in the direction of their bikes, "She looks just like the others do." Henry resisted Nick's nudging.

"I think she looks a little different," he said. "Her eyes are more open than they were."

"How can you possibly tell?" Jackson said, incredulous. "We saw her for like a nanosecond after she looked at us. Besides, we were scared crapless last night. There's no way to remember details like that."

"But, I remember," Henry was emphatic, "I remember."

"I believe you," Nick said gently and finally got Henry to turn back toward camp. None of them saw the blue light flicker as they walked away.

The goal for the day was to make it to Yakima, hopefully replenish some supplies and sleep in another hotel. Even though the power was out, a bed could still be slept in and it sounded wonderful. The promise of a bed was good incentive to get going. Thankfully, Yakima was less than 70 miles from their campsite. It was going to be an easy day of riding on mostly flat surfaces. Since the Sweepers had headed down I-5 there was a slim to none chance of meeting them or anyone else at least for the day.

The five of them walked their bikes back to the main road, looked both ways to be sure, and got situated on their seats. All of them were still a little sore, but the extra day's rest had helped. As they adjusted to the ride, no one was very talkative, mostly thinking about the woman in the woods. They were thankful for the cloud cover since it kept them from getting too hot. On this side of the mountain range, it was warm even for the first day of October.

The first couple of hours were unremarkable. Even mundane. They pedaled at a steady rate, swerved to avoid small pile ups on the highway. Only once did they have to stop and walk their bikes around a sizable accident that completely impeded their progress. To their surprise, other than birds, there weren't many signs of wildlife. Even the deer and small animals were subdued in this new stillness. However, it probably wouldn't take long for them to realize the main threat to their lives were no longer around. Nature would eventually take its course. At one junction, they saw a man standing next to his vehicle, he had been on the phone apparently in an animated conversation. His right ear pressed to his right shoulder, phone sandwiched between the two, both arms out to the side in a waving motion. A big splat of bird dropping painted the left side of his face. There were three large crows perched on his outstretched arms. Hazel stopped to survey this odd-looking ode to the human race.

"Any of you miss your phones?" she asked, interrupting the crows' tête-à-tête. They took off with a few choice "caws" at this disruption.

"Yes," Alice shook her head up and down vehemently. "Actually, I brought mine with me. It doesn't work. No signal, I've tried, but I have taken a few pictures of all the petriclyzed people. I wanted to document what happened. Create a record." She got off and dug in her backpack, withdrawing an iPhone that she turned on. She walked around the man with the phone and took a couple of photos. She turned the phone to show

Hazel the pictures she'd taken. The photographs were the work of a pro. The man with the phone was a solitary figure, giving a human face to the loss of the way of life. It could have been printed and hung in a gallery.

"How do you do that?" Hazel looked at her, awed.

"Do what?"

"Snap a photo and make it so artistic?"

Alice blushed and shrugged, "I don't know. I've always been into photography. I took a class in school. I didn't bring my nice camera, though, Henry said it would take up too much room. I guess he was right, but I miss it." She sighed and turned off the phone, putting it back in her bag.

"If we get some time and you don't mind, I'd like to see the rest of your photos," Hazel looked at her earnestly.

Alice assented. Then, "If we get to another sporting goods store like REI, remind me to pick up a solar charging pack. I didn't think to pick one up before we left. It would be nice to not worry so much about losing my battery power."

"Agreed," Hazel said.

The others dismounted also and decided it was a good time to take a stretch break and eat a light snack. They still had about forty miles to go, which would mean at least another four hours on the road. The guys worked on finishing the rest of the cheeseburgers. They loathed the idea of throwing any of them away. The girls agreed and helped themselves to a cheeseburger each followed by slices of pumpkin loaf and gingerbread loaf from their Starbucks stash.

Henry finished off four cheeseburgers and then started moaning about a stomachache. "It's your fault," Alice admonished him. He groaned and got resituated on his bike.

"Yeah, I know," he said, "but just like Thanksgiving, there's a certain satisfaction in eating too much and complaining about it. Give this one to me. It's probably the last time I will ever have McDonald's," he said this last part as if he were in mourning.

Alice gently patted him on the back, "Poor baby. No more fast food. No more acne from fast food. No more indigestion from fast food. What will you *ever* do if you have to suffer eating real food?" She laughed and rode ahead to join Hazel.

"Don't be too hard on him," Hazel smiled. "Soon enough we're going to be out of Starbucks delicacies."

"True," Alice surmised. "Hey Henry, I'm sorry that you won't ever have McDonald's again. Maybe in Yakima we can pick up some black clothes for your period of mourning," she laughed again and pedaled faster to get away from Henry who was making a beeline for her bike.

Hazel turned to Nick and Jackson, "You know, that almost makes me sad I never had a sibling."

"If it will make you feel any better, I can pick on you some more," Nick grinned at her.

"Hard pass," was the response. "You tease me enough any way, but it's just the right balance. Any less I'd think you didn't like me; more, and I'd have to kick your booheinie," she looked back at him and smiled, then they all pedaled hard, off the seat for more oomph, to catch up with Alice and Henry who were laughing at some joke further down the road.

They planned on waiting to stop again until they reached Yakima, but the stillness and humidity of the day weighed them down as they neared the city, each of them started to feel more unsure about getting there. Henry thought he saw blinking blue lights every now and then making him jittery.

"Are you guys getting a weird feeling as we get closer to Yakima?" Henry turned and asked.

"It seems really, *really* quiet," Hazel conferred. "The birds aren't even singing." As they looked toward Yakima, they saw a bright flash. "What was that?" Henry involuntarily ducked down.

"It wasn't blue if that's what you're worried about," Jackson said, getting off his bike. "I feel like walking my bike. Between last night and today, I'd rather find a way around the city. Personally."

"I think that's a great idea," Henry chimed in. "Who votes for going *a-round* Yakima?" He looked about him. Only Jackson held his hand up in agreement.

"I don't see how we can really avoid Yakima," Alice said. "None of us know the area. I don't want to lose our road. Besides, you can't let a spooky night make you crazy. Don't forget that we are armed, and we are together. Let's keep going."

"Fine," Henry moped. "I guess the sooner we get going the sooner we'll get through. There, I said it before you, Alice."

"Then, no need for me to repeat it," Alice said playfully, trying to help Henry get over his fear. They each grabbed the handlebars of their bikes and started toward the city. There were more cars now dotting the highway. Again, an accident had the entire road blocked. The only way around was a small path on the right-hand side. They had to walk single file through a tunnel-like enclosure. Light filtered in through the tight grove of trees on their right. They were completely walled in on the left. The tunnel continued on, following the curve of the highway, but it didn't let them back out into the open.

"Guys," Nick said quietly, "I don't like the look of this it feels too…"

"Man-made," Hazel finished. They all halted and looked frantically around them. There was no way to turn around and pushing their bikes backwards would be too difficult with the trailers.

"Be on your guard," Jackson warned. Henry undid the snap holding the gun in its place on his belt. Nick saw this move and did likewise. Then, they pressed forward slowly. Each new bend revealed a continuation of the tunnel and, as they walked, they began to realize that the tunnel must lead to the city limits. They now dreaded what they might find at the other end and breathed deeply to keep from letting fear get the better of them.

They rounded the last bend and saw the tunnel's opening about thirty yards in front of them. Their heightened awareness now had them fully ready for either a fight or flight situation.

Nick was the first to leave the tunnel, blinking in the sunshine willing his eyes to adjust quickly. Before they could do anything more, they heard a loud command from above them, “Hands up or we’ll shoot!” the deep bass voice, left no room, but for compliance.

Their hands went up, bikes resting against thighs. As their eyes adjusted, they could make out a tall wall that extended in each direction, the highway running underneath it in the middle. The wall was constructed of vehicles at least five high. A man with a high-powered rifle with a scope on top was looking down at them. The man moved again, and the light caught the glass of the scope. That was the flash they’d seen; these people knew they were coming. The tunnel was a way for them to control the situation.

“What’re you doing all the way out here?” the voice asked.

“Uh, we’re just headed through,” Nick spoke up, the others looking to him in relief.

“Where’re you goin’?” the other speaker boomed.

“Uh, we’re headed to Lewiston, Idaho, on the border of Washington.”

“I know where Lewiston is. Now, why are you headed to Lewiston on the Idaho border?”

“We have no parents and wanted see if my friend’s relatives are still there,” the others concurred.

“They’re all dead, kid,” the man said with something like bitterness in his voice. “You’re better off going back the way you came.”

“Please, sir,” Nick pleaded, “We just want to get through the city and be on our way. All of our parents are dead. Her grandparents probably are, too,” he indicated Hazel, “but we won’t know until we get there and see for ourselves.”

The man with the gun turned to confer with someone else. Then turned back and nodded at them, “We’ll let you in, but on one condition.”

“Anything, sir,” Nick said.

“You don’t go into any of the stores. You don’t go into any of the houses. You take nothing. You don’t take anything of ours and we won’t take anything of yours. Deal?”

"Yes, sir," Nick agreed.

"Best you stay here tonight. It's almost five now and you should stay inside the gates just to be safe." A couple other men had joined him, also heavily armed with long rifles. "Open the gates," he yelled behind him.

The five of them hadn't noticed that there were two large moving vans that blocked access to the city. These roared to life and were backed up so they could pass. Once they were through, the vans were moved back in place and turned off. Nick looked around him, whoever these people were, they'd taken the time to build a sizable wall and had cleared the roads of stalled or crashed vehicles in a really short amount of time. There were people all along the top of the wall, stationed at even intervals, but upon closer inspection, these people were frozen, deathly pale with traces of black. It looked as though the group in control had scoured the city for suitable "guards" that could be placed along the top to make it look like the city was completely guarded by its inhabitants. It was eerie to see these immovable images. Some had guns laying across their open arms or slung across their backs. Every once in a while, they caught movement, some of the guards were alive and spread out between the others. It had a disconcerting effect—the living among the dead.

The man from the wall joined them on the ground. "Welcome to the Yakima Annexation of Displaced Peoples. Name's Red—I run things around here," he said by way of introduction. "This here's Tony—he oversees our militia," the man on the right tipped his Stetson, "And this is Tom—helps me and Tony," another man in a brown trucker hat grabbed the bill in welcome. Both of their weapons slung behind their backs. Red had his gun still in his hands, muzzle pointed down.

"I'm Nick," Nick began. "This is Hazel," he lightly touched her arm, "That's Jackson," Jackson waved and smiled from the back of the line. "Henry," he pointed, "And his sister, Alice," she reached out to shake Red's hand. Red was surprised at the gesture but took it in his and shook it firmly. Red's was a reassuring grip, not clammy and limp and not overpowering like some do to exert their authority over others. Alice trusted him immediately.

"So, where're you all coming from," Red asked, picking up the pace a little leading them away from the gate.

"We're coming from Seattle," Nick, now the designated spokesperson, replied. He looked around him as they moved. The city was quiet, but not without a hustle and bustle here and there. People were going in and out of different businesses, scavenging for useful tools, supplies, and non-perishable foods. Those loaded down with items headed the same direction they were, some pulling wagons or using the bed of a truck that still had gas.

"Seattle," Red stopped short and looked at them. "When did you leave the city?"

Nick counted in his head, "Four days ago."

"You've made pretty decent time, then, on those bikes," Red indicated. "Did you come over the pass? Chinook, I mean?"

"Yes, sir. We came up and over day before yesterday. We camped for a day to give ourselves a break. Our butts aren't quite used to riding all day," he smiled at Red, some of the tension easing now that they knew Red and his compatriots didn't present an immediate danger. As Red explained later, they were a remnant of the population that once lived in the area before the Great Wave and the creation of FPNP.

"Was the pass clear? Lots of cars?" Red queried.

"Only one really bad wreck. We took a truck up from a campground 'bout five miles before the turnoff to go up and over. We had to abandon it just before the top of the pass because of the wreck. The road was completely blocked. Other than that, it was pretty clear. Any vehicles left on the road were easy to get around. It looked like most of the cars had run off the side of the road." Henry shuddered at this.

"Huh," Red said, more to himself. "How many people on the other side?"

"We didn't see anyone, sir," Nick said, omitting the Sweepers.

"We've been considering going to that side."

"Why? If I may ask," Nick said politely.

"Well, you see this area has lots of orchards and such, cattle ranches, some wheat fields over in Goldendale area and beyond that over to Oregon side, but it's all dependent on irrigation. So, without electricity, we can't get water to our crops. This side of the mountain is basically a desert. Bake your brains in the summer kind of heat, really good for growing produce, but only if there's enough water. Thankfully, our harvests are all in and stored in warehouses and grain silos, but come next year, there won't be any way to grow more food here. We won't have power to get water. On the other side of the pass, the growing season is, unfortunately much shorter, but there's a better chance of getting enough rain to grow crops. There aren't enough of us here anyway that would require a whole lot of land to produce enough to eat and save back for the following year," he finished his explanation as they started walking down a side street having exited the highway some time before.

Nick thought about what Red was saying, "Seems like a pretty good plan, actually. But have you considered the Willamette Valley down south of Portland?" He'd been there once and thought it was probably one of the best places for farming. Nice and warm in the summer with plenty of rain. Plus, it didn't seem too populated and probably would be less so now.

"We briefly thought of it, but too far away and too dangerous a trip to take all these people. We sent a scouting mission down and they came back yesterday. Portland is on fire, literally. Those who are still alive there have cordoned themselves off from the rest of the world. Large piles of cars like what we have, but in a smaller area. They took all the freeze-dried bodies they could find and lined them up one row after another. They turned the dead bodies into a maze. It also makes it appear that more people are there than actually are. We stole that idea from them. I'm sure you noticed we borrowed a couple of extras to round out our numbers at the top of the wall. At any rate, those crazies in Portland are defending it, armed to the nines. There's a pretty sizable group still left and will shoot at anything that moves outside their walls. They wouldn't even let our scouts past the area. They got chased down if they tried to enter and simply gave up. Those Portlanders didn't stop shooting until my group passed out of sight and out of range. That was our first idea, and we were just getting ready to send the scouts up the way to check the pass."

"So how are you going to get through the pass with that big wreck in the way?"

"We have a couple of bulldozers. We've been using them to clear the roads around here," Red turned to survey the area. "We've been able to syphon enough fuel from the different gas stations around here. We'd been filling up as many gas cans as we could before the power went off, but we figured we can refill tanks and canisters also by occasionally running generators. We run them sparingly, though."

"Sounds like you got it all figured out," Nick smiled. He liked Red, he reminded him of his father. A no-nonsense man who looked out for others to the best of his ability.

"And thanks to you, we now know that we can get through the pass just fine. Thanks," Red flicked a smile Nick's direction. "So, you really set on going to Lewiston?"

"Yes, sir. We are."

"Alrighty, then. We can talk more tonight after you all rest a bit. I'm taking you to our headquarters where everyone else hangs out when they're not on duty. We set up in the mall for now. Lots of open spaces for people to set up tents and have a little privacy. We go to stores to get things we need. Some are working solely on getting ready to head up and over the pass. More people showing up every day. We're pretty sure that eventually the trickle of people will stop. Our scouts tell anyone and everyone we're here so they can choose to come join us or not. We're thinking of staying in Enumclaw or even moving closer to Seattle for the winter and then exploring the area as we can for good farmland. Our scouts can gather or search for anything we need. With so many people gone, there's more than enough for the rest of us to live comfortably with a little extra work. Plenty of places for folks to live."

They walked another block and rounded the corner to the mall entrance. Many very large construction vehicles were parked in a side parking lot, like overgrown Tonka toys. There were at least six grain trucks full of wheat. Large semis with the trailer doors cracked open revealing crate after crate of produce of all kinds. Men were busy unloading more crates from several trucks that had just pulled in. The bulldozers were parked in a far corner along with a sizable crane that probably had been used to construct the walls around Yakima. Trucks, RVs, popup trailers, and coaches were making use of the larger part of the parking lot. Some people were sitting outside under awnings, clean laundry drying on makeshift lines. Kids ran in the patches of grass playing games. It was a whole community staying right here in the parking lot and running in and out of the mall main entrance doors which were propped open.

"We got horses and cattle, too, but for now we're keeping 'em safe on some of the closer farms. Eventually, we'll be reliant on them for transportation and plowing," Red said as they continued on.

Nick and the others were surprised at how many people were here, taking breaks from various job assignments, working on preparing for the winter and a possible move over the pass. It was more than they imagined seeing after days of being alone. As they first looked, there were at least three hundred people hanging out doing odd jobs or chatting, eating lunch, reading a book, playing a quiet card game.

"Where are all these people from?" Hazel asked Red. "Surely they're not all from Yakima."

"No. They're not all from Yakima. You're right on that one. When the ID2040 initiative was announced, a lot of people moved onto the Yakama Indian Reservation to keep from being forced to get the vaccine or the ID. The government was okay with letting them move just as long as the Natives were okay with them infringing on their land. The Tribal Council agreed to let them live there as long as they donated all their money and most of their belongings for the greater good. People were so afraid of the government by then, that they readily agreed and gave up everything they had in order to live on the reservation. The tribe was allowed to absorb the land owned by these people only if it was adjacent to the tribal land. Since the tribal lands are quite extensive already, they inherited a whole lot of good farming land and orchards.

"My wife and I decided to hedge our bets, too, and gave up the family farm to join the rest of the folks moving to the reservation. It was a prudent decision, needless to say. We had two daughters—one married with two kids who lived in Seattle. My other daughter stayed with us. Haven't heard from the one, but just looking around at what happened to all the others, I don't have to guess what happened to her and my grandkids. It's been extremely hard on my wife.

"When the stuff hit the fan last week, the people who had moved to the reservation decided they would move back to the cities again figuring that there'd be plenty of room and plenty of everything else. So, they started gathering here in Yakima pretty quickly. My wife and I were some of the first and being a well-known member of the community, they all started looking to me to make hard decisions. I try to run things like a democracy and let everyone have their say, but they're so frightened and so numbed by grief that it's been easier for a few of us to make the calls and then delegate. So far, so good. The Yakama Indians decided to stay put and work on reestablishing their former ways of life. Run things like they did way back before the government took their land. There aren't many of them left, but like us, they're ready to fight. I've spoken with their leader a coupl'a times and we are in agreement to help each other if those government yuppies decide to try 'n tell us what to do. After what they've already done, we'll make sure they get what's coming to 'em." By now they'd entered the mall, still walking their bikes. There were large skylights in the roof that let in a lot of natural light. In the atrium area many more tents were erected. Some individuals were sitting in camp chairs reading or relaxing. It was a pretty setting for a mall. The atrium was lush with vegetation and trees that were making their way to the light above. A few kids were hauling buckets filled with water for the plants. It would be interesting in a few years' time to see how nature reclaimed this area if left untended.

"A lot of these people are off duty at the moment. We have four shifts that patrol the streets and walk the walls," Red continued. "Right now, there's a large group out working on completing the wall. We cut the city in half simply because we don't have the manpower or vehicles available to construct a wall around the whole city. The entrance you came through was easy since it is the edge of town, but only a couple of blocks from here is where we decided to draw the line. We've had to move fast to get things done. We wanted to be as protected as we could in as little time as possible. So much we don't know right now."

"Why work on the wall if you're planning on going over the pass?" Alice asked.

"That's a good question, young lady," Red complemented. "The reason is, we plan on only taking the farmers over the pass to begin with. A lot of the rest will stay here for the winter. It's warmer this side, so safer overall. Plus, we know this area and know how to defend it. We don't know much, yet, about the other side."

"What if it's someone looking for help?" Alice followed up. "What do you do with them?"

"Well, if they're willing to work and contribute, we have no issues with them joining us. Like I said, our scouts tell those they run into that we're here. We figure the more people who are with us, aren't trying to kill us, the more chances we have of survival. Repopulating. I'm too old, but my one daughter just recently got married and when she starts having kids, I want a safe place for them to grow up."

"Makes a lot of sense, Red," Alice surmised.

"Here's a good spot for ya'll to set up for tonight," Red indicated a back corner under two escalators. "You can get situated and then maybe we can talk some more later. Plenty of light from the skylight here. I'm going to go back and finish my shift. Rest up now."

They slowly set up their tents and got their sleeping bags ready to go. They didn't talk much for a while, wanting to wait until they were a little out of earshot of the others. Hazel and Alice both laid down for short naps.

Nick, Henry, and Jackson decided to take a walk outside, check out the rest of the city. Dusk was already settling around them, the sun having disappeared again behind dark, foreboding clouds that promised rain; the smell of fresh rain already hitting hot dust floated in from the west. They breathed deep, it was a cleansing, refreshing smell.

"Pluviophile," Henry said.

"What?" Jackson turned to him.

"Pluviophile—one who loves rain or who finds peace of mind during rainy days."

"O-kay….," Jackson stared at him, then turned to Nick, "I think you did a good job back there. You didn't give away what we're actually doing, but you didn't give a bald-faced lie, either. I can appreciate that."

"Hazel's grandparents live or lived there. I'm just glad that they all didn't turn out to be crazies or anything," Nick breathed the fresh smell again. "We would have been seriously outnumbered."

"Yeah, I don't know about you, but there was a moment I was afraid they were Sweepers," Henry shuddered.

"Ditto," Nick said, "but did you notice that Red didn't mention anything about Sweepers?"

"I did," Jackson concurred, "however, they were very suspicious of us."

"I think they're just suspicious of everyone," Nick reasoned. "Since they didn't mention anything about the Sweepers, my guess is they haven't been through here and Red doesn't know about them."

"You think we should tell him?" Henry asked. "I mean, I would want to know if someone like that was out there rounding everybody up and either executing them or hauling them off in buses."

"I do," Nick kicked an empty soda bottle down the street. "It would be the right thing to do. I mean, I don't get the vibe that these guys are dangerous or anything."

"Exactly," Henry gave his approval, "I see them as good 'ol country boys who want to take care of the people entrusted to them. I could easily see myself wanting to be a part of the family." He looked across the high school football field they were walking next to.

"Well, maybe when we're finished with Denver we can come back and join them," Nick looked at him. "I mean, that's what I'm kind of enjoying about all this is that we have choices. Before, we were told what to do when and then punished if we didn't go along with it." Their conversation was interrupted by a staccato pop-pop-pop that reverberated off the near buildings.

"What was that?" Henry asked breaking into a run in the directions of the sounds. The commotion was coming from the southern gate nearest the mall. They heard more popping sounds, almost like Fourth of July, but as they drew nearer, they could tell it was gunfire that was being exchanged. But with who? They rounded the last corner that would bring them to the gate. In the dim light, they could make out Red, Tony, and another man crouching down behind a parapet, taking careful aim and firing several more rounds at a vehicle on the road. Henry and Nick could see several flashes of light as the occupants of the vehicle returned fire. Several men were at the gates on the ground, also taking up posts behind barriers where they had less of a chance of getting hit. Another pop and it sounded like a giant glass chandelier had fallen. The black SUV's windshield was now missing from the front of the vehicle. Several more rounds were fired and then all was silent, the volley ending just as quickly as it began.

Henry and Nick had their guns drawn, safeties off, fingers off the trigger, muzzles down while joining Red and Tony as they approached the SUV cautiously. Henry, Nick, and Jackson could see the driver behind the wheel and a passenger in the front, still wearing sunglasses, blood stains blooming across the white shirts, and dark suit jackets swept to each side, revealing empty gun holsters. Neither driver nor passenger moved.

After a moment to verify that these two men were no longer a threat, Red yelled, "All clear!" The boys approached with the others, still cautious. Fresh rivulets of blood seeped from several bullet holes; guns still clamped in their hands. Red opened both back passenger doors to double-check for others, weapons, or anything else that might be trouble.

"Anything?" Red asked.

"Nothing," Tony replied. "No IDs, nothing. Just a map." He unfurled a map of North Pangea and made note that there were big Xs through Seattle, Tacoma, Longview, and the Tri Cities (Kennewick, Pasco, and Richland). These were all major cities in Washington. Apparently, the Sweepers had already crossed off a number of them in their pursuit of stragglers.

"Whoowhee. Look at all this," by this time Tom had opened the back gate of the SUV and was rifling around. There were crates of ammunition, large service rifles, semi-automatics, scoped sniper rifles for long-distance disposal, bomb making materials, handcuffs, and extra gas canisters for the long drive.

"Take all that back to the command center," Red initiated action. "You boys can help, too," he said turning to Henry, Jackson, and Nick. Jackson was half in the driver's side door getting an up-close glimpse of the Sweeper, searching him while Henry searched the passenger, handing Nick the guns pried from the men's hands. Nick tossed them into one of the smaller crates, now very heavy, grabbed one handle to help the militia member carry it back to the mall, following Tom and Tony. When they got back to the mall, Tom led them to the Sears. This was where they'd set up their command center. Inside, there were many more firearms and ammunition boxes stacked neatly along one whole wall. Different sections of the store had been cleared and sorted into items for the trip over the pass. One area had been designated for food. There was a large variety of seeds stored in airtight containers labeled neatly with the type of seed it was. It was amazing how much these people accomplished in little over a week. It was a testament to Red's strong leadership and the willingness of others to work hard. Without his foresight and ability to take charge, these people would've been at a complete loss or would've lost valuable time with winter fast approaching.

"Thank you, boys," said Tom. "You can set your haul over there in the sorting area. Some of our guys will go ahead and catalogue what we've got and then make sure it ends up in the right place. Thanks for the help." They set their crates down where indicated, then made their way back to the mall and found Hazel and Alice, sitting quietly reading books they must've picked up from a nearby store.

"Hey, you're not supposed to take anything," Henry admonished them.

"Not to worry, big brother," Alice said looking up from her novel. "Red's wife took us to the bookstore and asked us if we wanted anything to read to help pass the time. We each took a couple of books, thought you all might want to borrow them, too."

"What happened to you guys? You look like you've seen a ghost," Hazel eyed them.

"You could say that," Nick started. Hazel and Alice sat up, full attention.

Nick took his seat, "We saw Sweepers."

The girls looked panicked.

"Don't worry," Henry eased them. "They're dead. Red and his guys exchanged gunfire and the Sweepers got the worst of it."

"Does Red know who they are?" Hazel asked.

"Not, yet," Nick told her. "When he gets back from his shift, we're going to tell him who they were."

"They had a map," Henry stated. "It had Xs over a lot of the cities in Washington. I think Yakima was maybe their last hit. They'd already got the Tri Cities which is south of here. It's the last major stop on the freeway before ducking back over to Oregon. Makes me wonder why Portland wasn't crossed off."

"Maybe there's several teams," Jackson wondered aloud. "I mean, did you see any buses coming up the road? If there were people in Yakima, why wouldn't they want to bring the buses and take people from here?"

"Maybe the buses are already full," Henry said.

"Or maybe these people here aren't the type they want working for them," Alice threw out. "I mean, these people are pretty self-sufficient. I don't think they'd like taking orders from a government who just wiped out most of humanity."

"I think you're probably right," Nick agreed. "Well, at least there's less of a chance that more Sweepers will be headed this direction. Or at least we can hope that those two were only coming up here to clean up and then catch up to the others. That's my guesstimation at any rate."

"I really hope so," Jackson said absentmindedly.

After Red's shift was over, Nick and Henry sought him out. They found him sitting in a camp chair outside a fifth wheel. The awning was extended and lined with battery operated white Christmas lights. He was leaning over a plate full of fried chicken, mashed potatoes and gravy. A warm biscuit in his hands.

"Pull up a seat, boys," he offered them two empty chairs. They thanked him and sat down. "So, you want to know who those guys were?" Nick and Henry looked at him a little surprised. They had come over to tell Red who the men were. Red caught their looks in the dim light. "Didn't think I knew about our government thugs, huh?" Both of them shook their heads no. "It seems we both know what these guys are up to. This wasn't the first time they've been to Yakima and my guess is it won't be the last until either we wipe them out or they get tired of trying. The people still on the Yakama Indian Reservation are giving them the same what fore, but they haven't been able to kill them like we have, just fend them off until they come back to try again later. We've traded the Indians firearms a couple of times to help out. Being on the same side and all. That's one of the main reasons we've worked so hard on our wall. We needed the leverage, get the upper hand, if you know what I mean. What we don't understand is why they keep coming to try and wipe us out. Why not just leave us alone?"

"They're called Sweepers," Nick answered. "Hazel and I found out about them when we went looking for our parents." He told Red a condensed version of the events and pulled out the email he borrowed from Hazel to show him.

Red looked over the paper and handed it back to Nick, "So, they're out to eliminate everyone who didn't become petrified, huh?"

Nick assented, "We call it the Petriclysm."

"Seems fitting," Red rubbed his chin with his free hand. "So, they're supposed to be rounding us up and exterminating us or keeping the ones they like, huh?"

"Yeah, it's probably a good thing you keep shooting at them," Henry encouraged.

"I agree, especially now that I know a little bit more. The first time they tried to come in they brandished their firearms and threatened us if we didn't let them through. We guessed they were trouble at that point. When we asked them to state their business, they said they were here on behalf of the Federation of the Peoples of North Pangea. They wanted to see if we were okay and if we needed any assistance from the government, as if they weren't the one's responsible for this petriclysm, as you call it. We let them know that we were doing just fine and that they could turn right around and go back the way they'd come. But when they decided not to leave and brandished their own fancy firearms, we drew ours. They fired first and that was the end of that."

"It was wise to not let them in," Nick said. "We wanted to make sure you knew who they were. Seems like you already had a pretty good idea."

"Thanks for taking the time to relay the information you do have. It's helpful and justifies the actions we've already taken and will continue to take if need be. By the way, did you happen to find a Sat phone in the vehicle? We found one last time and we think that's why they sent another team to check on the first two guys. We destroyed the phone, but they might've been able to relay a message before we took care of them." Neither Nick nor Henry had seen a phone. "Okay, then, maybe it'll show up when the guys are done sorting. I'll keep a lookout. It doesn't really matter since they'll probably just send another couple of government lackies to continue the cleanup work. I'm going to go take a nice cold shower now. You boys have yourself a good sleep and we'll see you off in the morning, if there's nothing else." Red stood and set the empty plate on the step of the trailer. Nick and Henry stood and shook Red's hand.

When they returned to the tents inside the mall, Alice and Hazel were waiting for them. "Where's Jackson?" Alice asked.

"I thought he was with you," Henry looked about.

"Well, we thought he'd gone to catch up with you. We haven't seen him since just after you left to talk to Red."

"Hmmm, maybe we should go look for him," Henry scratched the back of his head, looking to Nick for direction. At that moment, Jackson emerged from the other side of the escalators. "Hey, where've you been?"

"I had to go for a walk. Guys come here. I have to show you something," Jackson pulled something wrapped in plastic from his hoodie pocket. He went inside the nearest tent and the others followed, crowding around him. He opened the bag and pulled out something wrapped in toilet paper, slowly peeled back the layers and held up his hand. Something small and bloody was sitting in the middle of his palm.

"That looks like skin," Henry peered at whatever it was. "What is it?" he asked trying not to stare too long. Jackson flipped the item over, revealing three tiny dots.

"Ewww, what did you do?" Hazel put her hand to her mouth. "Is that..."

"It's the driver's BioID. After you guys left to haul things back to the command center, I hung back to see where they put the bodies. When you went to talk to Red, I went and got this off the driver's hand," he held it up, "Now watch." They all moved closer, staring intently at the little flap of skin. "There! Did you see that?" Jackson got excited.

"I didn't see anything," Henry looked confused. "Is this some kind of joke?"

"No, watch again," he encouraged. They continued to watch. The BioID flickered red, blazed, then faded completely. Jackson jerk his hand and the flap of skin and tissue fell to the ground.

"What was that?" Nick demanded.

"I'm…I'm not sure," Jackson answered. "But today when I was searching the driver, I saw it turn green for a second, then flashed red. I haven't seen it turn bright like that. No one else seemed to notice it, so I went back and took it. I wanted to see if I could figure out what it's doing. I mean, the guy is dead, and I've never seen a BioID do that in a live person."

"The blue lights," Henry said stunned. "It's got to be some sort of signal. What about his eyes? Did the driver's eyes look at you?"

"Not that I noticed," Jackson rejoined. "But you still don't know that that woman's eyes actually moved. It could've just been a shadow."

"No," Henry stated emphatically, "I know for a fact that her eyes moved. I can't believe you're still denying it. She looked right at you. Nick, don't' you agree?" Nick agreed.

"Whatever," Jackson flipped back at him, bending down to retrieve the BioID.

"What are you going to do with that?" Nick asked.

"I was going to try to figure out what it's doing," Jackson replied. "None of us have a read BioID, so we don't know for sure whether or not these IDs are known to do this. I'm pretty sure it's a signal somehow. My guess is it's just relaying to the servers somewhere that whoever had that particular ID is now dead."

"If that's the case, then maybe we should destroy it somehow," Nick put in. "Seriously, if it relayed that the Sweeper is dead and whoever is in charge knows where the Sweeper was going, don't you think they'd send another Sweeper here to check things out?"

"Maybe," Jackson seemed reluctant to get rid of the ID.

"You know, I think Nick is right," Henry said. "Jackson, you need to get rid of that thing. I also think we should tell Red about it tomorrow before we leave."

"No, don't tell him, please," Jackson begged. "It'll just make him more nervous."

"But if this thing is relaying to the mother ship that a Sweeper is dead, Red needs to know to expect more Sweepers to head this way," Henry reasoned.

"Henry is right," Nick agreed.

"Fine, do whatever you think is best," Jackson gave in, but not without bitterness at being ganged up on. "I'll just take this little guy outside and destroy it. We can ask whoever's in Denver what the deal is." He shuffled past the others and headed outside.

"I think we've had enough excitement today," Nick looked around. "Let's try and get some sleep. It's going to be a long day tomorrow." Henry filed out since they'd been standing in the girls' tent.

"Her eyes did move," Henry muttered under his breath.

CHAPTER 16

They woke to cloud cover and a light drizzle in the morning. The skylights were streaked with mist, pooling and running down the sides of the slanted windows. The five of them took their time packing, hoping the rain would quit before they headed out. No such luck, but Red showed up with five clear plastic ponchos that would cover them and most of their bikes. He also helped them with the tarps covering the trailers. Tom was ready to lead them to the south gate, the two passenger vans reversing to make room for them to leave.

Shaking hands with Tom in farewell, they walked around the shot-out SUV still parked at the entrance, the two bodies having been removed and thoroughly searched before being added to the landfill some ways out of the city. They mounted their bikes, thankful for the ponchos and headed down the road. They would have to be on the freeway now for some time and wanted to get this leg of their journey over before the Sweepers had time to send more reinforcements.

Once they were out of sight of the Yakima city walls, Jackson swerved to the side of the road and abruptly stopped. The others circled back to see what was wrong. Jackson motioned them closer and drew out a yellow clunky phone from his jacket pocket. He held it up to show them a Sat phone. Nick surmised that this was the phone that Red had asked him about the night before.

"What are you doing with that?" Nick asked, grabbing it from Jackson for a closer look. It was still on.

"I found it on the driver yesterday when I was searching the bodies," Jackson answered. "I didn't want to say anything to Red because he would've taken it and destroyed it. Look," he took it back from Nick and selected the map on the touch-screen. He turned it so they could see it. It was a regional map, showing the phone's current location with a blinking blue icon, on route back to the Tri Cities. Then he pinched the screen to show a larger swath of the country and more dots appeared. They were green, some slowly moving, others stationary in different locations.

"What are we looking at?" Nick asked, eyeing the green dots.

"Where all the other Sweepers are right this minute," Jackson said seriously. "We can use this to track their movements. Maybe even find where the buses are—get Felix and Ivy. Look, we just saved Red and everyone behind those walls," he pointed behind him. "Right now, all the other Sweepers think that the two guys who biffed it last night were successful in wiping out Yakima and are now headed back the way they came. Once we get closer to the Tri Cities, we can check to make sure no one else is around and once we're back on 410 we can turn off the tracking. I tried it for a minute last night in my tent. We can turn off the GPS on this phone, but still have the ability to track the whereabouts of the other Sweepers. You want to see something scary?" he asked. He zoomed out even further on the map and small pinpoints of green light lit up all across the continent. He turned to show them, "They're everywhere. The Sweepers. They're all over the continent and all over the world. Looking at the map today, though, I can tell that they are all slowly making their way to Denver. See how there aren't any green dots along the coasts? That's because they've already completed that part of the job. One of the Sweepers in Vancouver must've driven the phone some ways before turning it off. Created a diversion. Like they're already done sweeping and moved on."

"You could've told Red you had the phone," Nick said.

"Well, he didn't ask me. He asked you, didn't he? I didn't know they were looking for it until Tom said something this morning on our way out about not finding it. Besides, I didn't want to lose the ability to track the Sweepers' whereabouts. As long as we leave the GPS on for a while, Yakima is safe and look here, Seattle has no green dots anymore. They're done there, too."

"What about Portland?" Alice asked. "Red said it was very dangerous down there. Any idea what he might've been talking about?"

"No," Jackson said, zooming in on Portland, "Oh, woah!" He turned the phone to show them the Portland area. There were too many green dots to count. The dots were moving swiftly. While they watched the screen, one dot stopped moving and then went out. "Whatever is going on, it's not good," Jackson closed out of the map app and stuffed the phone back in his pocket. "I'm sorry I didn't say anything, but I didn't want to lose this phone. We have to hit up a Best Buy when we can. We need a couple of portable power sources so we can keep the phone charged." He hopped back on the seat of his bike and started pedaling.

"I need one of those, too," Alice reminded Hazel and shoved off, following Jackson. She caught up to Nick who looked a little angry. "Everything okay?" she asked him.

"Yeah, I guess," he turned to give her a reassuring smile, "it's just, Red was so nice to us that I don't like that Jackson kept the fact that he had phone from him. I think Red would have been amenable to the idea of us taking it. But now they're just going to worry since they didn't find it."

"Why don't you go back and explain it to him? That way they'd know, and we'd still have the phone. I doubt they would come after it. Who knows, maybe they'd really appreciate knowing that we're throwing the Sweepers off."

"You know, that's actually a really good idea," Nick said and arced his bike in a big U-turn. "I'll catch up to you," he yelled over his shoulder and started picking up speed. He disappeared around a bend before anyone could change his mind.

"What was that all about?" Henry asked Alice.

"I think he forgot something," was all she said. They continued riding. Jackson some way ahead not really wanting to talk to anyone.

An hour later Nick caught up to them. They had stopped for a quick break, drinking some water and eating a light snack. He stopped and got off, sweating from the extra exertion.

"Where'd you go?" Hazel asked him.

"I went and told Red the truth," he looked over at Jackson who avoided making eye contact. "He said to tell you, Jackson, thank you for taking the phone. It was a really good idea."

Jackson shrugged and mumbled something under his breath. He crossed his arms in a defensive posture.

"Look," Nick continued, "If I were Red and knew that the Sweepers carried a satellite phone, I'd be worried, too, if I couldn't find it. I would be worried that someone in the community had it and would bring more Sweepers if the signal didn't change soon enough. Really, he was glad to know where it was and that the plan was to take it back to the Tri Cities."

"Unless they were supposed to head to Spokane," Henry interjected. None of them had thought about this. Jackson pulled out the phone again and was checking something. He looked up.

"There are Sweepers already in Spokane. I think it's safe to say they were probably going to go back through the Tri-Cities," Jackson put the phone back in his pocket. "Look," he started, "I'm really sorry I didn't tell Red about the phone. I just didn't want to lose the advantage over the Sweepers." He turned to Nick, "Thanks for going back and telling Red. I'm sure it is a relief for him to know where it is." He looked down at his feet, guilt written on his features. He looked up again and at each one of them, "I promise I won't hold anything back like that again. We are a team, and we need to make decisions together. I promise."

"And I accept your apology," Nick said, extending his hand to shake on it. The others relayed their agreement. Henry slapped Jackson on the back and Alice and Hazel gave him friendly hugs.

"Oh, yeah!" Nick walked over to his trailer and brought out a long flat white box. "I almost forgot. Red's wife, Nancy, sent these along." He opened the box revealing twelve cinnamon covered cake donuts, "she made them fresh today." Each of them took two and ate slowly, letting every bite linger in their mouths for maximum flavor. "It was a thank you to you, Jackson, for a great idea for bringing the phone with us and for me for letting Red know where it was. I'd say it was a pretty good deal. There's two left," he held up the box. Henry gladly took one and Jackson the other after making sure no one else wanted them. Nick put the empty box back in the trailer and they set off again. They still had a very long day ahead of them.

It was 85 miles from Yakima to Pasco, one of the Tri Cities. They checked the phone several times to make sure that no Sweepers were in the vicinity. They all agreed that it had been a good idea to bring it with them. They arrived in late afternoon, completely exhausted, but wanting to get off the freeway and to pick up their route again this time cutting across on route 124, a secondary highway which eventually intersected PN Route 12/ state route 410. They would save themselves a lot more miles cutting cross country and help them avoid any more major towns or small cities until they got to Lewiston.

They found another large shopping center that had a Best Buy. Now that the power was out, Nick and Henry used a crowbar found in the trunk of an unlocked car to wedge the sliding doors apart. Once the doors were open enough to enter, they wheeled the bikes into the cash register area, then searched for solar charging powerpacks. Alice and Jackson worked together since each of them were in pursuit of the same item. Nick gave the store a cursory walk. He wrapped his hands around a game console controller, looking at the blank screen in front of him pretending to play, doing battle with the forces of evil in pursuit of defeating an enemy. He smiled to himself thinking that he was now living a video game in RL, every kid's fantasy. However, the reality was a little bit more shocking and the results a little too real. He meandered over to the computer section. A couple of the laptops coming to life as his fingers skimmed the mouse pads. Incredibly, they still had some battery life. One laptop started its ominous "I'm running out of battery" tone and then went blank. That was that. The death throes of a laptop. Henry caught up to him in this section. He was carrying a Nintendo Switch Lite in turquoise, Mario Kart, and a solar charged power pack. Nick looked down at Henry's full hands and smiled. Henry had the right idea. Even though they were on this mission, they could have a little fun now and then. He asked Henry to show him where the consoles were stored and chose a yellow one for himself, grabbed another Mario Kart, and the latest Super Mario Bros. game. On their way back to the registers, they each selected pairs of headphones for plug and play. No way did they want the noise from their games to become a risk hazard. To round out their shopping spree, Henry and Nick found matching cases in which to store their new devices and accessories.

When the others saw Henry and Nick's gaming devices, Jackson, Hazel, and Alice decided that they, too, would like consoles for a little bit of down time. Henry gladly escorted them to the appropriate area of the store and showed them their options. A little while later all five of them were similarly outfitted for the simple pleasures of video gaming on the go. They stored their new toys and headed on down the road. There was a gas station at their exit. They stopped and picked up more food to eat along the way. By now it was nearly dark. Jackson checked the phone one more time and was relieved that there were no new developments.

Several miles after taking the exit, they decided to find a place to make camp for the night. They found a secluded rest stop some ways off the road with enough trees to hide most of the light. A final check of the phone, now becoming a regular occurrence, showed that a small campfire would be okay. Hazel and Alice searched the surrounding area, gathering sticks and kindling for a fire. Nick and Jackson set up the tents while Henry found stones to ring a small fire pit. Once they were settled and their beds were ready to go, they ate a quiet dinner, enjoying some cups of macaroni and cheese they'd gotten from the gas station. Then they all retired to their beds, physically exhausted, but not quite ready for sleep. Each of them got out their new games and played under cover of sleeping bags until they were ready for sleep. The games were a welcome diversion from the stresses of the last week and several days.

CHAPTER 17

The next two days were uneventful. They cruised the rolling hills of farm country. Each small town as desolate as the next. Flying Vees of birds overhead broke up the tedium, honks of Canadian geese punctuating the stillness. Fourteen miles from Lewiston, they came through a winding ravine and joined the Snake river, sluggishly flowing past them in the opposite direction. It was a cool late afternoon, the road in shadow, sun glittering on the water. The sheer rock wall running parallel to the river, allowing only for the narrow road between the two. Clarkston drew nearer, being the town on the Washington side across the way from Lewiston. It was strange to be approaching a town, once twinkling with streetlights and house lights at this time in the evening, now dark and seemingly empty.

Jackson had periodically checked the phone in case Sweepers were headed this direction. The two towns having grown to a sizable population in the last twenty years. No green dots had moved any nearer. A large cluster still showed in Portland. None in Seattle or Spokane. Thankfully it seemed that the Sweepers were either not near them or sweeping through areas ahead of them; none had been seen heading back to Yakima. All of them hoped that Red and his company were finished with the wall and headed over the pass soon. Now that it was October, there was no guarantee that the pass would remain open for long.

The road they were riding down led straight through Clarkston to the bridge that would take them to the Lewiston side. The road bypassed a majority of the small town. There were a few major stores along the route, but none of them enticing enough to stop, except for the Starbucks. Alice had them stop and asked Henry to use his window breaker to let her in. The smell of fresh coffee and soured milk wafted out through the small opening. Alice was not in pursuit of more coffee, though; instead, she headed directly to the back room and emerged a few minutes later with a large paper bag filled to the brim with more loaves, muffins, and other goodies. She smiled, "I took a chance that they might have a freezer. They did! It was just starting to thaw so now we have a fresh supply. Anyone want to stop for a minute and have a bite?" They declined to stop longer than they already had, night was approaching, and they wanted to find a safe place to camp. They kicked themselves for not stopping at the campground located across the water from the ravine they'd come through. Chief Timothy? Something like that. Alice quickly stored the fresh supply of breads and started heading cautiously across the bridge.

Jackson stopped abruptly and had them double-back to the way they'd come, "I think there's a bike path here that goes under the bridge. Maybe we can ride it and find a more secluded spot to stop? I'm not comfortable in these towns. It's dark and I can barely make anything out." They thought this a good idea and turned back. They picked up the bike path that curved away from the road and under the bridge. It wasn't long before they found a clearing with some trees on each side for added protection. The river was in front of them and a sizable cliff behind them with large houses staring down through vacant windows. They set up for the night, not lighting a fire. It was cool, but not cold. They enjoyed some of the fresh breads Alice had procured and called it a night.

Nick was the first one to wake up and look out on a foggy morning. He was about ready to unzip the tent flap when he choked. Across from the tent sat an old man, naked from the waste up, fire blazing and fish smoking over the flames. The noise had aroused the others and now they all sat in their tents, not knowing whether it was safe to come out.

"Come eat, come eat," the old man beckoned them, a scraggly grey goatee flapping with the words. He was dark, cherrywood red, with black eyes, deep wrinkles at each corner. His legs were crossed in front of him and he beckoned again.

Alice, sometimes being the bravest one, eagerly threw on her sweatshirt, slipping on her sneakers and exited the tent. She took the proffered fish and sat down beside the old man to eat. Seeing that she was perfectly fine, the others silently joined this strange man, eating the smoked fish he gave them. The fish was delicious and was akin to eating an excellent, wholesome dinner after being on a fast-food binge for some time. They all sat watching the old man as he finished his fish. Then he stood and said, "Pack up and come," he motioned with his hand in the direction of the bridge.

They didn't ask him any questions and they didn't consult with one another as to whether or not they should do as this man had said. They simply got up, quickly collapsed the tents, stored their gear and followed the man. From the back he had a long salt and pepper grey braid that fell down his back. It swished ever so lightly from side to side trailing the old man's gait. He now had on a pair of leather sandals and carried a walking stick. The five of them followed, walking their bikes up and around the corner to the top of the bridge. He led them across it and down main street Lewiston. They didn't have time to assess their surroundings and couldn't stop for any supplies for fear of losing the old man or angering him. The old man did not stop, and he did not look back to make sure they were following him. He simply kept walking, picking up his pace as he came to another bridge that took them away from Lewiston. Once they were across the bridge, the old man grabbed a bicycle that was leaning against a post and got on. He started to pedal down the road; they all jumped on their bicycles to follow.

The old man moved faster on the bike than his years would suggest he could, his walking stick now resting on his right shoulder, his right arm loosely hanging over the top, keeping it in place. They rode for some miles, then exited the highway past a sign that said: ENTERING NEZ PERCE INDIAN RESERVATION. Nick gave a sideways glance at the others, but they were all too intent on following this stranger to question what was going on.

Just as suddenly as he'd begun, the old man came a halt and the others stopped behind him. He turned and looked at them each in turn, "Ta'c 'éetx papáayn. Welcome. We are the Nimiipuu people. I am Hin-man-too-yah-lat-kekt. Chief Joseph." At this, a small band of warriors emerged from the bushes and trees. Each man wore a leather shirt embellished with small dark blue beads and fringes, leather breechcloths with leather leggings, and supple moccasins. Their heads were topped with a single black feather and each carried a tomahawk in their right hands. The foremost man also carried a beautiful headdress, the ring of feathers white with black tips, an intricate head band with a red and black beaded design and white feathers with thin strands of red hung down on either side. This man handed his tomahawk to a nearby warrior and reverently touched his knee to the ground in front of Chief Joseph, then placed the beautiful head dress on the Chief's head. With this ceremony finished, Chief Joseph turn to the five teenagers and asked them to follow him one more time. Leaving their bicycles where they were, he led them across a small lea, to a tepee that was erected on the far side, smoke was threading out the top, Chief Joseph bent and entered; the others did likewise. The warriors who had followed them from behind, did not enter, instead, they situated themselves outside, spaced evenly around the tepee.

The old man sat back and looked at them long and hard before beginning, "Lewiston is not safe. Warring factions on each side of the river." He stated this as a simple truth, "You had safe passage because you were with me." He rested his hands on his knees.

Alice looked into his wizened eyes, "Are you a descendant of *the* Chief Joseph?"

He bowed his head in the affirmative, then, "I am his direct descendent, he was my great-great grandfather. He laid down his arms in 1877, almost 150 years ago. Today, we again pick them up." He rubbed his hands over the small flame.

"Why did you give us safe passage?" Nick asked. Added, "Thank you. We had no idea we were in trouble."

"You are on a mission. I can see in my mind's eye. Four days ago, I had a dream that people on wheels would come up the river. And here you are. You are they." He looked at Alice, "Long hair like fire." He looked at Henry, "Short hair like sunbursts," Henry self-consciously ran a hand though his hair trying to slick it down. Chief Joseph continued, looking at Nick, "Strong and steady, tall, blue eyes like ocean." To Hazel he said, "Self-willed. Compassionate. Do not act in your anger." Finally, he turned to Jackson, "You I do not know. You are hidden." Jackson looked around to gauge the reactions of the others. They smiled at him reassuringly. He was one of them and he was meant to be there. It didn't matter what Chief Joseph said. "You will stay here today; my warriors will scout your path and report back."

"We've already mapped it out. We're going to Boise from here," Jackson put in.

"You will not go to Boise," was the firm response. "You will go to Missoula."

"Missoula?" Jackson looked concerned. "But that's out of our way. It'll add days to our trip."

"You are going to Denver, I have seen this, too. You must go to Missoula."

"But it's out of our way."

"It is the only way."

The others looked at Jackson; he was right, going through Montana would take a lot longer. It was already October, which meant it could be much colder by the time they actually made it to Denver. Jackson was about to argue again, but a look from Nick and a small shake of the head told him that he was pushing his luck.

"Come," Chief Joseph said, as he got up and stepped out into the morning sunshine. "Grab your bicycles," he started walking in the opposite direction, through a copse of trees. Of the warriors there was no sign. They ran to get their bikes and quickly caught up to him as he led them to another large tepee standing alone, "You will stay here today. Rest. We will talk tomorrow morning." And with that he left them.

"Okay," Jackson said as he plopped down on the soft grass, "I say we make a break for it. This is too weird."

"It's weird, yes," said Alice agreeing.

"But..."

"But I trust him. Look, I don't know what's going on in Lewiston, but I got a really weird feeling going through town. Maybe he'll tell us tomorrow, but I really think he might've saved our lives this morning. Also, I don't think he's nearly as feeble as we might think. That man is a warrior through and through. He's dangerous, but good."

"I don't want to lose more time going a couple hundred miles out of our way," Jackson started to whine.

"Maybe we just go along with it and then when they leave us, we go the way we intended," Nick suggested. "Something says we don't want to make this guy mad. Did you see those warriors? They looked serious."

"And cool!" Henry interjected, excited at the experience to see real warriors and a real Chief. He was lying on his back staring up into the clear blue sky.

"Well, we could do that, Nick," Hazel started, "or we trust this Chief Joseph and go the way he is telling us to go. Yes, it will take longer to get to Denver, but is that a bad thing? It's not like we're really in a rush." She got up and rummaged in her trailer. She pulled out the Atlas of North Pangea they had consulted in REI. "We're to our first major point on the trip and now would be just as good a time as any to start mapping out the rest," she said flipping the page open to the full map of North Pangea. She found Missoula and traced with her fingers a possible route to Denver. She looked up, pleased, "Look here," she turned the map to the others, "Missoula might be the right direction to go after all. See, here is the freeway leaving Missoula." She traced Interstate 90, "It eventually crosses 15, then continues east to the I-25 exit."

"And I-25 takes us directly to Denver," Nick followed up. "It would drop us down from the north instead of coming from the west."

"And that might be the safest route," Henry summed up, "because it means we would be going through territory that would largely be ignored by the Sweepers; not a lot of population with which to contend. Turn on the phone Jackson and see if there are many in Montana and Wyoming." He flipped over to look at Jackson.

Jackson dug for the phone and turned it on. With a couple of quick swipes, he was surveying the map. "There's no green dots anywhere in Montana or Wyoming," he conceded. "But…" he paused. Then, looked closer at the screen. He turned the screen to show the others. There was a green dot on the screen hovering over Lewiston. The Sweepers were right where they'd just been. He faced the others, "He's right. On both accounts. There are Sweepers in Lewiston." Jackson looked at the green dot again, it blinked out. "It's gone! Do you think the warriors got them?" He looked at the others for answers. Finally, he turned the phone off and put it away.

"Maybe," Henry said. He peered around like they could jump out of the bushes at any time. "Why would they be in Lewiston? It seems kind of like an out of the way place."

"Maybe they were driving through on their way down from Spokane," Nick said. "They might send more Sweepers this direction, but for right now we have a reprieve. I say we thank Chief Joseph profusely the next time we see him and do exactly as he says. Who's with me?" Nick finished. They all agreed, then decided to unpack their sleeping bags and put them in the tepee.

The five spent the day wandering the area, watching the fast-flowing river splash the rocks in playful breaks. Several deer made their way down to the opposite riverbank to drink furtively from the ice-cold water. Alice and Hazel sat on rocks across from them trying to keep as still as they could in order to watch. The guys challenged each other to different activities. Sometimes they'd sprint as fast as they could from one side of the clearing to the other. On one of their races around the area, they came across a row of freshly dug mounds, two rows of twenty, forty in total. The mounds spoke of the tragedy of the Petriclysm even here. A stiff light-blue hand was slightly uncovered. This was the first time they'd seen anyone bury the frozen people. Henry and Nick scooped enough dirt to cover the hand again.

As they were settling down for the night, Chief Joseph and two warriors barged into the tepee. They didn't even have time to react before Chief Joseph yelled, "Where is it?!?"

Nick spoke first, "I'm really sorry, Chief, but I don't know what you are talking about." He looked at the others. Only Jackson kept his eyes averted.

"I know one of you has it!" the chief was enraged and getting angrier. "You brought them here. We destroyed them once before. Now! Who! Has! It!"

"Chief, are you talking about the sat phone?" Nick questioned, trying to figure out what it was he was looking for. Nick didn't want to anger their host, especially knowing that he'd saved them from Sweepers.

"No. No sat phone. ID. An ID," the chief responded. Nick looked long and hard at Jackson. Jackson's head was bowed.

"What did you do with the BioID you got in Yakima?" Nick asked Jackson quietly. Jackson didn't respond. Instead, he stood up and exited the tepee. A few minutes later, he reentered carrying something in his hand. He stood, eyes on the ground, his cheeks flushed, and held something out to Chief Joseph and let fall the small package he'd retrieved from his things.

Chief Joseph took what Jackson had and unwrapped it. The small flap of skin Jackson had cut from the Sweeper fell out. It was small and shriveled. The three dots barely visible in the decaying skin. A faint red light was emanating from the BioID. "You stupid boy," the chief spoke finally, throwing the flap of skin into the embers of the fire. It caught fire and then burst, a flame momentarily engulfing it. With that, Chief Joseph and the two warriors left.

They were stunned. Jackson had lied about getting rid of the BioID and it had led the Sweepers to Lewiston. They'd probably been tracked since leaving Yakima. There wasn't much to say at this point. Jackson knew it as well as the others. He'd broken their trust again and brought more trouble on them. He'd endangered innocent people as well. Without a word, each of them turned in for the night, sleeping as well as they could, hearing very little movement outside their tepee although they knew the warriors were patrolling the perimeter. Each of them feeling very thankful that Chief Joseph hadn't turned them out.

Chief Joseph aroused the five of them at daybreak. Dark purples and streaks of lighter blue were punctuating the night. There was another fire burning just outside the tepee and fish ready to eat.

"Eat, then pack, then talk," he said.

"Can I make some coffee?" Henry sleepily asked. Chief Joseph made the "as you will" gesture and Henry got started. The coffee was good with the fish.

Once they were all packed, the Chief brought them to the tepee they had first been in and indicated they should park their bikes and enter. They were surprised to see two other men inside, their hands and feet bound, their mouths gagged, white shirts rumpled and stained, black jackets trapped in back with their arms.

"Sweepers," Henry whispered. Chief Joseph confirmed this, then looked at Jackson. Jackson sat far back from the fire, arms across his chest, saying nothing.

"Yes, these men," Chief Joseph indicated, "Have been hunting down anyone still alive. And hunting you. They have told us their next move.

However, they will not be going." He said this last bit with finality. "Do you have any questions for these two men before you go?"

"One question," Jackson spoke first, chin tilted up in a defiant manner, "Where are the buses?" He looked at both men who eyed him back in return. Chief Joseph reached up to take the gag out of the first man.

"Wouldn't you like to know," he sneered. "Did you kill him? You little jerk?" Chief Joseph cut him off with a backhand to the face. "It was you, wasn't it? I'll kill you!" Then the chief reached through the opening of the tepee and beckoned. A warrior silently passed through. The Sweeper looked at him. He started trembling. Then he quickly spoke out of fear, "The last stop is Cheyenne." And with that, another look from Chief Joseph and the warrior lifted the Sweeper to his feet and hauled him out. The Sweeper started screaming and fighting his binds. The sounds got further and further away until they could no longer be heard.

"Any other questions," the Chief indicated the remaining Sweeper who was now sweating profusely.

"I have one question," Nick stepped up. "How did our parents die?"

The Sweeper didn't hesitate to respond, "They were injected with the same drug used for lethal injection. Don't ask me the name of it, I don't know. You're their kids, aren't you?" Nick showed this to be true. "Man," the Sweeper groaned, "For what it's worth, I am so sorry. I didn't sign up for any of this. You have to believe me."

"And yet, you did not stop," Chief Joseph finished. With another wave of his had a second warrior entered, picked up the Sweeper and frog-marched him out the door. The Sweeper went silently.

"It is time to go," the chief said, turning to them. "It is decided, you are to go to Missoula." There was no room for argument. Two warriors were ready to lead them to the highway that would take them on their way.

"Chief Joseph," Alice began tentatively.

"Ask your question," he said.

"How did your dream end?"

"You will see." And turned his attention elsewhere.

The two warriors quickly led them to the highway connecting Lewiston and Missoula. As they passed the turn off for highway 93, the road they originally intended to take, they saw that it would have been impossible to go that way even if they had wanted to. The road for as far as they could see was laid waste. Gigantic chunks of highway turned this way and that, parts of it turned up on end, holes where highway once had been. It looked like a war zone. Probably had been. They were too stunned to ask the men with them what had happened and doubted they would have answered anyway. The warriors pointed down the highway; the five mounted their bikes and were off. Nick turned to say thank you, but the warriors were gone.

CHAPTER 18

"What do you think they did to the Sweepers?" Henry asked, pulling alongside Jackson. "The one looked terrified when they took him out of the tepee."

"I'm pretty sure they will kill them if they aren't dead already."

"Are you okay?" Henry peered intently at Jackson. Jackson glared at him. Henry rolled away to give Jackson his space. He slid in next to Nick, "How are you?"

Nick looked at Henry gave him a quick smile, "Okay. Just thinking. I'm glad to know that my dad wasn't tortured or anything. And I think it really helps knowing that not all the Sweepers are vile automatons doing the work of the government. That last man? I could tell he was really sorry he'd killed our parents. It means something when someone says sorry and they mean it. You know?"

"Yeah, I do know, but I want to hear it from the top echelon. An apology for killing my mom and speaking of apologies," Henry screeched to a halt, turning to Jackson, "I think you have some explaining to do."

"I don't have anything to say to you," Jackson retorted.

"Actually, I think you do," Henry crossed his arms. "You lied about getting rid of that BioID. You could have gotten us killed. If Chief Joseph hadn't intercepted those Sweepers, we either would be dead now or on a green bus. So, yeah, you owe us an apology."

"I owe you nothing," Jackson shoved off.

"I think we should cut him loose," Henry pedaled after Jackson, cutting him off. Jackson came to a stop and got off just in time to meet Henry's fist. Henry swung with all his might, glancing off Jackson's right shoulder as he turned to deflect, the force of the swing sending Henry into a spin. He landed flat on the ground, staring up at Jackson. Jackson glared at him and kicked some loose gravel in Henry's direction. Nick extended his hand to Henry, pulling him up. Henry brushed himself off and lunged for Jackson. Nick stepped between them and held Henry back. "He could have got us killed!" Henry yelled.

"Stop," Nick tried to get Henry to calm down. Hazel and Alice were standing nearby watching the tussle.

"He could have got us killed!" Henry yelled again, the fight going out of him. He stopped struggling, tears welled up in his frustration. Henry brushed them out of his eyes. Softly, "You could've got us killed. Those Sweepers were tracking us because of *you*."

Jackson sighed, "Okay. I'm sorry. I really am. I didn't know. I thought I could use the BioID somehow. To help. I just…Look, I am *really* sorry."

"Do you really mean it this time?" Henry looked at him.

"I do. I'm sorry," Jackson said. "I promise I won't keep putting you in danger. Do you want me to just go?"

"Not yet," Nick shook his head, "but if you keep things like that from us again, you might have to."

"You gotta believe me. I had no idea it still worked. I'm sorry," and with that he went back to his bike, got on, and pedaled down the road.

"He won't do it again," Nick said, trying to reassure Henry.

Henry muttered, "I hope you're right. I hope we get to Denver before he gets us all killed." He started pedaling, shaking his head. "You know what I really want?" he picked up his earlier conversation, "I want to know why they can't just leave us alone. Those of us who survived. Why is it so important to find us?" He stopped talking and concentrated on the road ahead. The miles cruised by as the road became windier. The river next to them narrowed, the rapids increasingly swift until the rush of water was all they could hear. Once in a while, there were beautiful deep blue green eddies where they stopped and drank, refilling their canteens and using their LifeStraws to filter out any harmful bacteria. The trees were giant sentries overhead, keeping much of the sun from reaching the ground and hiding the riders in the shadows. By late afternoon it was time to stop. The road, following a pretty steady incline, added more strain to the already road-weary riders. They found a lovely place to camp by the river. The rushing water so calming that it was a struggle to get the tents ready before falling asleep.

In the morning they discovered that Jackson had gone. The impression of where his tent had been was barely visible. His bike and trailer nowhere in sight. Nick walked to the road hoping he could see which direction Jackson had gone, but there was no sign. Henry joined Nick, "Well, do you think we'll find him?"

"Only if he wants to be found. He might've gone back the way we came for all we know," Nick turned to pack his things.

"I'm really sorry. I didn't mean for him to leave."

"It's okay, Henry. Honestly, I think he's been looking for an excuse to be out on his own. If we find him, we find him. If not, I'm sure he can manage. Let's get ready to go." The cool air was an incentive to get moving. It was quick work getting ready for their day and the only excitement besides Jackson's disappearance were the bear tracks that Henry pointed out. Nick breathed a sigh of relief that the bear didn't go digging in their trailers or found them to be tasty treats wrapped up neatly in tents. They were on the road again in no time, each as silent as the other, concentrating on their own thoughts. The sun took several hours to reach the road where the warmth was welcomed by the steadily moving teens.

Nick cruised ahead of the others for some time. He enjoyed going faster and being the first one to round a corner. It gave him time to think and be alone, allowing his introverted self to recharge. He thought about those who were responsible for the Petriclysm and pondered Henry's musings from the day before. Why was it so important to round up and possibly get rid of those who survived? Why not let them fend for themselves? There were too few to really do much damage to either the environment or the government. His mind wandered further. Did the government keep doctors alive? What about engineers? Firefighters? Scientists? So far, they hadn't come across any doctors or those who could help in a medical emergency. Red only talked about the farmers and, if there were doctors among the group, he certainly didn't point them out. It was overwhelming to think about how many people it takes to keep a society functioning. One person or even a few aren't nearly enough to cover all the bases. So far on this trip, they had been very fortunate to not need medical attention, but what happens if and when they do?

He was brought out of his musings by a sound to his right. Nick cocked his head listening. He heard it again. A faint moan. *What was that*? He cruised to the side of the road and halted. The others caught up and Hazel started to ask what was going on, but he held up a hand to keep her quiet. They heard a faint moan in the woods. Parking their bikes behind a clump of trees to keep them hidden from the road, Nick led the others in the direction of the sounds. It came again, a little louder this time. His hand went to the pepper spray in case it was an injured animal. He still hadn't had his shooting lessons from Henry and was reluctant to handle his gun before then. The others followed silently behind.

Henry tripped and grabbed Alice, bringing her down with him. Henry let out a yelp of pain as he sat back holding his ankle. He looked around to find that he'd tripped over the tongue of a bike trailer hidden in the bushes. Alice disentangled herself and tried to help Henry up, but he fell back again. His ankle was definitely sprained. It was Jackson's bike he'd tripped over. It had been carefully concealed. Henry moved away from the brush on his hands and knees and sat against a nearby tree.

"Can you walk on it?" Nick asked, looking down at him concerned.

"I don't think so," Henry shook his head. "It's Jackson's bike and trailer."

They heard a muffled "Help" in the distance. "Wait here," Nick instructed, "I'll be right back. Hazel come with me. Alice, stay with Henry."

"Not like I can go anywhere," Henry's voice trailed after them.

Nick and Hazel hurried off through the trees. The moans were more distinct now. "Help," came the plaintive call.

"It's definitely Jackson," Hazel said as they made their way toward the noise. "He's in pain."

"Help!" came the plea, louder with more fervency. "Help me, please. Anybody," Jackson let out a sob as Hazel and Nick came through a final wall of bushes. There in the middle of a small clearing was Jackson kneeling, arms locked behind him. An unmoving woman standing in behind him firmly gripping both of Jackson's wrists. A knee digging into his lower back. Tears and snot flowing freely down his face as he sniffled trying to breathe. His body was painfully extended in a backwards C that didn't allow for any movement.

"Jackson!" Nick ran up to him. He grabbed Jackson's wrists unsuccessfully trying to free them from the petriclyzed woman's grip.

"Hurry!" Jackson sobbed, "You have to break her hands. I can't move." Nick withdrew the nightstick from his police belt and started beating the solid hands. A couple of fingers broke, and Jackson was able to wiggle his arms a little. "More," he said, trying to loosen the grip. Nick repeated the blows on both hands, eventually breaking enough of the woman's fingers to allow Jackson enough room to extract both wrists, one after the other. Once he was free, the woman fell over onto the soft forest floor. Jackson sat back on his heels, rubbing his wrists both of which were angry and raw. He wiped his nose and eyes, then looked at Nick and Hazel. He lost his voice momentarily in a shriek and pointed back at the statue. A bright blue glow emitted from the three dots in the middle of her forehead. "Quick," Jackson croaked, "the forehead. Hit it." It was all he could do to explain. Nick took the nightstick and with two swift hits, the forehead caved in and the blue light went out.

"What is going on?" Nick demanded, helping Jackson to his feet.

Jackson brushed the dirt and pine needles from his knees, "I was riding by and saw the blue light so I thought I would investigate and then she moved! Henry was right. They move! I turned away to run as fast as I could, but she was faster, like lightning speed. She put her knee in my back, grabbed my wrists and then froze again. I've been here since late last night. I left just after I knew you were asleep. That blue light came on several times. It was really bright. I don't know what it does, but it can't be good." They heard screeching tires in the direction of the road and four doors opened and slammed shut. The forest was still in twilight. Men's voices could be heard calling to one another as they came crashing through the underbrush.

"We need to hide," Nick hurriedly whispered. "Now! Follow me." The three of them crouched down and made their way deeper into the forest. The men's voices were getting nearer. They clearly heard the men talking to one another.

"Here," one man's voice echoed through the trees. "Here's she is." Nick's heart leapt in his chest. Did they find Alice? Where's Henry? Then he heard, "They broke her hands and bashed in her face." They were talking about the petriclyzed woman who had grabbed Jackson. "Got to be around here somewhere. No way that kid could have gotten free by himself. Fan out and keep looking."

Nick, Hazel, and Jackson ducked under a low-hanging tree, the branches thick and skirting the ground. "Don't you think they'll look under here?" Hazel asked, barely audible.

"If they do, we'll have to fight," Nick answered. "Get your pepper spray ready," Hazel complied and handed Jackson her firearm. He expertly flipped the safety and wrapped his hands around the grip.

They waited in the cool darkness of the pine branches. There wasn't much room to move. Nick stayed close to the edge of the skirt, watching for any movement. Hazel knelt and held the pepper spray in one hand and the night stick in the other. She focused on Nick, waiting for any signs from him. *Fight or flight; Fight or flight; Fight or flight* on automatic loop in her brain, bracing for confrontation. Jackson sat in a similar manner, waiting. The bushes just outside their hiding spot moved as a tall man dressed in all black stepped through. He stood mere inches from Nick who was sitting on his heels, ready to spring forward at a moment's notice.

The Sweeper moved to look under the tree when a scratchy voice came over a radio at the man's side, "We found a bike just off the road. All units report." The Sweeper dropped his hand from the tree branch and moved to grab the radio, unclipping it. "Yeah, uh, I'm about a hundred yards from the woman. No sign of anyone. Your call. Over." The man held the radio up to his mouth waiting for a response. The answer came back, "Head toward the road. Our quarry most likely headed back toward his bike. Over." "Copy." And the Sweeper turned away from where Nick was bracing for a fight. The steps faded. Nick let out his breath and sat back against the tree trunk.

"I think we should wait until we know they're gone," Nick suggested.

"We can't hear anything this far away," Hazel noted.

"No, but we can at least wait for them to put some distance between us and them before we go out to check things."

"What about Alice and Henry? Henry can't move," Hazel worried, "He tripped over your bike, Jackson. If the Sweepers found your bike they can't be far away." Her voice was tinged with accusation and anger.

"I…I…we're just going to have to wait. I'm pretty sure that Henry and Alice found some place to hide. They're resourceful. We just have to trust that they're okay," Nick tried to reassure her.

There was more movement on the far side of the clearing. Two Sweepers emerged from the wall of trees, having doubled-back from beyond their hiding place. "Should've kept the chief. He'd be good for tracking this stupid kid," he guffawed.

His partner responded, "Just think of how much trouble he would've been. Those stupid warriors would've chased us all the way to Denver." Nick, Hazel, and Jackson could see the two men clearly now as they walked past them. They were both dressed like the other man. Black clothes from head to toe.

"Although that headdress sure will be a nice ar-ti-fact for the boss's library," the words trailed the men as they moved on.

Hazel was crying now. Surely, they weren't talking about Chief Joseph. He had saved their lives. The Sweepers were only here because Jackson had kept the BioID. She looked at Jackson and could tell he was thinking the same thing. He wiped his eyes.

After what felt like forever, the three of them silently left their hiding place and cautiously made their way back toward the woman who had grabbed Jackson. No one was visible from the spot where Jackson had been caught, so they ducked behind another clump of bushes to make sure that the Sweepers were truly gone. They could still hear movement near the road. Four doors slammed shut, an engine roared to life, and gravel kicked up as the Sweepers continued down the road. Nick, Hazel, and Jackson waited a good ten minutes before moving again. Nick looked desperately around for any sign of Henry and Alice. Jackson took off in the direction his bike had been, and Hazel started looking for the other bikes. The three of them reconvened on the road. Jackson was angry. Nick was worried. And Hazel was relieved.

"I haven't seen any sign of Alice or Henry," Nick relayed.

At the same time Jackson was angrily spouting, "They took all my stuff! Left my bike completely destroyed."

While Hazel relayed that the other four bikes and trailers had not been discovered.

Nick looked at Jackson, "I don't care about your bike or your trailer. This is all because of you. If you hadn't kept that BioID, the Sweepers wouldn't have followed us to Lewiston. They wouldn't be on the highway now. Henry wouldn't have been injured tripping over your stupid bike. We wouldn't be in this mess if you had simply done what was asked of you in the first place. It's. Your. Fault!" He finished angrily and stormed off back into the trees to continue searching for Alice and Henry.

"Wait," Jackson went after him. "Wait! I'm sorry. I'm truly sorry." He was crying by now, the gravity of the consequences of his actions finally sinking in. Nick continued walking. Jackson stopped and sat down head buried in his hands as he sobbed. Wracking sobs shook his whole body. Hazel stopped in front of him, looking down.

"And now Chief Joseph is dead because of you," she couldn't help adding, then turned to follow Nick.

Nick and Hazel spent the next three hours looking for Henry and Alice finding no signs of them. By then it was early afternoon. Nick decided to retrieve their bikes and set up camp in the small clearing they'd found when following Jackson's calls for help. Hazel helped Nick bring each bike. They set up each of the tents. Nick was fearful the Sweepers would redouble their trek and decided against a fire. They still had some of the food they'd gotten at Starbucks and snacks they'd picked up along the way. Hazel and Nick sat silently in their camp chairs eating and waiting. Neither one of them voicing the fear that the Sweepers had found Henry and Alice.

"You should go get Jackson," Hazel suggested to Nick. "Regardless, we still need him, and he needs us."

"No," was Nick's decisive answer, "he's caused enough problems. He can fend for himself."

Hazel got up and walked away. She came back awhile later, Jackson following meekly behind her. She dug around in Alice's trailer and pulled out the camp chair for Jackson to use and found some food for him. Jackson was quiet, his eyes swollen from crying, his bottom lip quivering now and then in a threat of fresh tears.

Nick turned his chair away from Jackson, clearly showing how he felt about Jackson's presence. "Nick," Hazel started, he squinted at her, "We ALL make mistakes. Don't tell me you haven't. Jackson deserves a second chance."

"No, he doesn't. And it wouldn't be his second or his third," was the terse response.

"It doesn't matter how many times. We need Jackson."

"No. *We* do not. *We* need Henry and Alice."

"Well, *I* need Jackson. *I* need him to help rescue Henry and Alice and Felix and Ivy. *I* can't do it alone or even with just you." A branch snapped in the distance. The conversation stopped. Nick reached for the night stick; Jackson retrieved the gun he'd been carrying. Hazel didn't have time to react before Alice came crashing into the camp circle.

"Oh, thank God!" she exclaimed. "I've been looking all over for you! I thought the Sweepers got to you before they left." Alice reached out and gave Hazel a tight hug.

"Where's Henry?" Hazel wanted to know.

"Oh, we found a small cave kind of hidden behind some branches. I helped him get there before the Sweepers got here. They almost found us, but someone hollered over the radio and they turned back."

"Same thing happened to us," Hazel relayed. "I don't think they were very serious about finding us."

"No. They were serious about finding Jackson," Alice looked at Jackson, surprised to see clear evidence that he'd been crying. "What in the world happened? How did they know he was here?"

Nick explained how they found Jackson and got him loose. "I think it might have something to do with the blue light. They're using the BioIDs somehow to track. That's all I can think of."

"It makes sense," Alice concurred. "Maybe that's why they were only looking for one of us."

"Actually, a couple of us. They knew he had help getting free," Nick corrected.

"They destroyed my bike and took all my stuff," Jackson whined. "Alice, I am so sorry about all of this. It's all my fault," he looked at her hoping for an acceptance to his apology.

"You should tell her about Chief Joseph," Nick looked hard at Jackson.

"What about Chief Joseph?" Alice looked concerned.

"He's dead," Nick couldn't wait for Jackson's slow response.

"How do you know?"

"The Sweepers were talking about it when they passed by our hiding spot."

"They only said 'The Chief,'" Jackson argued. "You don't know for sure it was Chief Joseph."

"You're right," Nick glared at him, "But how many chiefs do you know?"

Jackson started crying again.

"It doesn't matter now," Hazel put in. "Nick, let it go. I want Jackson to stay with us if he wants to. Alice?"

Alice looked dumbfounded at the news that Chief Joseph might be dead. Her shoulders slumped, then she nodded in agreement. Looking directly at Jackson, "I hate that your actions created a lot more problems for us and for people who were simply trying to help, but I agree that we need you. Come and help me get Henry." She walked away. Jackson and Hazel followed her. They found Henry propped up against the back wall of the shallow cave. He seemed in good spirits, but his ankle was so swollen that it was impossible for him to put weight on it. Nick suggested they relocate their camp to the cave. It was more secluded and would allow them to have a small fire since the cave faced away from the road. Everyone agreed and returned to the clearing to help pack up and relocate to Henry's spot. Once there, Hazel had Henry sit on a camp chair and piled up enough stuff to elevate his ankle.

"How are we going to keep going?" Henry asked. "I can't pedal, at least for right now."

"You can ride," Jackson said from the opening of the tent. "I can pedal your bike. We can make a seat for you on top of the trailer. I'll pull you."

"That's a good idea," Nick said, "I guess Hazel's right, we do need you. But don't mistake that for trust. Trust is earned." With that he left to get cold water from the river.

CHAPTER 19

They slept late the next day and made a small fire for heat and to boil water for coffee. Henry was situated close enough to the fire to tend the French press since he had been self-proclaimed "The King of Coffee." The others were more than willing to relinquish the job to him.

The previous night they'd agreed to stay put for a couple of days in order to let Henry elevate his ankle. It was a welcome break after the terror of the day before. Hazel accompanied Nick to the river for water.

"How are you?" Hazel asked him once they were out of earshot of the others.

"I'm tired, Hazel," he responded. "I don't know what to do about Jackson. I hate the fact that he is still here. I know you want him to stay with us, but I'm just having a hard time with it. I don't trust him to keep his word. He's dangerous and I think he's got his own agenda. Know what I mean?"

"Yeah, I do, but I don't want to let him go off on his own. He already tried that and see what happened?"

"He only got in trouble because he let his curiosity get the best of him."

"But you would have done the same thing. Admit it."

Nick sighed, “Yes. You’re right. I would have gotten off my bike and checked it out, too.”

“What do you say about unhooking our bikes and riding a little bit down the road today? I think I saw a sign for a small town not far from here. It would give us a break from the others. Plus, if I’m right in my reckoning, it’s just about Henry’s birthday and we could scrounge around and find some gifts and maybe some cake or something to celebrate. What do you think?” she smiled at him.

“I think that’s a great idea. I could use a little break,” he smiled back. “Let’s get this water to the group and let them know we’ll be back in a little while.”

The others made no protestations against Hazel and Nick’s plan. Jackson knew he wasn’t wanted, and Alice was content with tending to Henry. Nick and Hazel hit the pavement feeling light without the trailers attached. Each of them wearing only the backpacks they’d brought from Anvac, mostly empty for a day of exploration and gathering. It was already colder than when they’d left Lewiston the day before and they’d donned their down vests for the day’s ride.

Both of them felt wonderful and raced each other at times as they made quick work of the few miles to town. Nick slowed down as they reached the city limits and pulled to the side of the road. Hazel drew up beside him. Nick was looking down the main street intently watching for signs of movement or for black vehicles that would give any indication that Sweepers were around. He kicked himself for not asking to borrow the sat phone.

“I think we should hide our bikes here and go on foot,” he advised as he got off and walked his bike to a nearby little shed. Hazel did likewise. Once the bikes were stowed, they cautiously approached the first building on the right.

The town was old and rustic. All the buildings on each side of the street shared walls with one another. Their painted facades that had faded over time. The eaves created a shaded boardwalk and log railings ran intermittently from one end of the storefronts to the other. Old-fashioned hitching posts were dotted throughout and had probably been used right up until the Petriclysm. It was an idyllic little town and had most likely been a stopping point for many tourists along the road. No signs of life were visible as Hazel and Nick approached the end steps that led to the first store along the walk. The bottom step gave out a small groan as they stepped up and their shoes made hollow sounds in the stillness as they walked long. They walked as quietly as they could to match the silence around them. Nick gave the entrance door a small shove as the warped wood stuck some. Once inside they noticed that only one customer and the cashier had been present at the time of the Petriclysm. They were old men, one leaning on one side of the counter and the other across from him had been caught in mid-conversation. They looked like they'd know each other well and had been jawing away the time. Nick thought it a much more pleasant way to blink out—talking to a friend versus what he'd seen in Seattle, tired drivers sitting in rush hour traffic on their way home. The busyness of city life juxtaposed to the quiet country life once lived in this small town.

Hazel started looking around. This store had apparently been a general store. All sorts of supplies were marked on shelves from one end to the other. There was an entire hardware area, a small section for electronics, non-perishable foods, and even a limited selection of popular novels. She thumbed through a couple of these and selected one for reading later when back at camp.

"We need to find a birthday card or something," Hazel said as she searched the racks located at the sales counter.

"I don't see any here, maybe one of the other stores will have some," his hands were full of marshmallows, chocolate bars, and two boxes of graham crackers. He was setting them on the counter while he opened his backpack and started putting them in. As he was finishing, the dark outline of a man approached the store entrance. Nick ducked and threw the rest of the food into his pack. "Hazel," he whispered as he crouched and moved toward the storage room at the back of the store. She looked up in time to see the door start to open and scurried to join Nick in the back. They stayed in the shadows and watched as the door opened further.

The man was half in the building when he turned and spoke to someone outside, "Yeah, there's a couple here at the counter. Silas, come help me get them out front." The door closed behind the speaker and shortly another man joined him. They started moving the man who was leaning on the counter, shifting him from side to side to dislodge him from his position.

The man named Silas spoke up, "I don't think these will work. They're leaning. Fall right over."

"Nonsense," the first replied. "We just need to lean them on one of those rails. Look more natural, know what I mean."

"I guess. Here, I'll tip 'im and you can grab his feet." The two men shuffled and grunted with the awkwardness and weight of the petriclyzed man. Once Silas got to the door, he rested the man's head and upper body on a knee while he managed to get the door open enough to start easing their burden to the nearest railing. Once that was completed, the two men reentered and struggled with the second man—the cashier on the other side of the counter—and then they were gone.

Hazel and Nick watched this proceeding and were very curious as to what these men were up to. There was no other exit from the store, so they remained hidden until they stopped seeing the men move across the storefront. Eventually, Hazel and Nick crept to the window to look out. They were in time to see several men getting into a black SUV before it headed out of town toward Missoula.

Nick spoke first, "What do you think they were doing?" He cautiously opened the door and peered left then right. All along the boardwalk, townspeople were standing. They recognized the two men from the store leaning against the nearest rail.

"They put people outside. See? None of them were here when we went into the store," Hazel pointed up and down the street.

"Right, but why?" And at that moment, bright blue lights lit up in the middle of all the statues' foreheads making the small town look anemically decorated for the holidays. The lights blinked on and off, some blazed bright as they had seen before and some were barely visible in the broad daylight. Nick lay flat on the ground and Hazel crouched. "We need to get back to the others," she whispered afraid that stone ears were listening in. Nick army crawled to the end of the boardwalk and they quickly retrieved their bikes.

Once they turned a bend and the town was no longer visible, Nick spoke, "I think they set them up to look for us. Or at least Jackson."

"I think you're right," Hazel agreed.

"So somehow the Sweepers can control the ID chips and use them," he thought out loud. "I wonder if we could hack into the system."

"What?" Hazel turned to him.

"I said, I wonder if we could hack the system."

"How?" she encouraged.

"I got it!" he exclaimed. "Let's get back to camp and grab the laptop and Jackson's sat phone. I bet there's a way to at least track these spies like Jackson's been tracking the Sweepers."

"Do you think so?"

"I'm not sure, but there's no harm in trying. We don't have anything to lose. It's obvious they're using these people as some sort of tracking device."

They raced ahead and got back to camp shortly. They parked their bikes near the highway and swiftly made their way back to camp. Jackson was sitting some distance from the others which made it easier to explain their situation to him. Nick didn't want Henry to know what was going on even though he was the most experienced with computers because they didn't want him to move his ankle. The sooner he healed, the better.

Jackson didn't let on that Hazel and Nick were nearby. He simply told Henry and Alice that he was going to go for a ride, too, see what Hazel and Nick were doing and asked if it would be okay to borrow Henry's bike. Henry was reluctant to let his bike out of his sight but gave in after Jackson pleaded a little more. Jackson promised to bring him a root beer or two as payment. They could stick it in the running water to cool it down. He grabbed the sat phone, the bike and wended his way to the highway where he joined Nick and Hazel.

Nick explained to Jackson what had happened with the two men in the store and how when they'd left the store the whole town was lined with petriclyzed people. They relayed to him how the blue lights had come on just after the Sweepers had left and the theory that Jackson might be able to access the trackers on his sat phone or use the computer to somehow get into the system. Jackson admitted that it was a long shot, but that it would be worth a try. He was thankful that he'd had the phone on him when the Sweepers took his things.

It was now a little past noon as they approached main street. Again, they stashed the bikes in the small shed. Nick carried the laptop and Jackson had the sat phone out and ready to use. Jackson checked the whereabouts of any Sweepers in the vicinity and noticed that there was only one green dot on the highway moving down the road. This corroborated what Nick and Hazel had said about the direction the SUV was traveling. No other dots were within a hundred miles of them. The three of them entered the same store Hazel and Nick had visited earlier. They knew there weren't any other individuals in the store, and they could sneak past the waiting statues outside by staying close to the ground. No blue lights were visible at the moment, which was a relief.

Once inside the store, Nick fired up the computer. Jackson was able to use the sat phone as a hotspot and the computer was soon up and running online. The Internet seemed to still be working, but from there, Nick had no idea what to do or whether or not there was anything to do. Hazel drew out the flash drive and handed it to Nick, "I don't know if this will help at all, but maybe there's something there." She shrugged as Nick took the flash drive and inserted it into the computer. The same files appeared as before, but Nick started looking closer at them. He skimmed several files on the virus and the vaccine and decided to open the folder with information about the BioID. There was a lot of history and then, "Bingo!" Nick double-tapped a file nested inside another folder labeled *Attributes*. "Here," he pointed. "It says *Alternative Uses*." He started reading.

"Anything?" Jackson stood over his shoulder for a better look.

"Nothing, yet. Why don't you see if there's another map on the sat phone? One that shows where all these BioID-ed, petriclyzed people might be."

"Okay," Jackson said, starting to look through more apps on the phone.

Hazel spent her time rifling through more shelves in the store. She still hadn't found a birthday card for Henry but had found a few things that might serve as birthday presents. One was a model car kit of the Dukes of Hazzard car—a 1969 Dodge Charger. She grabbed a few paint brushes and other recommended supplies listed on the outside of the box. Henry wouldn't have time right now to do it, but when things finally settled down and they could take a break, it would be a great way occupy some time. She grabbed a few other items including the root beers Jackson had promised to bring back and a couple of extra rolls of toilet paper, something they always needed.

From the far side of the room an excited Jackson relayed, "I think I've found it!" Hazel joined them as he turned the phone to show Hazel and Nick a different map. Jackson had zoomed in on the map to show the main street just outside the store. There were small black dots lining the street. "Look," Jackson explained. "I think this map shows the BioIDs. These black dots," he pointed, "Correspond nearly perfectly with the individuals outside. See?" Sure enough, they were in almost the exact same spot.

"But why aren't they blue?" Hazel asked.

"Probably because they aren't active right now." All of a sudden, the black dots flashed blue on the screen and all three of them crept up to the window and peered outside. The blue lights were flashing again. Jackson held up the sat phone screen and watched the street and map simultaneously. The blue lights on the screen grew brighter and then dimmed in the same way they saw the lights outside grow and dim. Then, the blue lights went out on the map and outside. The map returned to black dots. "They're pinging the IDs," he said lowering the sat phone. "I think they're using it to find people."

"Us," Hazel put in. "I think they're specifically looking for us. What happens when you zoom out on the map?" Jackson pinched the screen to zoom out. A map of North Pangea showed up. Spots of black were visible across the map. Some areas lit up in blue and then faded again.

"They're doing the same thing all over," he gazed intently at the screen, then swiped across it to show a different part of the world. Some areas were densely covered in black, places such as India and China, to use their former names. Places where the majority of the world's population had once been concentrated were now almost completely covered in black dots, so many they were indistinguishable from this vantage point on the map.

"Jackson, bring the phone over here. I think I've got something," Nick said from in front of the computer screen.

"What is it?" Hazel asked.

"Give me just a minute," Nick replied. "Jackson, find the Bluetooth address on your phone.

"Why? What are you going to do?"

"Just do it will you?"

"Fine. Here," he turned the screen to Nick. Nick copied down the address into a strange looking screen he'd pulled up on the computer.

"What program are you in?" Jackson looked at the screen.

"It's something I found on the flash drive. I think it will let us access the BioIDs. There were instructions and when I clicked the link, this screen came up. It's a walkthrough on how to hack the IDs. I think it only works if the person is petriclyzed, but we can find out later if we have time." Nick finished entering the data and hit 'run' on the screen. A strange series of bright green code ran up the black screen, reminiscent of DOS coding, running so quickly their eyes couldn't track what was happening. Then, the screen stopped, and a cursor blinked on a blank page.

"Well?" Hazel queried.

"Well," Nick blinked. "Check the phone, Jackson." Jackson did. He shook his head. The map looked the same. "Zoom in on one of the people outside and double tap it," Nick suggested. Jackson did and then gasped. Outside a blue light came on across the way, then, "No way!" Jackson jumped up excited. "Look!" He turned the screen, and they could see the storefront of the store in which they were standing.

"Stay down!" Nick grabbed Hazel and Jackson pulling them down. "If we can see the store, they can see the store." Jackson sat staring at the video feed. He double tapped the blue light and it returned to black, the light across the street went out again. Jackson tried a couple more along main street. The same process repeated itself.

"You did it!" Hazel congratulated Nick. "How did you do it? And what did you do exactly?"

"Your dad was a genius," he smiled. "He created a way to hack the phones by using the Bluetooth number on the device. It was a plug and chug program. I'm not a computer whiz by a long shot so his instructions walked me through the process. We now have access to all the BioIDs around the world. At least the people who are petriclyzed. We can pop in on other places to see what's going on or to turn off the IDs that have been activated."

Jackson had already been trying out this newfound ability and was watching the screen intently.

"What are you looking at?" Nick asked him. Jackson showed them the screen. They were looking at a lush green tropical paradise, the ocean waves crashing on a white sandy beach that looked so warm and inviting they could almost feel it. Sadly, the beach was littered with grey bodies in different modes of relaxation. Not a single living person walked the beach. Seagulls perched themselves on the tops of immovable heads and basked in the warm sun.

"It's Costa Rica," he said sadly. "It was one of my favorite vacation spots. Now look at it. Going to waste and all those people there who had simply been enjoying their day," he tapped the screen and the image faded.

"At least now we have a lot more ability to ride safely to Denver. Think about it, we can access different places before we bike through. We can check up on where the Sweepers are and what they're doing," Nick sounded relieved. "We won't have to worry so much about when they may use these cameras. What I want to know is how they did it. How did they get the IDs to work like that?"

"Same and," Jackson added, "can we do the same thing with those who are still alive? If we can access some of the IDs of the elite, just imagine what we can do."

"Henry's flash drive!" Hazel spoke up. "Remember, he has all their information. Maybe it includes their ID access numbers."

"I didn't find a way to access living individuals on the program," Nick said, while powering down the computer. "If we can maybe contact William somehow and see what he can do with this program. I bet he'd be able to figure it out."

"Or we can just petriclyze them with the kill switch and then access what's around them," Jackson piped up.

"We already decided we're not using that kill switch," Nick reminded him. "Besides, if we can hold them responsible for their actions, I would much rather have them suffer than be dead."

"No worries. I was just saying. You know," Jackson replied defensively. "At least we got this working. I can keep the map open for now and we can look through some of the other stores safely before going back to camp."

"Thanks," Hazel said, handing him the root beers. "These are for Henry. I heard you promise to bring him a couple. Now, I've got to find some birthday cards for him. We're planning on celebrating his birthday tonight at camp."

"Jackson, thanks for coming along and helping us with this. More and more I am really glad you took that phone," Nick squeezed his shoulder in appreciation. "And I'm sorry for getting so mad at you. Let's call it good and get out of here."

They successfully found a few birthday cards and gift wrap for Henry in another store and headed back to camp. When they got back, it was close to time for dinner. Nick and Jackson told Henry about the new map and showed him how they could access BioIDs around the world. They had to limit their time in order to save the battery. The sun was going down and charging batteries wouldn't be possible until the following day.

Hazel and Alice got Henry's birthday presents bagged in bright colored gift bags with lots of tissue paper. Alice was grateful to Hazel for remembering his birthday and for picking up enough cards that each of them could sign one for Henry. That night, they stuck a couple of candles in a plate of unwrapped Hostess chocolate cupcakes. Nick lit the candles and they stood around singing "Happy Birthday" before Henry blew out the candles. After the cupcakes were devoured, Hazel present Henry with his gifts. He particularly liked the Dukes of Hazzard model car and was excited about the future where he would have time to assemble it. They finished the night's festivities by making s'mores around the campfire. They ate so many that each of them was sick to their stomach and rolled to bed to sleep it off.

They stayed one more day before heading out. Jackson checked the phone on numerous occasions and could see when the Sweepers where checking IDs along the route they were following. He was able to detect a regular pattern as to when the IDs were pinged, which enabled them to plan their next moves according to when it would be safest to travel through the little towns dotted along the way. Jackson refrained from turning off the cameras when the Sweepers were using them to keep the Sweepers in the dark about the new ability to track them.

CHAPTER 20

It took them another three days to reach the outskirts of Missoula. By the time they reached the city limits, Henry's ankle had healed enough that he thought he could pedal, as long as his load was relatively light. The first thing was to find a bike shop or some sporting goods store where Jackson could get reoutfitted for the trip. They were more cautious using the sat phone to check for IDs sweeps as they had come to call them. It was the only item he'd had on him when the Sweepers found his things. Henry was very thankful that the Sweepers hadn't found the other trailers with the flash drives. He now kept the flash drive BioDie had given him buried in his pocket. He liked to pat it often to reassure himself that it was still there. Hazel and Nick also took to carrying the other two flash drives. Nick caried William's lethal Operation Covax and Hazel her dad's version.

They reached Missoula in mid-afternoon. Unlike their experiences in Yakima and Lewiston, they didn't see a single person out and about. The streets looked much like they had in every town they'd been through, cars piled up in intersections, people frozen in time on the sidewalk. Downtown was charming or would have been had there not been such a conglomeration of frozen people. Even after three weeks, it was still a disturbing sight to see so many people who had been affected by the government.

People who had simply wanted to live their lives, who traded some freedom for the ability to continue going to school or grocery shopping or working. Instead, these trusting people were now immortalized, permanently stuck doing whatever mundane activity they'd been doing those last few moments of their lives.

In the heart of downtown, a bicycle store still had bikes parked out front on display. Jackson found a comparable one to the Ghost he'd lost. Inside he found a bike trailer used for kids, but it would have to do since it was the only type of trailer available. There was an old Army Navy store at another corner. Jackson stocked up on gear. He was going to continue sharing the two-person tent with Nick and Henry. It was a tight squeeze, but in some ways more comforting. Jackson also unloaded a lot of Henry's things, storing them in his new trailer. At a corner pharmacy, Hazel found a good wrap that would help Henry's ankle continue to heal, while allowing him to pedal.

The highway took several strange turns in the heart of town. Eventually, the street signs pointed the way toward I-90, their next freeway. Unfortunately, it was their only choice at the moment. The route through town took them alongside one of the local high schools. When the Petriclysm hit there must've been a game in progress. Two football teams were on the field. Both lines of players squatting down, facing off. One player still had the ball in his hand and looked as though he may have been counting down to the snap. Three referees were all toppled in various places on the field. None of them damaged since they were on turf. The cheerleaders' pyramid had fallen over and only the head of the top cheerleader had broken away from her body. Nick looked away; it wasn't necessarily a pleasant sight.

Henry got off his bike for a closer examination, curiosity getting the better of him. He let himself in through the side gate of the chain-link fence and picked up the head, looking where the neck used to attach to the body. He turned to look at the face. The middle of her forehead glowed bright blue and her eyes dialed in on his. He screamed and flung the head.

He looked around him at the crowd in the stands. Hot dogs sat molding in hands, the popcorn long gone, as birds still hovered overhead looking for the last crumb, temporary tattoos peeling from the cheeks of members of the crowd dressed up to show their school spirit. An eerie glow filled the quiet space. One by one bright blue lights blazed in the middle of foreheads and from the right hands. The lights blinked one after the other, the crowd performing a wave with blue flashing lights. "We have to get out of here!" he yelled as he hopped and ran on his good foot back to his bike. "They're searching for us!" They made a bee line for their bikes and pedaled off down the street as fast as they could. Windows of houses radiated faint traces of light, then, without fanfare, all went dark.

Jackson had the sat phone and was monitoring the surrounding area. He'd gotten complacent and hadn't thought to have it available as they were making their way through the small city. The others just shook their heads. It was hard to always be on high alert and none of them blamed Jackson, necessarily, but from then on decided to take turns monitoring the phone.

It was a several miles down the freeway before they stopped again. "Hey, guys," Henry started, popping the top of an air-temperature Coke, the ice having completely melted some days before. He had the map of Montana unfolded across the top of his trailer. "What would you say to speeding things up a little bit?" he scanned further down the freeway. "The road looks pretty clear and the longer we're out here on bikes the more likelihood the Sweepers will catch us. Besides, my ankle is screaming at me, but we really can't afford to slow down now. Not after Missoula. Can we find a car to take? At least for a while?" This was the first time anyone had suggested using one of the cars on the road since the climb up Chinook Pass. Henry looked around, hopeful that the others would think this a good idea. To his relief they all agreed. Driving would afford them a small bit of comfort and added protection.

"Yes," Jackson said first, "I think it's a great idea. Let's start looking." The others also cheered the suggestion, packed up the rest of their snacks and started looking for a suitable vehicle. There weren't many to choose from on the freeway that would hold them and all their bikes and trailers.

The first vehicle they came across that could possibly work was a large white Ford Expedition that had run into the guardrail on the passenger side, the front corner was damaged, but the car still looked drivable. It was conveniently equipped with a bike rack for four bikes. Henry and Jackson worked on extracting the driver from the driver's seat, careful not to drop him. They set him against the cement median that cut the four-lane freeway in half; the driver leaning in an awkward way, head resting against the barrier his body at an angle, knees locked into a sitting position one hand now missing. Nick got into the Expedition and tried the engine. It wouldn't start. Out of gas. Henry started looking around for another vehicle, but neither of the next two possible options had fuel.

"They're all out of gas," Henry looked dejected. Then snapped his fingers. "Hey! I got it," he perked up. "We should take the next exit and find a gas station. There's got to be a car that has a full tank." It was a sensible idea. They luckily found another Expedition, this one blue, with a small open-topped trailer attached. The driver was not in the seat, he or she must've been paying inside when the Petriclysm happened. Nick found the keys still sitting in the ignition and turned them. The engine turned over slowly, then roared to life and everyone gave a cheer; the gas tank needle sliding to the F. They were in business. He got out and let the engine idle and helped the others load up the trailer.

Henry wasn't too keen on driving and preferred that Nick drive. Nick was more than happy to oblige only after asking the others if they wanted a turn. They all declined and said they'd get practice some other time. Nick slowly turned out of the gas station, maneuvering around a couple of parked cars, turned right and gently sped up the on ramp to join the nearly empty lanes. Nick was a cautious driver, which was good since there were still plenty of vehicles on the road making it an obstacle course. It took some time to adjust to pulling a weighted-down trailer. The vehicle reacted slower and needed more time to stop. Several times he had to remind himself that he was driving a real car with real passengers and not playing Mario Kart as he had become accustomed to do each night when they stopped.

Butte was the next major city on their route. It was a little more than a hundred miles from Missoula. Everyone was happy that they were speeding up their trip and giving their rear ends a break. The warm sun greeted them through the windshield. Big fluffy white clouds cast the occasional shadow across the road, the blue sky contrasted with the brown, scruffy hills on the left with pine covered hills on the right. The highway acting as a diving line between lush green and brown desert. As they left Missoula there were clusters of houses to either side, big maple trees lit up in brilliant yellow. Henry constantly checked for blue lights on the sat phone. So far, so good.

Alice enjoyed getting to sit back and watch the world go by. As a kid she had loved the long road trips her family would take. Usually they headed down I-5 to California. Her mom's sister and kids lived in San Francisco. As much as she enjoyed the drive there and back, the cousins were mean and usually enjoyed making fun of her hair color. Henry didn't like to go either, but tolerated things a little better, being the oldest one in the bunch he'd had an easier time. She looked over at Hazel who had wadded up her favorite green sweatshirt using it as a pillow up against the other window. Alice noticed that Hazel had dark circles under her eyes and guessed that she probably looked the same. They all needed a bath, desperately. Jackson sat alone in the third row of seats. He stretched across the entire seat, sitting sideways, face turned to the front of the vehicle. He was brooding again.

They ate away the miles, Nick sometimes slowed and purposefully listed from one lane to the other. Occasionally, Nick and Henry exchanged stories from their childhoods, finding that they had a lot more in common than they originally thought. Hazel eventually roused from her nap and suggested they stop at the next rest stop, stretch their legs and use the facilities, that is if they weren't already in use, her mind flashing back to the outhouse on the pass. She quickly buried the image and focused on the beautiful scenery out the window. Montana sure was beautiful and they could all see why it was called "Big Sky Country." It would have felt extremely monotonous had they continued to ride their bikes, though. Each one of them were secretly thanking Chief Joseph again, may he rest in peace. This being such an underpopulated area not only were Sweepers not around, the going was much easier on the freeways. Any of the pileups they encountered were, thankfully, not an impediment to progress.

The trees in the distance were dressed in bright colors in transition from green to gold to red, the sun hitting the tops of the trees adding a brightness to them. A breeze caused some leaves to lose their hold and float down to the water; a small river that ran parallel to the highway for a long time before veering off and away to the right. It was a beautiful fall day, and the drive was calming. Halfway to Butte they left the pine trees behind. The world opened out onto a high desert. Brown grass coated the rough ground; only a few scraggly pine trees dotted the landscape, determined to grow where they'd been planted. A light layer of snow blanketed the nearby mountains attesting to the fact that it was already getting cold and would only get colder as autumn drew to a close.

The next rest area was in the middle of a wide-open valley, the river running next to the highway the only change in the landscape. Henry checked the phone before giving the all-clear. They jumped out to see if they were able to use the facilities or if they would all need to discreetly turn their backs one at a time. There were no vehicles in the parking lot and, thankfully, both outhouses were free from petriclyzed squatters.

It was drawing toward late afternoon as the distance to Butte diminished. Ahead of them it appeared that a concentration of dark clouds was gathering over their destination, the sky turning blacker as they approached. Nick leaned toward the windshield to get a better view of the sky, the clouds looked like they were swirling, mixing with shades of grey and pale white. He started choking as the smell of burnt rubber and the putrid smell of houses on fire wafted through the vent. Those weren't clouds, it was thick smoke building fast and limiting the visibility as they entered the city limits. Henry was quick to turn the air on recycle, but not before each of them got a strong whiff of Butte. Nick turned on his headlights as they neared the city limits, two hazy beams to help them navigate the freeway. The setting sun was a red dot through the haze. It appeared that the entire city of Butte was engulfed in flames, buildings excreting columns of smoke out of broken windows, walls collapsing in on themselves in defeat, large sprays of fire shot up as a gas tank erupted sending debris flying through the air. Everyone involuntarily dropped down. Nick turned on the wipers to clear the windshield of the thick ash clinging to the glass. The closer flames outlined human-shaped shadows that looked like they were dancing in the licks of fire behind them—the remnants of the city's citizens.

"No blue lights," Henry peered through the window and looking down at the map. They passed the final exit to Butte. As they cruised past the onramp, a black SUV was merging onto the highway, shaving the side of the Explorer. The driver of the SUV looked over and grinned at Henry. "DRIVE!!!!" was all Henry could yell.

Nick stepped on the gas, leaning closer to the windshield attempting to see further, turning off the headlights. The SUV matched the speed of the Explorer as they continued on down the road, the SUV swerved to the left, Nick punched the gas and felt the Sweepers hit the corner of the rear bumper narrowly missing the trailer which had probably been the target. The Explorer teetered from side to side before all four tires landed firmly on the pavement again. His hands were tight on the steering wheel, going left, going right trying to stay just ahead of the black SUV.

"Just Drive!!" Jackson hollered from the back seat. He was turned around facing the SUV that had gotten in behind them, he could make out the gun in the driver's hand resting against the wheel. The trailer kept the SUV from getting closer, but it kept rocking from side to side threatening to jackknife if Nick couldn't find a straightaway soon. He found it and punched the gas, the speedometer pushing 80mph, but the SUV pulled out from behind them and was closing the distance. The two vehicles were nearly parallel, the black ash-laden SUV edging closer, forcing the Expedition nearer the median. The two vehicles rounded a bend in the road; Nick let up on the gas feeling the centrifugal pull, he skimmed the median as he came out of the curve, screaming past another pile up that loomed out of the blackness. There was barely enough room for the Expedition to pass. Time seemed to slow down as the black SUV slammed on the brakes and attempted to swerve in behind the Expedition. Making it only halfway over to the narrow opening, the black SUV collided with the pile up, flipping a somersault, bursting into a large blaze of fire, landing wheels up on the other side of the freeway. Jackson was watching out the rearview window, the bodies suspended upside down in the SUV, flames licking the exterior. With a final explosion, the SUV vanished in a thickness of smoke. The Explorer pressed on, swerving to avoid another vehicle and emerged from the wall of smoke, leaving Butte and the Sweepers behind.

CHAPTER 21

Nick's shoulders were hunched, and he had a death grip on the steering wheel. When they could no longer see the smoke from Butte, Hazel and Alice cracked their windows, thankful to clear the remnants from the car. Henry gently rested a hand on Nick's shoulder adding pressure reminding Nick to relax. Nick sat up a little bit and forced his shoulders down away from his ears. He let up on the gas and slowly came to a stop in the middle of the freeway, peeling his hands from the steering wheel, his fingers sore and stiff from gripping so hard. Nick got out, testing the road with his left foot. His legs were shaking from the adrenaline and he needed a few minutes to walk around and breathe the fresh air. He was standing on the side of the road hunched over. The stress finally getting to him. Hazel found a bottle of water from his trailer and handed it to him when he was finished. "Hey," she said, looking at him with concern, "are you okay?"

Nick nodded his head and took a swig of water, swishing it around before spitting it out. He took a deep, shuddering breath. "I'll be fine," he finally said. "Thanks for the water. We should probably get going. Who knows how long it will be before they send someone else?" They all settled back in their seats. Nick looked at each of the passengers in the rearview mirror for reassurance. Hazel smiled, catching his eyes in the mirror. Alice likewise gave him a reassuring look. Henry rested his hand on Nick's shoulder again and Nick turned to him, giving him a quick smile.

"On we go," Henry encouraged. There were still some hours to go before night completely overtook them. Hazel consulted the map again. The next stop was Billings. Two hundred and twenty-seven miles further down the road. Nick checked the gas. The Expedition should make it that far, but the daylight would be long gone before they got there. The terrain changed as they made progress, the Expedition climbed up into pine covered mountains. Low valleys breaking up the landscape, snowcapped mountains in the distance.

They lost the light little more than a hundred miles from Billings. Instead of stopping for the night, Nick drove cautiously, relying on the full moon to show him where to go. He was afraid to use his headlights again. So, he pressed on at nearly a crawl while the others all faded into a restless sleep. This allowed Nick to drive as he pleased; less pressure to go faster than he really wanted to. It took another three hours to get to the outskirts of Billings. Lights dotted the cityscape. "Hey, Henry," Nick said quietly, shoving Henry's shoulder gently trying to rouse him without waking the others.

Henry sat up a little groggy. He looked around at the others and whispered, "What's up?"

"We're cutting through Billings now. Look out your window and tell me what you see?"

Henry turned and studied his surroundings, half expecting to see more blue lights. "Well, I see lights here and there."

"Me, too. Are they blue?"

"Uh-uh," Henry shook his head. "Not blue. That's a relief, I'd say. But whatever you do, don't turn on your headlights and try not to brake much. That's what I say first." At this point they came nearer one of the lights. Henry pressed his face against the window, flattening it to try and get a better view. He spoke, fogging up the glass, "It's a small fire. Looks like it's in barrel. I see maybe four or five shadows around it. It means there's people here. I bet that Sweeper was headed this way to take care of them. I think you're mad driving skills saved their lives…at least for now."

Nick checked the gas gauge. It was on the E and the little gas pump icon lit up orange. "Hey," he roused the others. "We're about out of gas. I'm trying to milk this tank until we're nearly out of town. I'm hoping we have an easy time of finding another vehicle in the dark with a full tank of gas. Keep your eyes peeled for gas stations. And people. Stay alert." The other four sat up straighter, watching the city closely for any sign of trouble. It wasn't long before the Expedition began lurching, Nick took the nearest exit, they coasted to a stop at the bottom of a ramp.

They got out and unloaded the bikes and trailers as quickly and quietly as they could, talking only in whispers and only when necessary; relieved that no lights were visible in the vicinity. The area had been a hub for motorists before the Petriclysm. There were four gas stations, one on each corner. They made for the nearest Shell. Providence was smiling on them. At one of the pumps sat a sleek black Grand Jeep Cherokee with a small trailer just big enough to hold the bikes and trailers.

The driver was sitting behind the wheel, so Henry and Jackson worked together to get the driver out, keeping a watchful eye on the three dots on the man's right hand. The keys jangled but were around the middle finger permanently locked in a grip. Henry attempted to free the set of keys, eventually breaking the fingers to extract them. He handed the keys to Nick, who was already in the driver's seat, he turned the key in the ignition and the engine roared to life, settling into a low purr. All of them jumped in and checked for any movement outside. Henry handed Nick a Coke; Nick popped the top, relishing the tingle of carbonation on his tongue, appreciating the caffeine. It was going to be a long night. He put their new ride in gear and found his way back to the freeway.

Nick was road weary but did not want to stop anywhere in or near Billings, knowing that there were people here. He followed the dotted white line down the middle of the road, thankful for the full moon. He checked the rearview mirror again. Bright headlights behind flooded the car, illuminating the interior. His heart dropped. "Wake up!" Nick picked up speed and swerved around another large pile up on the freeway, then slammed on the brakes, reversing the car so it was just in front of the pile up, tucking in as close as he could get, parked parallel to the rest of the vehicles. He turned the car off making sure to keep his foot well away from the brake pedal.

"What are you doing!?" Jackson yelled at him. "They're going to catch up to us! Why didn't you just keep going!?" He was screeching by now, panic getting the better of him.

"Shut up!" Nick sharply yelled, turning to face Jackson. "Just wait!" The headlights drew nearer, then passed by, the taillights fading into the darkness. "Now," he turned to Jackson again, "You need to trust me! We weren't going to be able to lose them. I really don't want another race down the freeway like we had in Butte." He was frustrated and scared, tears forming in the corner of his eyes. Jackson crossed his arms and turned away from Nick.

"It was a good call," Alice said calmly. "We can wait here for a little while and then we can try to go on again. Okay?" She looked at Jackson, then Nick. Henry was facing forward, hand at his side, lightly resting on the butt of his gun.

Nick calmed himself then asked, "Did anyone happen to see who that was? What kind of vehicle?"

"Yes," Alice stated emphatically. "It wasn't Sweepers. All I saw was a small red car crammed with people. I don't even know if they actually saw us. They didn't slow down at all."

"Could you see who was driving it?" Nick asked, relieved to know it most likely wasn't a sweeper this time. Henry had the sat phone back out and was checking the Sweeper map. He showed Nick the screen. No green dots in the vicinity. They sat there quietly for some time. Finally, Nick got up the courage to start the jeep and continue their trip. There was no sign of the red car anywhere. Nick hoped they'd taken an exit back into Billings.

By early morning, Nick was finally ready to call it quits. They were near Sheridan, Wyoming having crossed the state line without realizing it. Nick was drawing closer to the city limits, looking for a place to lay low for the day. As the light gave him more ability to see further, a large clump of trees just off the freeway beckoned out of the low-lying fog. Those would be perfect, but there was a wire fence between the trees and the road. Nick slowed, looking for a gap. Ah ha! There was one, just ahead where a car had driven off the road tearing a gap in the fence. Nick came to an almost complete stop and eased the tires off the highway, he drove through the grass, bouncing up and down with the hidden dips. The movement was enough to wake the others as he made a U-turn stopping behind the trees. They could not see the freeway from where the Cherokee was nestled. Nick slid from behind the wheel to stretch his tired body.

"Where are we?" Jackson asked as he extended his arms out with a yawn, joining Nick for a quick jaunt around the small clearing.

"We're just outside of Sheridan."

"Wow! Wyoming already? That's great," his smile widened. "Hey, thanks for driving all this way, I'm sure you're tired. And, hey, I'm really sorry about yelling at you last night. I just sort of panicked."

"It's okay. You were scared, we all were. I didn't have time really ask, I acted because I had to. I'm tired, too. Like super tired. Will you help me set up the tent so I can sleep?"

"You got it. So, what's the plan?"

"I think sleep first, then we can sit down to figure out what we do next. We're almost there." Nick headed for his trailer and found the tent. He and Jackson had it up in a few minutes, now being very adept. Henry showed up with the sleeping pads and bags and helped Nick set up a bed. He had a couple leftover pumpkin bread slices in his hand, giving one to Nick. Henry was happy to be stopping to get some better sleep, his neck had a crick in it.

"Hey, guys," Nick piped up from the tent entrance, "I'm going to sleep for a while and then we should decide what we're going to do from here on out."

"I vote for pressing on as soon as we can," Jackson offered first. There was a light in his eyes that they hadn't seen for some time. Maybe the old Jackson was coming back?

"I'm fine with whatever," Alice stated. Hazel agreed.

"I guess we're talking about this now," Nick sighed and sat down on his sleeping bag.

"Yeah, well, I think," Henry began, "that we're now close enough to Denver that traveling at night might be our safest bet." He got up and rifled around in his trailer for the atlas.

"We can't go on right now anyway unless one of you wants to drive," Nick said, now having lain down, arm resting across his forehead, his right eye peeking at them.

"But what about the no headlights thing?" Jackson asked. "It makes it more dangerous to drive at night without them and with them we become a target."

"Right, but I agree with Henry," Nick started, "and we were very fortunate last night that there was a full moon."

"Yes! And as long as the sky stays clear, the moon will be out for a couple more days at least," Henry interjected. "See here," he pointed at the atlas, his fingers tracing the mileage page again. "We're only a little more than 400 miles from Denver. Nick's right that the closer we get the more Sweepers we might find. Eventually they're *all* headed that direction."

"How far is Cheyenne?" Jackson asked.

"Let's see here," Henry paused. "A little under 200 miles."

"Sooooo, we could be there by tomorrow morning?" Jackson looked hopeful, thinking of Ivy and Felix.

"Yes," was Henry's short reply.

"So, if we get to Cheyenne tomorrow morning, maybe we can sneak around and see if those buses have come through, yet, please?" Jackson pleaded. The others all looked at Jackson. They understood his desire to find his friends. It really went without saying.

"Of course, we'll help," Nick said. "So, if you're all okay with hanging out here until it gets dark, I'm going to sleep so I can be ready to drive again," Nick collapsed back down on his sleeping bag, the warmth now building in the tent; in no time he was asleep.

"Thank you, Nick," Hazel said to his sleeping form. The girls got their tent set up. Everyone settled in for a morning rest.

The roar of a diesel engine punched the stillness, revving its engine, belching black exhaust in dual plumes from large double smoke-stack mufflers each time the driver hit the gas. The truck crawled down the freeway, stamping the gas at random intervals. Nick was the first to jerk awake and throw his shoes on. He snuck to the edge of the trees to see what was happening. There was a very large, matte grey truck idling on the freeway mere yards from where they were hiding. Nick crouched low trying to get a better view. Jackson and Henry soon joined him one on either side.

From where they hid, they could see a very large, burly man who was in desperate need of a shave sitting behind the wheel of a jacked-up truck. He wore a red bandana that was tied around his forehead. He sat, patting down his dirty jean vest until he found the pack of smokes he was looking for. He lit one and rested his arm out the window, pulling it in only when he needed a drag. Then, the boys' attention was drawn to what the man in the truck was waiting for. There were four other men who were looking through the few cars that were still on the road. One man, also dressed in a jean vest and red bandana, long stringy hair falling down his back was forcefully hauling a driver out. He dropped the driver and the driver's leg broke; the man sent the pieces skimming down the highway with one swift kick. He then rummaged through the shorts the driver was wearing, found the man's wallet and began taking anything of value. He took the driver's gold wedding band, then turned his attention to the car, opening the glove box, then the center console, checking the backseat, and finally popping the trunk. He found a Rubbermaid container, popped the lid looked in then hauled it to the truck slinging it into the bed. The other men, dressed in a similar fashion, were doing the same at various points, hauling anything of value and throwing it into the truck. When they were done canvassing the area, the four returned to the vehicle. Three hopping into the back and one into the passenger seat. The truck's engine revved, sending twin plumes of exhaust into the air, the men brandished mean looking rifles as the driver hit the gas continuing on down the road toward Sheridan.

"What in the world was that?" Henry was the first to speak.

"Scavengers," Jackson said without a moment's thought. "It's a really good thing we decided to hide here for the day. Stay out of sight."

"Yes," Henry bobbed his head emphatically, "A very good thing. I don't think I want to mess with those guys." They were about to return to their tents when the truck they'd just watched meander down the highway came flying from the other direction. The three men in the bed of the truck were ducked down low, their rifles aimed ready to fire. The truck flew past the three boys in the bushes, followed only seconds later by a big blue Chevy with several men, all armed to the teeth with similarly mean looking weapons. Several shots were fired from the blue Chevy. A return volley was lobbed, and the chase continued on down the road and out of sight.

"What was that?" Hazel asked taking a spot next to the boys. Alice squatted down next to her brother.

"We're guessing the guys in the grey truck were scavengers," Henry offered.

"Or raiders," Jackson upped the ante after watching the display on the road. "They just got chased off by another gang or something. Maybe they encroached on the others' turf." He shrugged and turned his attention back to the freeway. After a little while, the blue Chevy could be seen making its way languidly back toward the city. The guys were all laughing and joking. Apparently, their chase had been successful.

"Let's hope that's the last we see of anyone today," Nick got up to return to the land of slumber. "We need to head out as soon as it is dark. Pray the skies stay clear. Good night." He let the tent flap fall and disappeared.

CHAPTER 22

The Grand Jeep Cherokee eased back onto the freeway a couple hours after dark. It was important to wait until the moon had risen enough to provide ample light for the night's drive. Neither the blue Chevy nor the grey truck had been seen again and, as far as anyone could tell, no one lived near the freeway. Most of the cars were off to either side of the road making progress that much easier. Everyone was excited about the night's drive knowing that they would soon be in Cheyenne and very near the end of their trip. Jitters rippled through the car as Nick concentrated on the road. Jackson was extremely eager, making plans for a potential rescue. He was sure they would be there in time to intercept the buses before heading on to Denver.

Nick could tell the jeep wouldn't make it as far as Cheyenne. Thankfully, it was an uneventful night's drive, but hours before daylight, the jeep chugged its final mile then died in the middle of nowhere. Not even a single car was visible on either side of the four lanes. It didn't take long to realize that the bikes needed to be unloaded; the last part of the trip would end the way it had begun. Nick estimated they were probably a good sixty miles from Cheyenne.

After several days of enjoying the comforts of traveling by car, it took some time to get going and for their rear ends to get reacquainted with bike seats. Henry's ankle was still a little sore and he didn't feel like pedaling terribly fast, but Jackson zoomed ahead, urging the others on. They capitulated and eventually matched Jackson's speed.

Night was waning when the Cheyenne skyline emerged on the horizon. Jackson pedaled harder with wild abandon. They had made it! He was ready to find Felix and Ivy and then take down the people behind the nightmare they'd been living in since September 23. The others tried to keep up, but Jackson paid no heed to where he was going or what he was going to do once he got there.

"Jackson!" Nick hollered. "Stop!" Jackson made no indication he'd heard Nick. Nick pedaled as fast as he could to catch up, then passed Jackson, cutting him off forcing a stop. Nick was breathing hard; Jackson glared at him. "Jackson," Nick started, trying to catch his breath, "we can't just go barreling into a city where we know Sweepers might be. We need to be cautious. Hide our bikes maybe or walk some place where we aren't totally in the open."

Jackson blinked as if he were only just now aware of Nick's presence. "Oh, uh, yeah. Sorry there," he sputtered. "I was just. I don't know, looking for the buses. I wasn't thinking." He got off the bike and started walking it down the highway. The sun broke the horizon as they crossed a bridge, spanning a small lake. Looking for a good place to leave the freeway and seeing no immediate exit, Nick encouraged them to ride a little bit further, keeping eyes and ears open for anything that might indicate where the buses were being kept, that is, if they were still in Cheyenne.

Henry was diligently searching the area on the phone. No green dots were visible and very few black dots could be seen. He pinged a few of the IDs, but the video feed didn't provide any information that was useful. He turned the phone off to save battery life.

Another mile further down, the freeway intersected with an east-west freeway, the exit and on ramps creating a four-leaf clover. To the left was an industrial area where lots of tractor-trailers sat idle. Jackson gave the warehouses, big garages, and vehicles sitting in the dirt lots a cursory glance and indicated that they needed to get a closer look. They veered off the freeway, carefully dismounting, walking their bikes through the short brown grass that ran along the edge of the roadway, careful not to flatten a tire. Below them were two sets of railroad tracks that tunneled under the freeway and would put them in close proximity to the warehouses. Henry half slid down the embankment with his bike, as did Jackson and Alice. Nick and Hazel were both wearing their hiking boots which offered them a little more traction. They stored the bikes in the middle of the darkened tunnel. Then continued to the far side of the tunnel entrance to get a better view of the nearest building. It was blue, the wide shop doors open on either end.

The razor wire running along the chain-link fence deterred them from getting closer to the building, but the rumble of a large vehicle starting up from somewhere inside the blue building gave them pause. They watched intently as a green bus slowly emerged from the doorway shadows. The five of them waited for another bus to appear, but only the one drove out.

"Only one?" Jackson questioned. "Where are the rest?" He waited, watching. From their vantage point, they could not make out who, if anyone was on the bus. Then, several people emerged from a side building and began boarding, the bus rocked slightly from side to side.

"Are they there?" Hazel asked Jackson. "Do you see Felix and Ivy?"

"I can't tell from here," Jackson squinted trying to make out a shape he recognized. "They might be on there. I don't know. Can you see any more buses inside the building?"

Henry looked as hard as he could, shifting to try and get a better view, "I can't see anything, just some shadows crossing in front of the open door at the other end."

"We can't really wait any longer," Jackson said. "We need to do something." While they watched, three black SUVs pulled out of another building they hadn't been watching. Sweepers. The vehicles sped out of the lot, kicking up dust in their wake. The SUVs made quick progress and were seen entering the freeway above them and speeding off down the road headed toward Denver.

"No green dots," Henry piped up watching the map on the screen. "Either their phones are off, or they know we've been watching. Think about what happened in Butte. Nothing on the screen."

"I think you're right," Nick said. "Might as well turn it off for now. We're so close it's not really going to matter."

"Okay," Henry turned off the phone. "I have an idea," he spoke up again. Jackson eagerly turned his attention to him, keeping one eye on the bus and the blue building. "So, you remember how Red used the vans as a gate in Yakima? I think if we found a couple of cars, we could cut the bus off and hop on and free all those people there," he pointed at the small group getting ready to leave.

"I like it," said Jackson. "Let's go."

"Wait," Nick stopped him, "What are you going to do with the rest of the people?"

"Free them, too, duh," said Jackson getting ready to sprint.

"Guys," Hazel interrupted, "They're getting ready to leave. If you're going to do this, you need to hurry."

"You go on ahead," Alice encouraged, "We'll catch up."

The three boys looked at each other and took off running back through the tunnel. Henry ignored the outcry from his ankle. They had no time to unhook the trailers or care about being seen. They pushed their bikes and trailers up the embankment, hit the pavement, and pedaled as fast as they could down the freeway, keeping their eyes peeled for two suitable vehicles that could be used to stop the bus. A half mile down the road from where the bus was expected to get on the freeway, they found a small pile up. The bikes were ditched on the side of the road and each of them scrambled from one car to the next looking for a car that would start. There was no time to try and haul drivers out of vehicles, Nick and Jackson simply reached in and turned keys in ignitions. None of them started. Jackson grabbed at his temples, looking around in despair. That bus would be on the freeway in no time and they would miss their chance. Then, "Jackson, over here, help us get this car into the roadway." He looked over to see Henry standing at a driver side door attempting to push the car to block the lane. Nick was at the back pushing, leg muscles taut with the exertion.

"Throw it in neutral," Jackson yelled, jogging over to help. This was their last chance. Henry reached in and moved the shifter down to the N. The car started rolling. Ten feet and the car crashed into another one. There was still enough room for the bus to get through. The boys hurried to the next vehicle and quickly pushed it into place. They stood back to gauge the efficacy of these two vehicles and agreed that this should do the trick. They ran and ducked behind another vehicle to await the bus's arrival.

It wasn't long before they heard the unmistakable rumble of the big green bus. Nick thought back to Anvac, how each day his dad would arrive home and they would spend the evenings together talking or reading until lights out. He swallowed a lump, not having thought of his father for a while. The memory cemented his determination to stop the bus and to help free Jackson's friends.

The bus rounded the bend and applied the airbrakes, stopping several feet from the vehicles impeding its progress. Jackson motioned to Henry to let him borrow the gun. Henry was reluctant to hand it to him but saw that arguing now would be futile. Henry handed it to Jackson, then said a quiet prayer that Jackson wouldn't do anything rash. The bus door swung open, the driver looked like he was wrestling with his seatbelt and with his attention diverted, Jackson leaped on to the bus, gun trained on the driver.

The driver, an elderly black man with short white hair, gold wire rimmed glasses pushed high on the bridge of the nose, a blue sweat-stained shirt stretch thin over his protruding belly, looked at Jackson and looked at the gun, then slowly raised his hands the seatbelt forgotten. The driver spoke in a soft, kind, deep bass voice that reminded one of dinners at grandma and grandpa's, "Well, son, what can I do for you?"

"I'm not your son," Jackson said, all the rage he felt coming out in those four words.

"Well, then, just tell me what you want," his calm words causing Jackson to pause.

"I want Felix and Ivy," Jackson responded, regaining his determination.

The driver looked in the large rearview mirror at the few passengers seated throughout. "Ivy? Felix?" he questioned making eye contact with a few of the riders. They all shook their heads, then turned back to Jackson. "I'm afraid they're not here."

Jackson slightly lowered the gun and turned to survey the faces staring back at him. His face fell as he realized that his friends were not among the riders. Henry and Nick came up behind Jackson. Henry gently took the gun from Jackson, then looked at the driver.

"My name's Henry," he said.

"Abram," the driver replied, holding out his hand for Henry to shake. Henry awkwardly shifted the gun to his left hand in order to shake Abram's; it felt like soft crinkled tissue paper.

"Hold on, hold on, hold on," Jackson butted in. "We aren't here to be friends or be friendly," he admonished Henry, grabbing the gun back from him. "We need to find Ivy and Felix. Any idea where they might be?" he looked sternly at Abram.

Abram sighed, "Son, this here is the last bus to Denver. The other two left three days ago. This one broke down and we were just waiting for it to get fixed. Them Sweepers brought a mechanic over from Denver to fix it." He indicated the few riders behind him, "These are the only ones who wouldn't fit on the other two buses. They got the better ride, I'd say, lots more leg room. If your friends were picked up somewhere, they already in Denver by now." Abram looked at Jackson sadly.

"Sir," Nick spoke up. "I'm Nick, my friends and I have been heading to Denver for what seems like forever. I would like to be able to get to Denver in one piece and since we know you are headed there, we can do this one of two ways. Either you name your price to take us the rest of the way dropping us off somewhere inside the city or we hold you at gun point and you still drop us off. Take your pick."

"Well, now," Abram sat back thinking a bit, chuckling to himself. "So, you either pay me to take you or you force me to take you. Where do I sign up?" he said drawing the question out slowly; he eyeballed Nick and then looked at the gun still in Jackson's hand. "Before I decide which of these two mighty fine options I choose, I want to know one thing. Why are you going to Denver?"

"Our business is our own," Nick said, recalling the words of Frodo to the gatekeeper.

"I see that you are determined not to tell me. If that's so, then I'm determined not to take you," Abram crossed his arms defiantly. "Gun or no gun."

"Fine, if I tell you our plans, will you take us?"

"Yes."

"Wait! Don't," Henry stopped Nick. "What if he tells you-know-who what we're up to. We'll never get it done."

"Son," Abram started again, looking at Henry, "if your goal is to take down all these crazy people who decided to wipe out almost 8 billion people, I would say, get those cars out of my way and let's be off."

Nick's jaw dropped, "Wait, you knew?"

"Nick, them Sweepers have been looking for you all for a couple a weeks now."

"How did they know about us?" Nick climbed onto the bus taking the first seat, noticing Alice and Hazel standing outside the bus, he beckoned them to join the group. "Abram, this is Hazel and Alice."

"Pleasure, ladies. I was just starting to tell these gentlemen how I know all about your little posse. First, let's load up your gear and then we can be on our way," Abram looked at each of them in turn, "I'll take you for free, as long as you put that gun away." His eyes flicked to the gun still in Jackson's hand. Henry took it from him and slid it back into his belt, snapping it in place. "I will get you through the security checkpoint and find a suitable place in the city to drop you. I will continue on my way and say nothin' but a prayer that you accomplish what you set out to do. Your secret is safe with me. I wouldn't mind seeing these guys brought down a peg or two myself. Deal?" he stretched out his hand. Nick took it, sealing the deal.

"What about all of them?" Henry pointed at the other passengers. "What if they say something?"

"How would ya'll like to get off the bus here and now and go your separate ways?" Abram yelled up at the rearview mirror. There was a general outcry from the few passengers who stood on shaky legs indicating that they would all very much like to get off the bus and leave. Henry, Jackson, Nick, Hazel, and Alice stepped aside to let these poor individuals out. Each passenger made a run for it, afraid that Abram might change his mind. "Load up," Abram smiled.

Nick and Henry opened the back of the bus and loaded the gear, Jackson and Hazel helped from inside the bus. Once everything was loaded, the boys moved the vehicles blocking the bus's path, and they were off.

"Pull up a seat or two," Abram began, and they trundled down the highway, "To start, well, now, I hear a lot. They think I'm with 'em, you know?" Abram smiled, indicating the bus. "I was a bus driver in Seattle. They kept me and a couple other drivers around from the transit authority to drive these old things from one city to the next after they were done rounding up all the live ones and deciding who lives and who dies right there. It's been a miserable business, but I kind of like my life and have faith that it can only get better from here on. This here is my third trip to Denver from various points. I have one to go before I'm released."

"How did you escape the Petriclysm?" Nick asked.

"The Petriclysm did you say? Ah, all the stone people? Fitting, fitting," he thought for a moment, "Well, I was in East Anvac. Once the thing happened, these Sweepers as they call themselves, must be an official title or something, came knocking. Asked for bus drivers. Said I was one, so I was recruited. I saw some pretty gruesome things down at Pike Place before they loaded up the first selectees."

"I saw Felix and Ivy get on the bus," Jackson interrupted. "Felix is Guatemalan, has a slight accent, glossy black hair, cut short. Very square jaw and eyes almost black, maybe a little too close together, large nose that came to a point, almond colored skin. He. He's tall and muscular. Uhhhh," Jackson paused his mind's eye racing through the description, "He was wearing dark blue jeans and a white polo shirt. Ivy is lighter skinned than Felix, but also Hispanic. From Cuba! Long black hair that goes to her waist. Wearing a pink tank top and black leggings. Tennis shoes. Uh," he closed his eyes again. "Black. The shoes were black. They both speak Spanish fluently so they might not have used English. You couldn't help but notice that they were good looking," Jackson finished, opening his eyes, looking, pleading with Abram to recall them and tell him they were safe.

"I know who you are talking about. Yes. I recognized them from East Anvac, but you know how it is. In the ghetto, you keep your business to yourself."

"Yes, we know," Nick said. "Hazel, Jackson, and I were all in West Anvac. Although we didn't know there was a West and an East. We just thought it was Anvac."

"So, back to the question," Nick started again.

"Wait!" Jackson stopped him again holding up his hand. "Felix and Ivy. What about them?"

Abram turned his wise old eyes on him, "They were on the first bus to Denver. They are already there. For about, let's see maybe almost a month."

"What do they do with them in Denver?" Jackson asked.

"That I couldn't tell you. I only have the directions they give me. I've only been there twice. There's a depot where I drop my passengers and then they get sorted. After that, your guess is as good as mine. Now," turning back to Nick, "you remember a guy named BioDie?"

Nick swallowed hard. "Yes," his tongue stuck to the roof of his mouth.

"They found him on account of that really nice car you dropped off. He exchanged certain information about you in order to be left alone. He didn't know which way you'd gone but knew where you was headed, suggested they try heading to Boise. Something about a flash drive. That's all I know. 'Cept those Sweepers been looking all over for you."

Nick groaned and sat back in the seat. It was over. The Sweepers had been out looking for them and they definitely would be searching the city for a group of kids who wanted to take down the new one world government. And they knew about the flash drives. After all of BioDie's help and encouragement to use the kill switch and he blows it by saving his own skin. *But almost anyone would trade the info to be left alone* thought Nick. *I would have done the same thing if I were him.* Even though Nick was disappointed in BioDie, he couldn't fault him for wanting to live. BioDie—William—was too fat to be much use to those in control. The intel was all he had to offer.

"Even so," Nick said with resolve, "we need to get to Denver. Whatever happens we still need to try." He turned to Jackson and asked, "When did you see William? Before or after you saw the buses leave Pike Place."

"After."

"So, Bio—William—had already told them about us," Nick thought aloud. Turning back to Abram, "Abram, thank you. No matter what, we're still going to give it a try. Who's with me?" The others reaffirmed their commit, but Jackson stared out the window lost in thought.

CHAPTER 23

I don't know today's date, but I do know that are about a hundred miles from Denver. We met Abram, the bus driver who agreed to take us the rest of the way. I am so glad that even in this hostile world, we can still find trustworthy people who are willing to help. He hopes we are successful in our endeavor. Unfortunately, things have been complicated because William told the Sweepers about what we were up to just after we left Seattle. They're on the lookout for us and have been this whole time. I'm glad I didn't know that till now. I would've been terrified to keep going. The really bad thing is they know we have a kill switch and that our intention is to use it. I don't even want to think about what they would do to us if we are caught. I'm guessing death. Honestly, even after all we've been through and everything we've seen, I still want to live. Life itself is something. I see why William would want to trade what he knew in order to live and be left alone. I hope for his sake that he relocated somewhere where the Sweepers won't be able to find him.

Knowing that the Sweepers know about us definitely complicates things, but I am still determined to go through with this. Maybe even more so now that I've gotten better acquainted with the atrocities those in power have committed. The Sweepers are just the lackies. They work for those in charge. I still don't actually know who these people are, but Nick and Jackson were looking at the flash drive that Henry got and they seemed to know that everyone was some sort of powerful person before the Petriclysm.

I feel really bad for Jackson. He came all the way from Seattle with the goal of rescuing his friends Felix and Ivy and still can't find them. Abram confirmed that they'd been taken to Denver. So at least they are still alive. Or were.

I can't even think beyond Denver. There's still so much to find out before we can actually do anything. I just hope we can do something. If I had to plan for life after Denver, I think I would really like to go off somewhere and find a nice little house to live in. Plant a huge garden, grow stuff to eat since there won't be the convenience of just going down the street to the grocery store. Maybe I'll choose someplace that's close to a larger city where I can go and scavenge for food and clothes when the one's I have wear out. At least that's one thing, we won't run out of certain things for a long time if ever. I'll see if Nick wants to come along. Or maybe the two of us will go back and live in Red's community. Whatever I, or we, decide, I do hope Alice and Henry will join us. I'm not sure if I really want Jackson sticking around, though. I get the feeling he's kind of over it and wants to be on his own again. Sometimes I think we should've just let him go off on his own after we rescued him in Idaho. He's caused enough grief as it is and I'm not sure he's done yet.

Denver is close. I hope these aren't my last words, but if they are, I want whoever finds this to know that I loved my parents very, very much and I enjoyed my life up till the Great Wave. My closest friends were Nick followed by Alice and Henry in that order. I always wanted a dog and to be able to spend all day wandering a neighborhood or reading a good book with a hot cup of tea. It's been a good life and I really hope there's more to come.

The last leg of the trip to Denver lasted little more than two and a half hours. Henry pointed out areas of interest. There were large fields and tent housing constructed around the perimeter about twenty miles from the city. He supposed these temporary buildings housed the people who had been made to work the fields. The harvest was already in, but tractors were tilling the earth to get it ready for the next planting season. It made sense that the elites needed people to work the menial jobs to keep their new utopia afloat. Jackson wanted to stop, but Abram convinced him it was more expedient to topple the top gurus, then find his missing friends. Several miles outside the city, Abram pulled over.

"We there already?" Henry asked, letting his knees drop from the middle of the seat in front of him, sitting up.

"Not yet, but you need to store your gear before we go any further. Unload it. See that tumbled down old shack there? Put your stuff in there. You won't be able to get into the city with it. The guards will come aboard and ask for names—have something ready to tell 'em. They will make sure you have nothin' else but the clothes on your back and the shoes on your feet. So, grab what you need and make sure you can keep it hidden." Abram opened the door letting them out.

It was hard parting with the bikes and trailers. After so much time it was like parting with old friends. Nick rummaged in his trailer and grabbed a snack to eat before entering Denver. Henry grabbed the Karmann Ghia model keeping it well hidden in its plastic bag, the flash drive already hidden deep in his pocket. Each of them grabbed their fake BioIDs plus the four extras. Hazel pocketed the gold coins and tucked her journal in an inside pocket. Nick wanted to bring the computer, but couldn't find a good hiding place for it, so had to leave it. They hid everything under the seats. The springs creating perfect hidey holes.

The large gates leading into the city loomed uninvitingly ahead twelve feet high at least. They were shut fast with guard shacks on either side. The bus rumbled up to a large white line, stopping on the word STOP. Abram handed the first guard some paperwork that stated his business in the city. The second guard came aboard to check each passenger to make sure they had nothing more than the clothes on their backs and the shoes on their feet, too lazy to conduct a final round of pat downs. The five of them remained absolutely quiet, eyes on the floor. They breathed a sigh of relief when the guards gave Abram the okay to proceed. Abram put the bus in gear and waited for the wrought iron gates, crowned with spikes to slide back on the tracks to admit them. Once through, they heard the gates close with a final resounding clang as the bus continued down the road.

"Okay, folks," Abram said from the front seat, "I'm guessing the important building is the old state capitol building. I can drop you near there if you have a mind."

Nick sat up a little, "That sounds like a workable plan, but do you happen to know anything about where they keep the servers?" He turned to Hazel and asked for the blueprints.

"Servers?"

"Yeah, it would be a large building that houses lots of computer stuff. It's what kept the BioIDs going. Looks like this," he showed Abram the printout.

"Oh, yeah, that building. Well, seems to me them Sweepers were talking about it one night. The people in charge done away with it seeing that it wasn't being used anymore."

"They got rid of the servers?" Henry asked. "Then why did we come all this way, then?"

"Wait, Henry," Nick stopped him, "it makes sense. They wouldn't need *those* servers anymore. They must have a different set for those still alive."

Henry realized this, "Of course, duh, the servers we're looking for wouldn't be nearly as big."

"Right. So, I think Abram's got it right," then turning back to Abram, "The old capitol building would be capital." He smiled at his turn of phrase. "By the way, Abram," Nick leaned over the seat sitting on his right leg, "How are you going to explain showing up with an empty bus?"

Abram smiled, "I already got that figured out. See, I also have paperwork that allows me to leave the city with an empty bus. There's still people need hauling in Vegas, so I was selected to head right on out and over to get more. Once I'm out of sight, I'm headed somewhere else. Don't ask me where since I don't know. I got almost a full tank and one place to get more. Then I'll see where the good Lord takes me. They weren't too smart to save the paperwork for *after* I dropped off my load of passengers." He chuckled at the Sweepers' seeming stupidity. Nick was glad that Abram had an exit strategy and wouldn't be around in case they got caught.

"Hey," Jackson moved closer to the front of the bus. "Where exactly have you been dropping off passengers?"

"At the old bus depot for processing, like I said before," Abram looked over at him.

"And where is that?"

"Halfway between here and the Capitol building."

"Could you drop me there first? Please," Jackson asked politely. "I really need to find Felix and Ivy."

"But what about us?" Henry asked him.

"What about you?" he retorted. "You've got three other people with you. Felix and Ivy have no one."

"But it's not even a guarantee that they're anywhere near here," Henry attempted to reason with Jackson.

"Just let him go," Nick stepped in. "He won't be any help to us if all he's after is finding his friends." Jackson scowled at him. Nick turned to Jackson, "Catch up to us when you find them, okay?" Jackson shrugged. "Go ahead, Abram, and drop him off near the depot. If that's okay with you."

"Sure, but I'm going to have to stay some blocks from the depot. I don't want to get caught around that area with a bus and not be going the right way. If you know what I mean," Abram turned left at the next intersection.

"Thanks," Jackson mumbled. "I can walk as long as you point me in the right direction." He avoided looking at the others. After a few more blocks, Abram pulled to the curb, opened the door and pointed the way. Jackson got off without a word.

"Now," Abram said watching Jackson' back fade from view, "on to the Capitol. I'm gonna have to do the same with you all. You're going to have to walk a couple of blocks. I need to keep as low a profile as I can in this big hunk o'green junk." He chuckled again and drove on. He turned into a small alley that ran beside the Crown Plaza Hotel and parked behind an old crumbling red-brick wall. "This here's about the safest place I can drop you. Lots of the buildings around here are used for official purposes now, and even before the Petriclysm as you call it. The court houses are here, plus the Police Department where all them Sweepers like to congregate. They commissioned old police cars, painted 'em black and cruise the city and surrounding areas checking for people who aren't supposed to be here." He turned in his seat to face them, "I really do wish you good, good luck. I hope you live to tell me about the rest of your adventures whatever they may be. When you think of it, come find me. I may head up to Vancouver, B.C. way. Heard there's a community there that would welcome me. I want to hear all about how you took 'em down." Abram opened the bus door and each of them got off, giving him a big hug on their way out. The doors closed with a rubbery pop, the air brake released, and Abram shoved off. The four of them watched as he turned the corner. They would never see him again.

CHAPTER 24

"I guess we should get started," Nick looked around at the unfamiliar city. He dug out his fake BioID and fitted it the way William had shown them. The others did the same then checked each other to make sure the BioIDs looked good and that no air bubbles were present under the silicon. They would need these in order to pass for citizens in the city. They stood rooted to the spot where Abram had dropped them. Not exactly sure how or where to begin. Now that they had been successful in getting to their destination, the next move wasn't quite so clear.

"Uh, maybe we should start walking," Henry suggested. "That way," he pointed in the general direction of the State Capitol. The nearest corner was Tremont and 14th, several blocks from their intended destination. Some people were milling around, waiting for the stop light to change, checking BioIDs out of habit, eyes flicking to the forehead or hand. After thinking that only the elite were left alive in the city, it was surprising to see very common people in work attire mingled in with some who very obviously came from money and privilege. Denver was looking more and more like a regular city, how they used to look before the Great Wave and the fallout from the vaccine. The streets were bustling, people en route to various places. Some were sightseeing as if this was the first time they'd been to Denver. The four of them were standing there trying not to gape at the novelty of seeing people, seeing cars drive down the road unimpeded. They attempted to look like they belonged there.

It was a surreal sight to have living, breathing, moving people milling around. Henry and Hazel were both a little unsure of how to act, not having been confronted with strangers who weren't either trying to survive or out trying to get them. Nick grabbed Hazel's hand and started walking across the street when the light changed. Others were crossing with them, Henry and Alice didn't hold hands, but walked side by side matching the gait and attitude of the passersby who seemed completely unconcerned with their presence. Nick noticed that every person they saw had three dots either on their forehead or on the right hand. Real BioIDs that were still active. He'd been right. Not all of them were part of the elite.

The four of them continued down the one-way street past the old firehouse No. 1, which had been converted into the Firefighters Museum. Henry couldn't help but look in. Off to the right was an antique white fire truck. He would love to be able to come back for a better look. He slipped out to the street and caught up with the others. They came to the end of the street and saw the dome of the capitol building in the distance. They made the for the building, but as they passed a small convenience store, Henry asked if they would wait for him to go in and get a couple bottles of water. His BioID account should still have money attached to it. The others okayed this stop but waited nervously for Henry to rejoin them. A few minutes later, Henry emerged from the store with a huge grin on his face. "What?" Alice questioned him.

"I asked the person behind the counter if she could tell me my balance," his grin getting bigger.

"Well?" Alice prodded.

"I'm a millionaire!" he exclaimed. "I think BioDie, I mean William, went in and added bookoo bucks to my account! I bet he did the same to the rest of yours, too." They guessed he was probably right about their accounts being sizable as well.

"I bet it was so we could pass easier once we got here," Nick stated. "I'm going to go in and get a snack and something to drink, too. I'll ask for my account balance, just to check our theory."

"Well in that case," Hazel started walking toward the door, "Maybe I should check, too." Nick put out a hand to stop her.

"Remember the Sweepers are looking for the four of us. Two of us getting snacks and asking for balances probably won't tip anyone off, but if three of us or all of us go in one right after the other, that might look kind of suspicious. Tell you what, let me know what you want, and I'll pick it up for you. Henry share with Alice, you got enough stuff there for right now." Henry reluctantly gave his sister a large bottle of water, a bag of chips, and one of the two candy bars he'd picked up as well.

"Umm, I'll just have a blue Gatorade and a Kind bar if they have it," Hazel requested. "I'm not very hungry, but I need to make sure I don't get dehydrated. Thanks."

Nick walked in and a few minute later came out carrying a small bag. He couldn't help grinning either. He looked at Henry and said, "Turns out, I'm much richer than you."

"What?" Henry playfully stuck out his lower lip, "How much did William give you?"

"Turns out I have about 10 million at my disposal," he laughed again pulling out the Gatorade and Kind bar for Hazel. "I got a couple more if you need them." The next two blocks led them past the courthouse, the detention center, and the city council buildings to open up onto a wide grassy plaza surrounded by trees. Off to the right was a Greek amphitheater and a memorial across the way. The Capitol's dome shone golden in the early afternoon sunlight. The walk along the sidewalk skirting the amphitheater was nicely shaded. It was surprisingly warm for a late-October afternoon. The trees were just starting to change color and drop their leaves. In the distance, several caretakers were sending gusts of brown leaves drifting in a determined direction wearing backpack leaf blowers and bright orange earmuffs for protection. The only benches were in the middle of the greenway surrounded by beautiful beds of late blooming flowers. The benches were a little too conspicuous, they were looking for a semi-out of the way place to sit and rest before deciding what to do next.

They came to a broad walk inlaid with large squares made of red brick. To the right was a grassy area with more trees that could possibly offer them better coverage. Henry read the sign, which stated very explicitly that the grass was off limits on Mondays and Wednesdays. "What day is it?" he asked. The others stood and thought for a few minutes, trying to reckon how many days they had been on the road, knowing they'd left Seattle on the 27th, but still they couldn't recall what day of the week that had been either. Finally, Hazel retraced their days all the way to the Petriclysm, which had happened on a Thursday. As far as any of them could recall, today was either Monday or Tuesday. Henry looked across the grass and spotted several people parked under trees and figured they would be safe enough if others were also sitting there. Following the curve of the sidewalk to the right it brought them closer to the capitol building while hiding them from a direct line of sight. Turning a little to the left, they ventured across the grass and found a large tree about thirty feet from the road that ran in front of the building. They hoped the servers were there or at least a computer that could be used to launch Operation Covax. The tree they chose faced the sidewalk they'd left. People strolling casually by.

It felt really good to sit down and stop for a few minutes. They'd been on the go since the night before and only managed a short nap on the bus into Denver. Each of them was exhausted and couldn't really begin to think about next moves yet. They didn't even know if this was the right place to be and had no clue how to go about looking for Christopher MacPherson or Calvin Hastings, the president of North Pangea. It was strange to be this close and yet still feel so far from their goal. They had been so intent on getting here and knew so little about the city that it was overwhelming to try and figure out their next move.

Henry pulled out some water and a small round of Oreos as they settled down for a respite. "Well," he started, "What do you think we should do? After walking around a little bit and seeing the people here, I we're right to not use William's kill switch. I mean, even the person at the convenience store had a BioID and somehow, they're still here, which means there are a lot more innocent people than we thought. Just like you and Hazel pointed out." He directed this statement to Nick, "It's not just the elite here. It's a whole city—all the moving parts of what keeps a city going."

"Or at least the parts needed to serve the rich. They don't lose the conveniences of the modern world," Alice added. "I can't see wanting to kill these people. They didn't do anything to cause the Petriclysm. They seem to just be living their lives. I think we should stick with Hazel's flash drive."

"Yeah," Henry started thinking aloud. "But BioDie gave me that red flash drive for a reason."

"Isn't is just a whole bunch of dossiers on the ultrarich and powerful?" Hazel asked.

"Yes…but, if there was some way to program Operation Covax to only shut off certain people…Maybe there's a way. But I'm not *that* good with computers," Henry admitted. "I mean, I tried hacking a couple of times and BioDie taught me a few things, but I…well, hang on…Let's think about this." He leaned back against the tree, arms behind his lead looking up through the canopy.

"Maybe we can sit here for a while and rest, take naps in shifts for the time being. If we need to, we can get a hotel room. I'm rich enough now," Nick relaxed. "I could really use some sleep and time to think, too." The other's nodded.

"I'll take first watch if you want," Hazel said, taking a swig of her drink. "I got more sleep last night that the rest of you. I've been so tired I could sleep anywhere, and I did." The other's thanked her and stretched out on the cushy grass. Within minutes, Nick and Henry were sound asleep. Alice lay with her eyes open for a time, but eventually fell asleep for a little while, too.

CHAPTER 25

A couple hours passed. Henry was the first to wake and discover that all four of them had been sleeping. He nudged Hazel, "Hey, what happened to being our bodyguard?" He joked as Hazel sat up.

"Oh, my," she shook her head waking more fully. "I am so sorry I fell asleep. I guess we're lucky that no one took notice of us."

"Look!" Henry pointed through the trees, Nick and Alice waking to the sound of his voice. They turned in time to see three figures furtively making their way toward the Capitol building. One of them looked very much like Jackson. The other two could only be Felix and Ivy. He'd found them!

"What do you think he's up to?" Alice asked suspiciously.

"Maybe he's looking for us," Henry got up and was about to yell across the grass at them, but Alice pulled him back down.

"Don't," she warned. "He didn't look like he was looking for anyone. I've seen that look on his face before."

"What look?" Henry was confused.

"A very determined look," she said. "He's up to something. We should probably follow him. Find out what he's doing," Alice stood to leave. The others got up, grabbing their drinks and snacks and skimmed the walkway by staying hidden in the shadows of the trees. They watched Jackson, Felix, and Ivy run across the street, then veer to the left of the building, ducking into the trees. "Hurry," Alice encouraged them. They looked both ways down the street, then ran following Jackson's path. They glimpsed him again as they rounded the side of the building; this side being completely in late afternoon shadow. The four of them tried not to bring attention to themselves, running at a moderate pace. They hadn't forgotten that Sweepers were on the lookout for them. As they ran, Hazel was ahead of Henry. The silver flash drive fell out of her pocket. Henry scooped it up as he passed by, stuffing it into his pocket. They came around the backside of the building, seeing Ivy slip in through a single side door, Felix and Jackson already inside. Nick raced to the door and caught it just as it was about to close. He turned and looked at the others, waiting for them to catch up. He hadn't wanted to take any chances that the door was locked. Hazel, Henry, and Alice followed while he held the door, bringing up the rear. The door closed softly behind them the door locking. How did Jackson get the door open? There was no evidence of broken glass.

It took a minute for their eyes to adjust to the dimness of the hallway. There wasn't anyone around that they could see and there was no sign of the others. Nick looked at the signs at the stairwells for any clue as to which direction they needed to go. Henry found one that directed traffic to the basement and subbasement. He was about to suggest going down when they heard a door close above them, so decided to head up, hoping to catch up to Jackson.

The door at the second floor was locked; they continued to the third floor. The door had been opened recently and hadn't closed all the way. The four of them snuck into the dimly lit hallway looking for clues. There were raised voices coming from the far end. They moved in single file, staying as close to the wall as they could. The door to the right was ajar and light was flooding a small section of the hallway. They stayed just outside the edge of the light, crossing to the other side to see better. They saw a man in his mid-40s with dark brown hair and a dazzlingly white smile looking at someone speaking just out of view. Hazel dug around in her pocket and withdrew a photo. It was the one she had taken from MacPherson's office that first day after the Petriclysm. She turned the photo to catch some of the light, then showed the photo to the others, flipped it over and pointed to a name. It was Christopher MacPherson. The man they had been looking for. Their attention was drawn back to the conversation. They recognized Jackson's voice who could clearly be heard yelling now.

"Why did you kill my mom! She did everything you asked her to do even when she didn't want to! Why didn't you override her BioID? You couldn't even do that? Are you that selfish? One person, one GD person who needed a reprieve more than anyone else. SHE WAS MY MOM!!!!" he ended, out of breath and out of steam.

"Are you finished now?" was the calm, condescending reply. Jackson refrained from saying anything else for the moment. "I see you found a couple of friends," the man indicated Ivy and Felix. "Busted them out of their work detail. Hmmm? How'd you do that you little sneak?"

"Looks who's calling me a sneak, Chris, you filthy no good…"

"God, to put it mildly," MacPherson looked at his nails in a bored manner. "Essentially, I have the ability to do whatever I want, fry a BioID if I see fit, I created the technology, you see. Central Pangea has given me carte blanche over North Pangea now that Calvin has relocated to Rome. I'm in charge here. See that button over there?" the button was not visible from the open doorway. "All I have to do it hit it and you'll be taken care of."

"Go ahead," Jackson retorted. "I'm faster than you and I'd be on you before you could take one step toward that button, you miserable, murdering monster."

"I am no murderer, I'm a savior," was the annoyed response. "I should have used my powers of persuasion on your mother to force you to get the BioID. Then I could have taken care of you a long time ago. There were trial runs, you know?"

They could hear Jackson breathing hard, angry.

"I see," MacPherson continued. "Nothing left to say, huh? Well, I have something for you," he made to move, and Jackson lunged for him, in one swift movement, MacPherson had Jackson's right arm pinned behind him, pushing up. Jackson's shoulder blade was fanning out, threatening to dislocate again. "You listen here, you little punk—" he turned to Felix and Ivy, "don't even try it—" he turned back to Jackson, "I got something to show you." And he shuffled with Jackson to a point in the room where those waiting in the hallway could not see what was happening. They heard Christopher's voice, "Yes, please send her up. Thanks." The click of a phone being settled into is cradle. Around the corner from the office, the ding of an elevator was heard followed by doors sliding open. A blonde woman who'd made a garish attempt at looking younger walked around the corner. Hazel caught herself. This was the same woman she'd seen in the other picture in MacPherson's office. Probably the one Calvin Hastings had mentioned in his email. She didn't notice them in the shadows and walked directly into the office.

The next thing they heard was a pitiful cry that came from Jackson, "Mom?"

"Jackson," was the terse response. Then, "What are you doing here?"

"I, I…I came to," he broke down crying. Jackson's mom was visible in the doorway, Jackson's arms extended, wanting to embrace the mom he thought was dead. When his mom didn't reciprocate the action, he lowered his arms back to his side, wiping his nose and eyes.

"Again, Jackson," his mother said, exasperated as if she were dealing with a toddler. "Why are you here?"

Please don't tell them Hazel thought. *Please don't give us away. I'm so sorry that this is all your mom can say after you thought she was dead.* "I came to rescue my friends," Jackson finished jutting out his chin in defiance. "I found them at the sorting area. They were helping sort clothing and jewelry that was found in some of the bigger cities. I…I," he paused again, choking down another sob. "I thought you were dead," he lowered his head; his mother making no sign that she was glad to see him.

"Well, I'm not dead," his mother finally said. "I came here with Chris to help work on some new technology. Finding ways to keep those left alive from repopulating too fast. If it's too fast our whole project will have been for nothing."

"You weren't going to come and find me?" Jackson asked. He was audibly crying by now. Hazel's heart broke for Jackson, listening to the pain at finding his mother alive made worse by this rejection. A mother who did nothing to find him or save him. She was glad that she couldn't see his face right now.

"Jackson," his mother began sternly, letting out a sigh, "sometimes these things are bigger than you or me. I would have eventually come and gotten you. I was pretty sure you knew how to take care of yourself."

"But," Jackson choked, "Mom," was all he could say.

"I'm very sorry to interrupt this touching family reunion and all," MacPherson crossed the doorway and stood next to Jackson's mom, "but what *are* we going to do now that he's here and with friends." He looked toward Felix and Ivy who stood dumbfounded, knowing they were in a lot of trouble.

"I can just go," Jackson said. "We can go. We can leave the city and never come back. Just tell me one thing," Jackson made to move toward the door. "Why did you do it? Why did you kill more than 7 billion people?" The others in the hallway pricked their ear at this question.

His mom spoke up, "We didn't *kill* anyone, we simply shut them off. Like a computer. Consider it the elimination of an invasive species. Computer virus. You name it. Overpopulation was destroying the environment. All we did was fix the problem. Now the environment can heal itself and we can control how many humans there are from here on out." Jackson looked disgusted and made to leave.

"Not so fast, young man," MacPherson blocked his path. "I can't let you go now that you've been reunited with your mother," his tone patronizing with a warning. Whatever he had planned, Jackson and his friends were in a lot of danger. Hazel could sense Henry's desire to barge in on the conversation and do whatever he could to help Jackson. Taking down Christopher MacPherson would be an extreme pleasure, but Hazel reached out to calm him, telling him to wait. MacPherson turned to Jackson's mom, "So, Catherine, what should we do with them?"

"Can't we just let them leave?" she asked. "Jackson won't do anything, and he'll keep his friends in check. I'm sure. He'll leave like he said he would. Won't you Jackson?" she turned to him, her tone warning him that anything else could cause them both trouble. There was a hint of concern in her look; a pleading that he would comply. She did care about him, at least a little.

"You know, Catherine, I really don't think that's an option right now, do you?" he wrapped an arm around her, snakelike, and then around Jackson, bringing them both in for a little squeeze. "You know," he said, "he could *earn* his freedom. We have that new little experiment downstairs in the lab. I need another test subject. If he volunteers, I'll let him, and his friends go when we're finished."

"No," was the short, decisive reply. "No. You are not running my son through that protocol. It needs more work. I won't allow it."

"Then maybe I can use one of his friends first. Otherwise, I'll have to call up a few of my best Sweepers. They deserve to have a little fun now and again," he winked. "Jackson here can be outfitted with a BioID and then my Sweepers can decide what kind of statue they'd like in the vestibule of their hotel."

"No, Christopher," Catherine responded firmly. "You let him, and his friends go, and we can find someone else. He's my son. End of story." But MacPherson was not about to let it go. He pointed to three chairs and instructed Jackson, Felix, and Ivy to sit. Then he walked over to an intercom. A scratchy voice from some other part of the building came through. "Yes?" "Send up some guards. I have a little problem that needs to be taken care of right away." Drawing out the word "problem." "Yes, sir, I'll send them up now." And the intercom clicked off.

Nick realized that they were now in a very precarious position. He was sure that MacPherson had called for Sweepers to come and take care of Jackson, Ivy, and Felix. Jackson's mom had no control over what was going to happen next. She'd already sat down out of view, waiting. A couple of times she tried to plead with MacPherson, but knew it was useless. He was going to have his way regardless. Nick felt in his pocket for the flash drive. It was still there.

Before Nick, Hazel, or Alice had time to react, Henry took off down the hallway and into the stairwell. It was too late to follow him. The Sweepers were now getting off the elevator, headed for the open door. The first Sweeper entered, kicking the door wider, flooding the hallway with more light, which caught the three listeners unaware, full in the light from the office. The last Sweeper noticed them sitting there and pointed his gun at them. "Looky, looky," he sneered. "Hey John, look what I found." The Sweeper named John stepped back out of the office and smiled. The Sweeper with the gun motioned with it to the three indicating that they were to get up and head into the office. Nick, Hazel, and Alice complied stepping into the light. Jackson was surprised to see them, but looked relieved, too.

"Well, well, well. I should have known that your son was part of the four we were looking for," MacPherson looked smug. "We've been looking all over for you guys and here you are. William was right, you are resourceful, and he didn't lie about where you were headed. I'd love to know how you got here, but I don't have time for chit chat." He turned to Jackson's mom, "Looks like we have enough test subjects for a trial run."

"No, it's not ready," Catherine tried again.

"Now," MacPherson added with finality. "Take them down to the lab. I'll be down in a few." The Sweepers turned to go, MacPherson snapped back around, "Wait!" He lifted his finger in the air. "I almost forgot something. Now, who has the flash drive? Come on. Cough it up or there's going to be a very unpleasant search. I know one of you has it." Nick moved first digging in his pocket. He procured the flash drive. He dropped it in MacPherson's outstretched palm. "Good little boy," he said setting the flash drive on the desk and pulling a hammer from the drawer. Two swift downward strokes and the flash drive lay in pieces. "Alright then, let's go to the lab."

The Sweepers used their brawn and guns to get the six teens to move. They crowded into the elevator. The Sweeper nearest the door hitting B2. The doors swished closed and the elevator started its descent with a jerk. It was a slow-moving elevator. Hazel watched the numbers laconically turn—2—1—B—B2. The elevator stopped and the doors opened. They were pushed into an enclosed hallway made of cinder block, their motion triggering the overhead lights. They were marched down the hallway toward a heavy metal door with a small mesh-screened glass window. A Sweeper hit a panel in the wall that opened up revealing a keypad. He hit seven numbers, the light flashed blue and the locks disengaged. The lights came on when the door opened. They were ushered into a large lab that looked a lot like the lab Hazel and Nick wandered through that first day when looking for their parents.

MacPherson arrived shortly after they entered the lab. He was now dressed in an official looking white lab coat with Dr. MacPherson stitched in elegant blue embroidery above a small pocket on the left-hand side.

"Okay, then, where to begin," he rubbed his hands together. Nick pictured MacPherson as a more sinister version of Dr. Frankenstein positive that he was about to create his next monster. MacPherson looked over each of them, like he was evaluating specimens, then pointed at Nick. "Let's start with you. Yes. Oh, and Jackson," he spun around, "be sure to pay extra special attention, since you'll be next. Come," he waved. "Come here," he reached for Nick. Nick's feet were glued to the spot. He moved only after a Sweeper came from behind and gave him a big shove. Nick flew forward and fell on his hands and knees. He was staring down at MacPherson's feet ensconced in ugly brown loafers that seemed out of place. "Get up!" was the short command. Nick stood, shaking himself off, ready for whatever came next.

He was forced to sit in a chair that resembled a dentist's chair, but this one had straps. MacPherson did the honors himself and made sure that Nick had zero wiggle room. He first strapped down each arm, the straps digging into his skin. Then, the head strap was applied. Nick could only move his eyes. Finally, MacPherson, anchored each of Nick's legs. He was now completely immobilized; the others held at gun point. Then MacPherson went over to a cabinet and withdrew a syringe and a small vial filled with clear liquid. He expertly tilted the vial upside down, filling the needle. He squirted a little out to get rid of air bubbles, then plunged the needle in to Nick's arm, depressing the plunger. The clear liquid entered his arm with a burning sensation, the fire traveling in all directions. Nick bit his tongue to keep from crying out.

"What did you do to him?" Jackson yelled, he had one arm clamped in a Sweeper's strong grip.

"Oh," MacPherson seemed pleased with the question. "My dear boy, I'm just trying the latest MERS vaccine on our young man here. What's your name, boy?"

"Nick," he answered through clenched teeth, the pain now reaching every part of his body.

"Nick," MacPherson repeated. "Nick here just got vaccinated. Now I'm guessing he was one of the antivaxxers who used to live in some ghetto, so this is the first time he's ever experienced this. I'm so sorry my dear boy, I know it's highly unpleasant," MacPherson's voice had changed from the condescending power-hungry man they'd heard in the office on the third floor, to a softened, matter-of-fact educator who was working on his bedside manner, but coming out as a patronizing adult addressing someone beneath him. "Now," he continued, "for part two." He searched in another drawer and found a small machine that none of them recognized. He held it up for examination, "This here is the tool we use to install the BioID, now set for the BioID2. It's the latest version of the original technology that everyone all over the world wanted free of charge. Oh, how wonderfully it worked and now they're all gone, just like lice when you apply the right shampoo. It really was a brilliant plan," he smiled. "Before I implement round two, Nick, tell me, what is your last name? I need it for my records." Nick tightened his jaw, refusing to talk. "Ah, ah, ah, now," MacPherson reprimanded him. "If you want to get out of this alive, answer the question."

"Webber," came the mumbled answer.

"I didn't hear you," MacPherson goaded in a sing-song voice. "One more time. A little louder for me."

"Webber!" Nick nearly shouted.

"Webber, Webber," MacPherson rolled the word around, thinking. "As in Alex Webber?" Nick's body language betrayed him. "So, your Alex's son. Fitting, don't you think?" he stopped, waving the device in his hand. "This was your daddy's crowning achievement."

"I thought he invented the vaccine?" Nick questioned.

"Oh, yes, he did that, too, but it wasn't quite what it needed to be until he worked very closely with Jackson's mom, you see. He liked to tinker with the technology, too, to see how he could use it to create more effective vaccines. He didn't realize what he'd stumbled upon until it was a little too late. I'm sorry we couldn't keep him around longer." MacPherson patted Nick's shoulder. Nick started thrashing from side to side attempting to avoid whatever it was MacPherson held in his hands. It was at this point that MacPherson noticed the three little dots in the middle of Nick's forehead. "Well, well, well what do we have here," he bent over for a closer look. "Ve-ry clever. This must be William's work." He got closer to Nick's forehead and searched the hairline for the edge of the silicon. He soon found it and peeled back the fake BioID. MacPherson flung it onto the counter and then proceeded. "Oh, I forgot," he stopped. "Which would you prefer? Forehead or right hand?"

Nick wiggled his right hand and squeezed out between his lips, "Hand." MacPherson turned to Nick's hand and centered the BioID marker. He rested his hand on the trigger and looked at Nick, "Brace yourself. This is going to hurt." Nick started thrashing again, moving as much as his restraints would allow. MacPherson tsk-ed and cooed, "Now, now, now…"

"NOW, NOW, NOW!!!!" came echoing from the far side of the lab almost as an afterthought of MacPherson's last repeated words. MacPherson pulled back from Nick's hand. The voice yelled again, "Now! Hit it now!" It was Henry's unmistakable voice reaching them from somewhere in the back recesses of the lab. The Sweepers had jolted into action to locate the owner of the voice. MacPherson looked annoyed at having been interrupted, but the next thing he knew, all the Sweepers were petriclyzed in position, some fell over, shattering from the momentum of their run. They were instantaneously translucent blue with black veins. Everyone was stunned. They hadn't seen the Petriclysm happen, only the aftermath. They were shocked at how fast the Sweepers were turned to stone.

Henry came running from the back of the lab, exultant as his success, then stopped short. MacPherson was still standing there, very much alive. "Wait, but I thought..." Henry trailed off dumbfounded.

"Ha!" MacPherson grew angry, tossing down the device in his hand. "You thought you could get rid of me? Huh? Well," he reached up and peeled back a fine silicon covering from his forehead. The three dots coming away with it.

"You, you have a fake ID?" Henry gaped.

"Let's just call it protection," MacPherson rolled it up and stuck it in his pocket.

"Get him!" Jackson yelled, but before anyone could react, he was already out the door at a full run. The elevator doors swished open as he hit the button, still on the subbasement level. The doors closed just as Jackson got to them, his fingers barely missing the opportunity.

He ran back to the others. Hazel was unstrapping Nick who then grabbed his fake BioID from the counter and tucked it in his pocket. He rubbed the spot where MacPherson had injected the vaccine.

Henry was still angry that MacPherson hadn't been killed, but the others congratulated him that the Sweepers were no longer a threat. They started to ask Henry what he had done, but before he could answer, another individual joined them from the back of the lab.

"William!?" Hazel looked surprised. "What are you doing here?" she reached out and gave him a big hug.

"William," Nick started, "What…how?"

"I'm so sorry I told the Sweepers," was the first thing he said. "I had to say something otherwise they were going to kill me. Then after I told them, they came back and forced me to come here and work on their next ID. God, I am so glad you're all alive. Will you forgive me?"

"Of course," Nick said giving him a hug, "I probably would have done the same thing, too. So," he was afraid to continue, "Did you just petriclyze everybody else who had a real BioID?"

"Nope," Henry jumped in. "You know that flash drive that BioDie—William—here sent me? Well, I was right! It was a way to select certain people to biff it. Here's your flash drive, Hazel," he handed it to her. "You dropped it when we were running to catch Jackson and I didn't have a chance to get it back to you. William changed the code to mimic his first kill switch, but with modifications. Obviously." She put it safely back in her pocket, thanking providence that it had fallen out when it had.

"So, you're saying, you just chose who got petriclyzed? People like the ones we saw walking down the street or the woman working in the convenience store are okay? Still alive?"

"Yes. They should be, plus, we still have all that money BioDie—William—put in our accounts. We're rich! Oh, yeah, he upped my limit to match yours," he smiled slugging Nick in the shoulder. Nick winced; he'd hit the injection sight. "Ooops, sorry," Henry apologized.

"What about my mom?" Jackson asked. "Catherine Hastings? Did you turn her off, too?"

Henry answered, "I saw her name on the list and had William bypass her, too. He knows your mom, Jackson, but he didn't want to save her. She's done some terrible things. And she wasn't coerced like she told you. She did them willingly."

"But I listened to him," William interjected. "Your mom is fine." Jackson sighed in relief.

"What do you say we get out of here," Nick looked around. "I'd personally like to be above ground. They all agreed and headed to the first floor.

CHAPTER 26

The sun was still out, but the day was almost spent. There were many people still walking around the Capitol building. Nick was glad to confirm that not everyone was a statue, but there were a few new ones here and there. Some passersby made note, but most had gotten so used to seeing them when they'd first arrived in Denver, that it wasn't such an unusual sight as to draw much attention.

"Where's MacPherson?" Jackson wanted to know. "We still need to get him."

"My guess," William answered, "is he's either in his office or he's long gone."

"Let's head up to his office. I want to have a look around even if he isn't there," Jackson walked over to the elevator doors and pressed the button to go up. They waited quietly for the elevator to arrive, the doors opened with a ping and they all stepped in. A moment later, the doors slid open onto an empty hallway. The light in the office still on. Jackson led the group and was the first to enter MacPherson's office. The door was wide open, drawers had been quickly opened and papers shuffled around. Whatever he'd been after, he'd grabbed it and left in a hurry.

The phone on the desk was ringing, William leaned over it and hit the speaker button to answer it. A shrill male voice came on the line, "What the hell, Chris! You better have an explanation for this. Sweepers all over Rome have turned to stone. What are you thinking running your experiments still? We told you to stop. Enough people are eliminated that we need to keep everyone else we have left, including the bottom feeders you always ragged about. If we lose too many more, our way of life is going to be drastically altered. Do you hear me? Chris? Hello? CHRIS!!! Answer me!! I'm still in charge of you. I'll send someone to take care of you if you don't answer me this instant! Say something Chris or I will turn you to stone." William reached over and hung up on him.

"Who was that?" Nick asked.

"Calvin Hastings. Former President of North Pangea. Now vice president of Central Pangea," William grinned. "Looks like we were pretty successful and Mr. MacPherson, 'scuse me, Dr. MacPherson, is going to be in a world of hurt once he arrives in Central Pangea. If that is indeed where he is headed. He might be running around the city trying find anyone left he might be able to boss around. Wherever he is right now, he's not as powerful as he was just a few minutes ago. All his goons—some must also be in Central Pangea—are all now frozen assets. Now, let's have a look around and see if we find anything important this creep didn't take with him."

There was a door behind the large imposing desk. It was closed. The letters stenciled across the frosted glass in metallic gold read "The Library". Jackson was curious, knowing that MacPherson's interest in books was very limited. He approached the door with caution and turned the handle. There was no resistance and the door opened silently. He felt around on the wall inside the room for a switch, found it, and flipped the lights on. Jackson took a staggering step back. Henry caught him and peered over his shoulder. The color faded from Henry's face, making his freckles stand out even more. Then he and Jackson entered. The others assembled just inside the door for a looksee and were equally as appalled. The room was not a library, it was a museum.

The room reminded one of the Greek statues in the British Museum, arranged artfully around the room, but unlike the statues created from a slab of marble or poured from bronze to resemble their human counterparts, these forms were marble created from flesh. MacPherson had created his own art collection by sending Sweepers scouring the cities and towns to find human forms in the shape of well-known works. Unmistakable were Rodin's Thinker, a young man immortalized in the famous pose had been stripped of his clothing and placed upon a pedestal. Beneath the translucent body was a placard that read *The Thinker by Christopher MacPherson*. An armless, headless winged Nike resembling the original displayed at the Louvre was placed on a pedestal next to the Thinker. Whoever the woman had been she now had a pair of large extended wings made to match the blue hues. A flowing white dress had been carefully draped to cover her nakedness. There were many more, filling the length and breadth of the large room. Bodies chosen, broken, and dressed as imitations of classical art. At the far end of the room was a Centaur. The top half of a bearded man, trapped forever in a bend to the right, was attached to the body and neck of a horse. The horse was cold, stiff, and marble-esque like the humans surrounding it. In his sickness, it appeared that MacPherson had also injected this horse with the vaccine and given it a BioID just for this monstrous creation.

Hazel cried out in alarm as she recognized a bust with a distinctive feather headdress, red strands flanking the temples. Even the features of the man's face resembled Chief Joseph. Jackson reached up and removed the headdress. "I'm going to take this back to the reservation. It doesn't belong here," he folded the headdress and held it like a newborn in his arms.

All stood staring at the macabre collection of still, translucent bodies. Hazel and Alice wandered the gallery, reading the placards. Sad for the individuals who stood here now as works of art, their humanity completely stripped. One display stood out in particular. It was a group of three—two adults and one little girl—still dressed in the clothes they must've been wearing at the time of the Petriclysm. A family. The faces were locked in frozen screams, looks of terror etched across their features, the little girl clinging to her mother. It almost looked like they were aware of what was to come. One could almost see the tears on the little girl's face. The small placard below the grotesque scene read *"Art of Death" Phase 1 First Trial by Christopher MacPherson and Catherine T. Clayburn.*

"What in the world," Nick finally said in the stillness. Hazel came up beside him and stood close enough to just touch arms.

"They look terrified," she said.

"They probably were," was the sad response.

"He is a very sick man," she said. "I really wish that the kill switch had worked on him."

"Me, too," he wrapped his arm around her. He needed her nearness as much as she needed his.

After touring the entire room, finding no books they regrouped in MacPherson's office. William dug through the desk and found a laptop stuffed in the back of a bottom drawer. He opened the laptop. It came to life, not even password protected.

"Looks like someone forgot something important," William started poking around.

"Anything?" Henry asked, trying to peer over William's shoulder.

"Nothing much, yet," William said still looking through the computer's hard drive. "Oh, ho, here we go." He hit several more keystrokes, then showed them a screen. "Bingo!"

"What is it?" Henry looked at the code.

"Access to all the remaining active BioIDs. All of them."

"You mean, like in the world?" Henry looked hard at the lines of code.

"Yes. Like in the whole world."

"So, we could actually use Operation Covax and select who to wipe out. Like we did with the Sweepers?"

"Only one problem," William turned the screen back.

"What?"

"This is simply a list of ID numbers. No names. We only have lists of the most important people and we'll probably still need them for a while," William said. "And it won't work on MacPherson since he doesn't have a real BioID and who knows how many of the others also have fake IDs," William was now poking around some more.

"So," Hazel broke in, "What about just using the virus on my dad's flash drive. Just shut down the system. Now?"

"We could," William agreed, "but them what happens to our money? The civilized parts of the world still rely on currency. We're probably going to need it if we plan on going to Rome."

"Rome?" Hazel looked at him.

"Rome."

"Why would we go there?"

"Duh," Henry said. "We have to finish the job."

"And Rome is the only place where they store all the matched names to ID numbers," William finished.

Nick looked at William, then asked, "Any idea what MacPherson was doing to me?"

"Yes," William sighed, "he was running his Phase 3 experiment. It's a sterilization through vaccination program. He hasn't finessed the combination of vaccine and BioID2 yet."

"So, wait," Henry looked up, "Did MacPherson make Nick…" he trailed off.

"There's no way to tell," William shook his head sadly. "MacPherson was interrupted. There's still a chance that Nick is just fine."

"Well, no matter," Nick said, "I'll be okay." He tried to smile. Tried not think how his future may have been instantaneously altered.

"How would MacPherson get here to there?" Henry asked, now firmly ready to move on and get MacPherson.

"Let's see," William paused. At that moment they could hear the distinctive sound of a helicopter gearing up for takeoff, a rotor system accelerated, blades spinning faster. They crowded in front of the big office window. A black helicopter was seen between a couple of nearer buildings rising into the sky. It turned east; big gold letters "CP" glinted as the helicopter flew toward the east coast. "That should answer your question. There he goes now."

"Where's my mom?" Jackson asked, remembering that his mom had been here, too.

"Probably with MacPherson," William stated. "I'm sorry Jackson. She wasn't who you thought she was."

"Did you know when I saw you that she was still alive?"

"No, I didn't find that out until they brought me here to work."

"So back to my question," Henry interrupted, "How do we get to Rome?"

"We'll figure it out," Nick smiled.

EPILOGUE

November 15

It was so nice to sleep in a cushy bed last night. I had a hot, hot bath before crawling in and took another long hot shower this morning before joining the others for a nice continental breakfast. It's nice to be rich. I'll have to thank William personally later.

We were all pretty disappointed that MacPherson got away. If anyone needs a kill switch, it's that man. It was fortunate that Henry found the flash drive I'd dropped. In my haste I had no idea it'd fallen out of my pocket. Henry said it was a split-second decision to run and try to find a place to access the mainframe computers. I'm glad he found William. None of us knew he was here, but we're really glad that he's on our side. He would really like to go back to Seattle to make his car models and stare at the Karmann Ghia parked in the alley behind his building, but he knows that if he doesn't go with us, he'll never truly be free. It's kind of nice to have an adult around. Sometimes it's hard to make the right decision when it comes to certain things.

Jackson, Ivy, and Felix left early this morning. They're going to pick up three of the bikes we hid in the shack. Ivy is going to take my bike. I'm really going to miss it, but our travels aren't going to be taking us back that direction, at least for now. Jackson doesn't want to go to Rome. He's very hurt by his mom's actions and the fact that she kept so much from him. I'm sure it stings knowing that she didn't even bother to come looking for him or his sister for that matter. He doesn't want to see his mom again. I don't blame him. He's going to go live in Vancouver. Ivy and Felix want to stay with him. We wished them safe travels. I don't think they're even going to try driving any cars. I think it will be good for Jackson to have a little extra time to think. They are determined to go through Lewiston so Jackson can find someone to give the headdress to. He's still hoping to find Chief Joseph alive. I am, too. The passes will be closed soon or at least by the time they get there and then they'll be stuck. I wish them safe travels. I really hope that Abram is in Vancouver when Jackson gets there. Abram would love to hear how things turned out thus far. I am really thankful we've gotten to this point. If it wasn't for William and Red and Chief Joseph and Abram, we would have been in a world of hurt. If I could send them thank you cards I would. All those books about kids without adults lie to the reader. Just to let you know.

How did Jackson free Ivy and Felix? Well, it turned out to be a relatively easy thing. He still had two of the fake BioIDs. He found Ivy and Felix walking between two large warehouses that were being used as sorting facilities. One of the other jobs the Sweepers did was to haul all sorts of things of value or possible use from other places. Ivy and Felix were assigned to sort through all the things they brought. Jackson simply waved them over, slapped the BioIDs on their foreheads and calmly walked away. I'm glad he was able to find his friends. I might've been friends with Ivy and Felix and better friends with Jackson, but you have to have more in common than just seeking revenge. I'm kind of glad Jackson won't be going with us.

Nick is scared that he may not be able to have kids now because of what MacPherson did to him in the basement. I still have hope that he'll be just fine, but we're not willing to do anything to test it, yet.

Alice and Henry are going with us, too. Alice would much prefer to stay here but is going since Henry is adamant that he's going to stop MacPherson "No Matter What". I think we are all on board, but right now, it's time for a little break. Nick and I are going to ditch the others today and do some sightseeing. With all the Sweepers gone and MacPherson already headed to Europe—Central Pangea—we have a little breather. The sun is shining, the day is cool, but not cold, and I get to explore Denver with my best friend.